OUT OF THE Shadows

HUDSON SECURITY

CHRISTINA SOL

For Todd, Lucy & Jackson

CHAPTER ONE

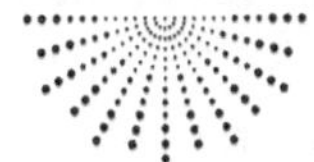

"Cameras will go dark for three minutes. Acknowledge," Sabrina "Bean" Ventura said into her headset, voice sure and steady. While she received confirmation from each team member, her finger hovered over the Enter key. "On my mark: five, four, three, two, one, mark."

As she pressed Enter, her gaze swung to her top left monitor. The three video feeds she'd overridden were playing the prerecorded material she'd programmed. A glance at the center monitor showed her team was on the move. Swift and silent. And most importantly, undetected.

Leaning back in her chair, she tried not to stare at the timer counting down on one of the screens, but it was impossible. No matter how many times she'd done this—and she'd done this countless times—her heart still hammered in her chest. She never took for granted the lives that were relying on her to keep them safe. She checked the two live drone feeds and their thermal sensors to ensure there weren't any unexpected visitors approaching the old warehouse. Orange-and-red figures indicated her team of six, plus the one they were there for.

So far, so good.

"Confirming the package is still in the warehouse's southwest corner by the west exit," Bean said. The four Hudson Security members on the team were elite, and the two FBI agents joining them tonight were skilled. However, they had just over two minutes left to retrieve the package, plant the fake, and then get the hell out of there.

"Copy, B," a familiar voice replied as the six heat signatures converged on the lone, motionless one in the corner. Gavin Frazier, head of Hudson Security and her boss, was the acting team leader: Alpha One.

Bean's head was on a constant swivel between all seven of her monitors. Her eyes narrowed on a slight movement off to the side of the building. Zooming in, she bit back a curse. Her fingers flew over the keyboard as she pulled up the warehouse's floor plan. "West exit is no longer viable. Repeat, west exit is no longer viable. Two bogies approaching."

"Copy. Package retrieved by Alpha Six," Gavin said. "Switch to Plan Bravo?"

A glance at the countdown timer had her grimacing. "Negative. Plan Charlie. North exit, then circle to the east. River evac." Her heart thumped hard in her chest. "You have sixty seconds until the cameras are back online. Get the hell out of there."

"Copy."

Bean's pulse was loud in her ears as she watched the team rush toward the north exit as the two unknowns entered the building. The team cleared the warehouse, and the drone feed showed them sprinting for the nearby forest. The two unknowns were still standing just inside the warehouse door. They hadn't moved toward where the fake package had been planted, and it seemed that so far, they hadn't noticed that anything was amiss.

However, the team wasn't yet in the clear. Between them

and the forest was a clearing the size of a football field with three cameras that would be coming back online in under fifteen seconds. They were running in a pack with Alpha Two and Four leading the way. Alpha Six was in the middle carrying the package, with Three and Five flanking them. Alpha One took up the rear. They were nearing the edge of the surveillance cameras' range, but not quite close enough to be out of range. She willed them to move faster.

Bean eyed the timer again, and her knee bounced beneath her desk uncontrollably. "Ten seconds. Nine. Eight. Seven. Six. Five. Move your ass, Alpha One. Three. Two. One." She sucked in a breath as the cameras went live. She waited a heartbeat for the alarms to sound.

Nothing.

Letting out a loud sigh, she slumped into her office chair. "You're clear, Alpha Team."

"Thank fuck," Gavin murmured. "That was close."

Too close. Blowing out another breath, she relaxed her shoulders and rolled her neck. She took a swig of her fluorescent-green energy drink and grimaced when her stomach churned. Too much caffeine today.

Pulling up the map of the area on her screen, she refocused. "Once you hit the river, head downstream. Bravo Team is about a klick away and will meet you." She tapped her headset, opening up the comms. "Confirm, Bravo Team."

"Copy, B," a deep voice replied. "Alpha Team, this is Bravo One. Status of the package?"

"Package is secure." Gavin paused. "Alpha Three is tending to the package right now, but we're going to want medical ASAP."

"Confirmed," Bean said as Bravo One muttered a curse. "There are EMTs standing by at the boat launch. Hustle, boys."

The next few minutes ticked by ever so slowly. There

were still no alarms going off at the warehouse, nor any communications or signals coming from the two unknowns signifying they'd realized anything was wrong. They hadn't bothered checking on the package—thank God, seeing as it was a fake—before they began patrolling the perimeter of the property. But Bean wouldn't breathe easy until both teams were back at the boat launch.

A full eleven minutes later, Gavin spoke the sweetest words into her headset. "Bravo Team, we see you. Signaling."

"Copy that, Alpha One," Bravo One said. "We see your signal. Coming in."

Bean listened to the teams' low murmurs. As usual, there was no idle chitchat. It was all business. "Alpha Team and the package are secure," Bravo One said. "We're hauling ass back, B."

With three clicks of her mouse, Bean redirected one of the drones—which were still monitoring the warehouse—and spotted the teams' Zodiacs. Another click had the drone scanning the length of the river with its thermal detector. "Looks like you're in the clear. Only wildlife detected along the river." The screen with the feed of the drone that had remained at the warehouse showed only two heat signatures. "The warehouse is still quiet."

"Any ID on the two bogies?" Gavin asked.

She shook her head even though he couldn't see her. "Negative. I can't get the drones any lower or they'll be detected."

"Continue to monitor until we get back to the launch. Our part is done. And, Bean, everything you have on these fuckers—and I mean *everything*—gets sent to the feds. These assholes are going down."

Bean's eyebrows rose in surprise. She'd worked closely with Gavin for just over eight years. The man was the epitome of calm. Missions could get completely screwed up, but he always remained steady. Intense as hell, but steady. It was because she'd worked closely with him for so many years that she heard the tension and fury in his words now. And *that* was unlike him.

The package had been their mission. The rest of it—the red tape and legalities—were the responsibility of the various agencies they worked with. Gavin was a strong proponent of need-to-know. Of all the intel Hudson Security gathered—and there was always a *lot* of damning information—only the necessary items were shared. But Bean also knew that this package, this mission had hit her boss harder than usual. "Copy, Alpha One. Comms will remain open until you dock."

Two hours later, Bean dumped her headset onto her desk and stretched. Her lower back protested each and every movement. After a loud groan, she took a swig of her energy drink and wrinkled her nose. She looked longingly at the opposite side of her living area, knowing that her bed was just down the short hallway from her home office setup. She was closing in on forty hours awake—the three catnaps she'd snuck in were long forgotten—and knew she was about to crash. Hard. She was familiar with the signs: trembling hands, jittery vision, and the damn brain fog. But it didn't matter, because they'd completed the mission.

The package was safe.

No.

As much as she tried to distance herself, after the last couple of hours, she no longer could. Her stomach rolled. The "package" was a three-year-old little boy. Thankfully, he was safe and had been reunited with his family. But he'd incurred substantial injuries that made her vomit. Literally.

The Hudson Security members of the Alpha and Bravo teams were on their way back home to Hudson Island via helicopter. They were forty minutes out. They generally did a debrief immediately post-mission, but the way her insides were shaking, she wasn't sure she'd make it.

Just a couple more hours, dammit. Cringing, she chugged the remainder of her energy drink as her computer dinged an incoming video call.

Stifling a groan, she accepted the call. "What's up, MacKay?"

Oliver MacKay, boss number two and Hudson Security's second-in-command, was based in London.

"Hello, B— Whoa. You look like hell."

She glared at him. "You want to try that again, MacKay?" She tried to put effort into always looking professional, but she'd been awake for way too long, not only because of the mission that had just wrapped, but also because of a bunch of research crap she'd done for MacKay. So he could shove it.

"Shit. Sorry. No. I meant, um, I'm just not used to seeing you all . . ." He waved his hand at the screen.

She rolled her eyes. Yeah, her hair was piled on top of her head, and instead of her usual blouse-and-blazer combo, she was wearing a ratty, oversized sweatshirt. Still, she leveled her best glare at him.

"Sorry, B. You look fine. Tired but fine."

Shaking her head, she held up her hand. "Stop talking, MacKay. Seriously."

"Yeah. Sorry, again."

"What's up?"

He cleared his throat. "How'd the mission go?"

"Good. We'll be debriefing in about forty-five. You want me to patch you in?"

"Please. But that's not why I'm calling."

"Oh, goody."

One of his dark-brown eyebrows arched, and she bit back a curse.

"Sorry. I wasn't supposed to say that part out loud," she muttered, flashing him a toothy grin. "As you so eloquently mentioned, I'm tired."

"We're even, then."

"Not even close, MacKay." Letting out a sigh, she leaned back in her chair. "What can I do for you?"

"I wanted to thank you again for recommending Tiny. Do you think he'd be interested in joining full-time? Better yet, would you trust him to join the fold?"

Bean frowned. Alexi "Tiny" Kirilov stood at a whopping six-eight and looked more like a gym bro than a freelance hacker. She'd worked with him numerous times before she'd joined Hudson Security, and she'd occasionally pulled him in on an as-needed basis—more so over the last year as her workload had increased tenfold. He was a talented hacker, though she was better. But did she *trust him* trust him?

"I take it by your silence that the answer is no." MacKay's British accent sounded extra snooty.

"I wouldn't exactly say that," she hedged.

"Let me rephrase. When you work together, do you block his access to some things and spy on his shit?"

She scoffed. "Of course. It would be completely stupid not to." When MacKay groaned, she hurried to add, "But I do that for everyone who's not already in. And even some of those who are but don't have high enough clearance. You and I both agree that people only need to know what they need to know. And even then, I like to know what they do with whatever info they've been given access to."

"B, I'd like to offer Tiny something more permanent. He's been reliable, and his intel's been accurate. Besides, it will take some of the pressure off you."

A wave of exhaustion washed over her, and she scrubbed her hands over her face. "Fine. I'm more than happy to pass off some projects to him." Lower-end projects that were beneath his skills. Call her a control freak, but she wasn't willing to give him more. Not just yet anyway. At least, not until she had to.

"Thanks, B."

"That doesn't mean I'm not going to monitor his ass, though."

MacKay chuckled as she stood. Her vision flickered and then tilted violently to the side. She toppled to her right but caught herself on the edge of her desk.

"Bean!"

Blinking furiously, she willed her vision to clear, willed the fog that had overtaken her senses to lift. With a deep breath, she lowered herself back into her chair. Her hands shook and she shoved them under her thighs. "I'm fine, MacKay," she said, glancing at the man on her monitor.

Holy crap, was that trembling voice *hers*? She tried again. "I'm fine."

"Bullshit, B. What's going on over there?" The concern on his face was palpable.

"Everything's fine, MacKay. I gotta go, but I'll patch you in for the debrief. Talk soon."

Before he could comment, she cut off their connection. He immediately called back, but she declined the call and silenced her ring notification.

With a loud groan, she sank deeper into her chair. It was no secret she'd been burning the candle at both ends. She'd fainted earlier in the week, but thankfully, she'd been home alone. This time, she'd almost face-planted in front of one of her bosses. Not okay. As much as she hated to admit it, maybe bringing on Tiny wasn't a bad idea.

CHAPTER TWO

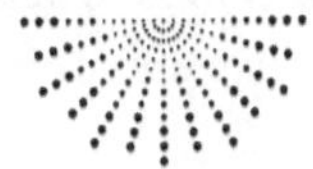

Gavin Frazier ran his hand over the scruff on his jaw and adjusted the headphones over his ears. The muffled noise of the helicopter was soothing in a fucked-up kind of way. Their mission had been successful, but damn if his stomach didn't tighten when he recalled the poor little kid. A glance at the faces of his teammates sitting around him showed they felt the same.

Anson McClintock was the three-year-old son of tech billionaires Edward and Rita McClintock. They'd each founded a social media network—two of the most popular sites in the world—and their marriage had made global headlines. After Anson was born, they'd gotten him his own around-the-clock security detail.

But Anson had still been kidnapped.

At his own damn third birthday party.

The McClintocks had been determined to handle the ransom negotiations privately, but after two days, the kidnappers had begun sending videos of them cutting the toes off the toddler's right foot. After the third video, the McClintocks had called Hudson Security.

Within twenty-four hours, Gavin's team had located the child. Another twenty-four hours later, Anson had been reunited with his family and was currently at the hospital undergoing treatment for his injuries.

Gavin's gut clenched. The fuckers who'd taken the toddler had attempted to cauterize his foot with an iron. The boy had barely been conscious when their team had found him hidden in a warehouse in the foothills of the Cascade Mountains.

Within those first twenty-four hours, Hudson Security had gathered a ridiculous amount of intel, enough to find Anson and put his kidnappers away for life. Gavin had told Bean to hand everything they had to the FBI. The two men responsible for kidnapping the child were members of the McClintock family's security detail.

Gavin would personally do everything in his power to make sure the damn feds crossed all their T's and dotted all their I's. They'd snatched a kid—a baby, really—and tortured him for the hope of twenty million dollars. No way were those fuckers going free. Not on his watch.

A buzzing in his pocket yanked him from his thoughts. As Gavin pulled his phone out, he glanced out the helo's windows and caught sight of Hudson Island's lights in the distance. Seeing the island he'd called home for the last decade lifted some of the tension he'd been holding in his shoulders.

Glancing at the text message, he frowned.

MACKAY

Check on Bean. Was on a video call with her and she looked like shit. It looked like she almost passed out.

Unease stirred in Gavin's gut. He acknowledged his second-in-command's message, but before he could delve deeper, they were landing. Within twenty minutes, his team was gathered in Hudson Security's largest conference room. There was a split screen on the Smartboard. The top two boxes showed Bean's home office and MacKay's office in London. Their in-office crew of eight took up the lower half of the screen.

Gavin's eyes narrowed as he took in Bean. Her long, dark-brown hair was slicked back in a ponytail, and she wore one of her customary button-up blouses. The only thing that was different from her usual attire was that she was wearing dark-framed glasses, which wasn't unusual since they'd all been up for way too many hours to count.

After working closely with Bean for the last eight years, he knew when she'd hit the wall. Her deep-blue eyes, which lightened and darkened depending on her mood, got shaky. It was always concerning when that happened, but the woman looked like her usual put-together, badass self. If MacKay thought she looked like shit, then they must have had a bad connection.

Dismissing MacKay's concerns, Gavin got down to business. "It's nearly four-thirty in the fucking morning, so let's make this quick." After giving a concise recap for MacKay's sake with his team chiming in here and there, Gavin turned to Xander Bonetti, one of their top security specialists. "I'd like you to meet with the McClintocks later this afternoon. I talked to Edward briefly tonight about their security personnel and recommended they clean house. Edward wants us to take over the personal security for his son and wife tomorrow. He's also requesting we take the lead on hiring long-term security for them. However, he's insisting on keeping his own core security personnel. A team of five led by Adrian Polanski that he apparently 'trusts with his life.'"

Xander frowned. "He wants to keep the people that were in charge of hiring security for his kidnapped son?"

Gavin shrugged. "Apparently, Edward, Polanski, and the other four guys go way back. And I quote, 'It wasn't their fault they were duped.'"

Groans and muttered curses filled the room.

Xander shook his head. "When the fuck are people going to realize that longevity doesn't equate to loyalty?"

"So Edward trusts Polanski and his guys with his own life, but *not* with the lives of his wife and child." Bean's eyes rolled. "People are freaking strange."

"Like I said," Gavin began, commanding everyone's attention, "I briefly talked with Edward. Obviously, he was preoccupied with getting Anson back and with his son's condition. Xander, when you meet with him later, try and push him to reconsider keeping his current security. Team Two, you guys are going with. Since Anson will be in the hospital for at least a week, and Rita says she'll be staying with him the entire time, I don't think we need to assign an additional team to the two of them right now. We'll reevaluate assignments when the kid gets released from the hospital."

Xander and the three men who made up Team Two nodded, and Gavin turned to the screen. "Bean, I'll need you to run deep background checks on all the new candidates for the McClintocks ASAP."

"Copy," she said, then a smirk lifted her lips. "Oh, sorry, MacKay, you're muted. Hang on . . . Oh, damn. Sorry, my feed froze, and I can't unmute you."

MacKay flipped her off. The corners of his lips twitched as chuckles and snorts sounded throughout the conference room. One, they all knew her last sentence was a blatant lie. And two, the grin on B's face was the definition of smug.

Wrangling the group back in line, Gavin doled out a few more assignments and then leaned back in his chair. "Good work today, everyone. Now get some rest, and we'll check back in at fourteen hundred hours." As his team nodded and rose from their seats, he called out, "Bean, call me on my cell in five."

Following the group out of the conference room, Gavin said his goodbyes and made his way to his office. Flopping down onto his leather couch, he let out a tired groan. He loved the thrill of going out on missions, and while he hadn't had the opportunity to go on many lately—he had teams of younger, highly qualified men and women who were more up to the task—he hadn't been willing to stay behind on this one. Images of that tiny kid flashed in his mind. Then they were replaced by images of other children. Other kids who'd been tortured and beaten . . .

Bile churned in his belly, and he scrubbed his hands roughly over his face. He hadn't been able to rescue those other children, but he'd been able to rescue this one.

His ringing cell phone pulled him from his grim thoughts. Yanking it from his pocket, he answered the video call.

When Bean's face filled his display, his eyes narrowed. "You okay?"

"Sure thing, boss. Why wouldn't I be?"

He didn't buy her chipper, carefree routine. Not for one second. The woman was neither.

"Push your glasses up, B." Her right eyebrow arched, and he fought a groan. "Please."

She shoved her glasses to the top of her head and glared into the screen. "Happy?"

No. Not at all. Because the darker edges of her blue eyes trembled ever so slightly.

He quickly took in the area behind her and spied a bright-red sweatshirt lying on the table. He'd bet his company that she'd been wearing that grubby sweatshirt when MacKay had spoken with her earlier. And he'd also bet there was a reason she'd changed back into her usual professional wardrobe after hanging up with the guy.

Gavin tried not to sigh but wasn't sure how successful he was. "You hacked into MacKay's messages, didn't you?"

Her eyes widened the tiniest of fractions. If he weren't so attuned to Bean's face, he would have missed it.

"I don't know what you're talking about."

He tilted his head and arched his own eyebrow. "Really?"

"Whatever," she huffed, readjusting her glasses. "Besides, it's rude to say someone looks like shit. I thought British people were supposed to be prim and proper."

"You know MacKay's neither of those things. He's just worried about you, B. You almost passed out?"

She snorted. "No. He may have been a tiny bit right about the looking-like-shit part, but he was dead wrong about that."

Gavin wasn't quite sure he believed her, but it was nearly five in the morning, so what the hell did he know? "Good work today. Seriously. I don't know how much longer the kid would have lasted if you hadn't found him so quickly."

She sobered and let out a sigh. "I hope he'll be okay."

"Me too. He'll be safe with Team Two watching him."

She nodded. "I'll get on those background checks for the new security staff ASAP."

"I know you will. Get some rest first, though."

"Night, boss."

"Hey, B," he said before she could cut their connection.

"Yeah?"

He glanced behind her. "That 49ers sweatshirt back there may be a piece of shit"—he smothered a grin when she rolled her eyes. He was an unapologetic Seahawks fan, much to Bean's disgust—"but *you* don't ever look like shit. Tired or not. No matter what that dumb Brit says, got it?"

Bean's eyes went owl wide. "Uh . . . thanks?"

What the fuck, Frazier? He wanted to clobber himself in the head. Why the hell had he just said that? "Night, B," he said, forcing a smile before quickly disconnecting.

He frowned and scrubbed his hands over his face. Damn. He must be more tired than he'd thought.

CHAPTER THREE

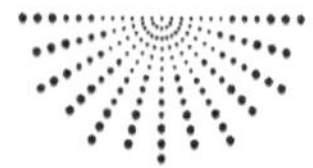

Roughly thirty-three hours had passed since the mission debrief, and Bean's office clock declared it nearly two in the afternoon on Wednesday. She'd managed to catch a few hours of sleep after the mission, but she'd been working nonstop since. She'd handed off two projects to Tiny—a client who had a stalker they needed to trace emails and calls from, and a company looking for someone internal who was sabotaging their IT security. She was still swamped though.

From extensive background checks on the prospective new members of the McClintocks' security detail, to shoring up Hudson Security's firewalls, and little fires popping up here and there, it was safe to say her plate was full. If she could just get a couple more hours added to the day, she'd be able to knock everything off her to-do list.

Squirming in her office chair, she snorted as she dialed out, her phone ringing in her ear. *Yeah, right.* If she had two more hours in the day, she'd no doubt fill it with more work.

Work-life balance? Not a thing for her.

The phone continued to ring, and she was a split second

from disconnecting the call when a man's deep voice answered. Nerves took flight in her stomach as she cleared her throat. "Hey, Doc. It's Bean at Hudson Security. I hope it's okay that I called your cell." She fiddled with her pen, absently doodling while she spoke. While there were a number of doctors at the local clinic, Doc Buchanan was the head physician as well as the father of one of her colleagues. She and Doc were friendly when they saw each other, but still, she hoped she wasn't overstepping. "Is this a good time?"

"Of course, dear. How can I help you?"

She softly pressed the pads of her fingers against the edge of her right cheekbone and winced at the sharp pain. "I know it's last minute and all, but is there any chance I could get in for a quick appointment to see you today?"

He was silent for a moment, and she swore she could feel his unease through the phone. "Of course. Is there a specific time you're thinking?"

Glancing at her computer monitor, the calendar blurred. *Shit.* She blinked a few times, and thankfully, her calendar came into focus. "Would now work? I could be there in fifteen minutes. Twenty tops."

The last thing she wanted to do was drive into town. *Especially* to see a doctor. She also didn't know how she was going to sneak out of the office without anyone seeing her, but Bean knew if she didn't get checked out, she'd go down the internet rabbit hole and self-diagnose herself with a fatal aneurysm within an hour.

"Can you tell me what's going on?" Doc's soothing voice, the concern in his words, had her throat going thick.

"I'm sure it's nothing, but I . . . um . . . fainted, and on the way down, I must have hit the corner of my desk." She cleared her throat as she cringed. "With my face."

"I see. When did this happen?"

She glanced at the clock on her monitor. "About half an

hour ago. When I came to, I was on the floor, but I don't think I was unconscious for more than a couple minutes. I want to make sure I didn't break anything in my face or give myself a concussion." And hopefully figure out what the hell was wrong. This was the second time this week she'd passed out.

"You know, Bean, I was about to head over to the gym. Why don't I swing by your office and see you?"

"You know that you're a horrible liar, right, Doc?" A smile tugged at her lips. She knew the man belonged to De La Rosa Gym, which was located next to Hudson Security, but she didn't believe him for a second.

He chuckled. "Perhaps. Truthfully, I don't think you should be driving. So I can come to you."

Though relief had her shoulders relaxing, she asked, "Are you sure?"

"Bean, my dear, the fact that you called me is telling. I'll see you in twenty."

"I'll let security know you're on your way. Thanks, Doc," she said before hanging up.

Bean quickly sent an interoffice message to both Mel at the front desk and the guys monitoring the security gate about Doc's arrival, then she leaned back into her chair with a groan. Well, more like a whimper. Her face was on fire and her hands trembled. Whether that was from her fall or the impending visit with Doc, she wasn't sure. The man hadn't been wrong. She avoided doctors of every stripe as much as humanly possible. But if she *had* to see a doctor, Doc was the one. The man was efficient, quick, and to the point.

Bean wasn't a fan of needles, hated being poked and prodded, and that heavy-duty disinfectant smell that was universal in every medical facility never failed to make her stomach turn. Her earliest memories were flashes of her sitting in a bright, sterile room working on various projects while a handful of doctors in white lab coats studied her every move. But regardless of her hangups, she needed to figure out what was wrong. Get it fixed. Then move on.

Fifteen minutes later, her desk phone buzzed. The display indicated it was Mel at the front desk. "Yes?" Bean asked, pressing the speaker button.

"Doc Buchanan is here to see you."

"Thanks, Mel. Please send him back."

Scanning her monitors, Bean began closing out the screens that contained confidential information, which was basically all of them.

A knock sounded at her office door. As the last screen went dark, she called out, "Come in."

"Hi, Bean," Doc said, a warm smile on his face as he closed the door behind him.

She rose and stepped toward him with her hand outstretched. "Thanks for seeing me, Doc." After shaking his hand, she gestured to her office's seating area—aka the comfy couch she often crashed on during long cases and missions. "Please, have a seat."

Instead of sitting, he set his bag on the coffee table and tilted his head to the side as he studied her face. "I'm not going to lie. I was surprised when you called. But considering the shiner that's blooming, I'm glad you did. Would you be more comfortable doing the exam on the couch or sitting in your office chair?"

Neither. She frowned. "Couch, I suppose."

"Have a seat." He pulled an oxygen monitor, blood pressure cuff, and a stethoscope from his bag and sat on the coffee table across from her. "Pull your sleeve up, please."

Undoing the button at her wrist, she rolled up the sleeve of her blouse. Moving the material to her shoulder, she stilled when Doc's hand settled over hers.

"What are these from?" he asked, his gaze on the two large bruises on her biceps.

Her frown deepened, and for a moment, her words lodged in her throat. "I, um, passed out a few days ago at home. I think I hit the edge of my dining table on the way down."

Concern was evident on Doc's face as he fit the cuff around her upper arm. "Any blurry vision or headaches?"

She contemplated lying, but that defeated the entire purpose of seeing Doc. "Yes to both," she said with a soft sigh. "But the blurry vision was for just a few seconds, and the headache's nothing big."

His lips pressed together as he placed the stethoscope's earpieces into his ears. "Try to relax," he murmured, taking her blood pressure.

The cuff tightened around her arm, and she tried to think calm, pleasant thoughts, but it was pointless. The hiss of the cuff deflating matched her spirits.

"One-thirty-eight over eighty-eight. A little high." Placing the cuff back into his bag, he pulled out a package of exam gloves, hand sanitizer, and a clear bag that contained a tray and multiple plastic boxes. After sanitizing his hands, he put on a pair of gloves and scanned her face, asking, "May I?"

She nodded and then winced as he gently prodded her bruised cheek.

"How many times have you passed out?"

It took all her willpower to hold still. "Just the two times. I thought the first time was a fluke, but today . . ." She shrugged. "I figured it was better to give you a call."

"Well, I'm glad you did," he replied, removing his gloves.

After shining a flashlight in her eyes and checking the bruises on her arms, he had her stand and do a number of exercises that reminded her of field sobriety tests she'd seen done. Seemingly satisfied by her actions, Doc gestured for her to sit back on the couch. Then he donned a new pair of gloves, opened the clear bag, and quickly assembled a mini phlebotomy station.

Her stomach rolled. Violently.

"We'll do a quick blood draw and should have the results back in two to three days."

She may have nodded. She wasn't sure. All she knew was that it took every bit of concentration to remain calm. When he disinfected her arm with an alcohol swab, she wanted to yank her arm away from him. When he came at her with a giant needle, she wanted to stab *him* with it. Instead, he jabbed it into her arm.

Breathe. Do not *puke on the man.* The seven little words replayed in her mind like a mantra. A mantra that was failing miserably.

Her heart pounded as he swapped in a second vial into the blood-draw-needle contraption thing. This needed to be over. Now. Just as the bile started to creep up her throat, he removed the needle and placed a piece of gauze over the tiny puncture.

"All done. Hold that, please," he said while he placed the vials into a container. "Now," he continued as he taped the gauze to her arm, "let's talk about you passing out."

Let's not. "Did I break anything in my face?"

The corners of his lips twitched. "I would say no. The bruise is already a nasty shade of purple, and I imagine it's going to look even worse tomorrow. While I don't know much about what it is you actually do here at Hudson Security, I assume that it can be highly intense. How are your stress levels?"

Uh, hard pass. "Do you think I have any signs of a concussion?"

The look he shot her said he knew exactly what she was doing. But thankfully, he went along with her subject change.

"Your pupils are responsive, and your balance is good. However, you did lose consciousness and mentioned blurry vision. Even though you lost consciousness before you fell, there's truly no telling how hard you hit your head. I wouldn't rule out a slight concussion. As such, you need to take it easy for the next forty-eight hours."

She nodded. *That* she could do. "No problem."

Doc narrowed his eyes. "You do realize that part of the taking-it-easy bit means limited activities and avoiding loud noises and crowds?"

"I'm not much of a gym goer or hiker, so limited activities won't be a problem. And as for crowds?" She shrugged. "It's safe to say that I'm not exactly a people person. So I'm good there." Understatement of the year.

He shook his head. "Limited activities also means temporarily halting things that require a lot of concentration." He nodded to her workstation. "Reading, screens . . . basically all computer work."

Her eyes widened. Hell, her mouth may have even fallen open.

Doc chuckled. "Try twenty-four hours, and we can see how you feel after that."

"You're kidding, right?" When Doc shook his head, she rushed on, "My job—there are critical things that need to happen and—"

"And you lost consciousness for an unknown amount of time, fell, hit your face, experienced blurry vision, and you currently have a low-grade headache. Correct?"

She pressed her lips together and shot daggers at the man.

Doc chuckled. "Glare all you want. Am I wrong?"

She huffed out a resigned sigh. "Fine. I'll need to make arrangements."

"Good. Now, the last time I saw you, we talked about

your diet of processed foods and energy drinks. Any improvements there?"

Rolling her eyes, she let out another sigh. "Pretty sure you know the answer to that one, Doc."

"Your diet's still piss-poor then, huh?" He tsked and shook his head, but the humor in his expression softened the rebuke.

"But the good news is I've actually been drinking more water." Which was true. However, *more* was a bit misleading since her hydration starting point had basically been zero. Baby steps, right?

"Good. And the energy drinks?"

"Those are still part of the rotation, but I did switch to the less sugary ones. Also, for every couple of energy drinks I down, I drink a bottle of water. I swear." Granted, they were the smaller half bottles, but whatever. Water was water, right?

He simply stared at her for a moment, and it took everything she had to not squirm. "Bean, you have to ease up on those drinks. All that caffeine and sugar—even the sugar-free varieties—are just not that good for you. But the increased hydration is a plus. Your new goal is one bottle of water to one energy drink." He rushed on when she opened her mouth to protest. "At least *try* one-to-one. When was the last time you ate today?"

She frowned. She'd missed lunch for sure. Had she had breakfast?

"Bean, my dear, it's nearly three o'clock. Skipping meals can be a factor in your passing out." He nodded to the container holding the vials of her blood. "My guess is your blood work is going to show that you're anemic. The bruising and fainting are all indicators."

"What's the treatment for anemia?"

"Depends on what kind of anemia. We'll check your

thyroid too, but iron-deficiency anemia is the most common. In a nutshell, you might not be getting enough iron in your diet."

Her frown deepened. "Eat better, then?"

Doc nodded. "I'd also suggest minimizing stress."

Her head was shaking before he finished speaking. "Look, my job *is* highly stressful, but I love it. It's often time-sensitive and intense, but it can also be absolutely thrilling."

"That's all great, Bean, but you also need to decompress, which is something I don't think you do. Outside of work, what are your hobbies? Interests? Do you go hiking?"

Heat rushed over her cheeks. "Despite living on Hudson Island and working where I do, I'd say I'm not exactly the outdoorsy sort."

"Well, how about yoga or meditation?"

She barely held back a scoff. "Not my thing."

Doc's brow arched. "Have you actually tried either?"

"Yes," she said, drawing out the one word. "The guys once got me a package over at the Pacific View Resort with all sorts of yoga and meditation classes." She'd taken one class of each, and while the yoga class had been more challenging than she'd anticipated, she'd been bored out of her damn mind. The meditation class? Ridiculous. Fifty minutes of just lying there on a supposedly comfortable mat that was anything but. Breathing. While the lady next to her fell asleep. No, thanks.

"How'd it go?" Doc asked.

"Well . . . I did one meditation and a beginner yoga class. Then I ended up swapping out all the remaining classes for two massages, a facial, and their signature Pacific View Resort Mixology Session. And don't worry, that class used all organic booze and fresh ingredients for the mixers, so it was totally fine." She flashed him her most innocent smile.

Doc chuckled, shaking his head. "I've heard that's a fun

class. They also have a cooking class if that's something you're interested in. Bottom line, Bean? You need to find a hobby that has nothing to do with work. That has nothing to do with computers or screens or tech. Tell me about your social life. Do you get together with your friends much? Unwind with them?"

This conversation needed to end. ASAP. "I spend a lot of time at work, so I mostly have work friends. Everyone gets together outside of work too." Not that she joined them that much. Maybe once a month. Maybe. Not that Doc needed to know that.

"Good. Like I said, it's important you take the time to relax. Do you have family in the area?"

She went cold. That too-familiar hollow feeling settled into her gut. Shaking her head, she willed her expression to remain neutral. "I'm not close with my family." It had been over a decade since she'd seen her parents in person.

He nodded, again studying her. "I'm sorry to hear that. But you know, sometimes it can be for the best. Sometimes absence is better than toxicity."

Her stomach clenched as she took in what he'd said. Releasing a breath, she let the wisdom of those six words wash over her. "Thanks, Doc."

"Of course, dear. Now, seeing as we don't know the actual results of your blood draw yet, do you want my unofficial medical opinion?"

Her brow furrowed as she tried to read him. "I don't know, do I?"

"Probably not, but I think you're working yourself into an early grave. You're exhausted. You forget to eat. When you do, there's zero nutritional value in what you consume. And you're stressed. You're only thirty-two, but you're a heart attack waiting to happen. I think the fainting spells are a precursor to something much more serious."

"Holy crap, Doc," she murmured, worry curdling in her belly. "It can't be *that* bad."

"You've passed out twice." He gestured to her arm and then her face. "You're lucky you only have bruises. What if the next time you pass out, you crack your head even harder? Then what? You wait for a coworker to stumble upon your unconscious body?"

She blew out a breath. "Geez, Doc."

"It may seem like I'm being dramatic, but if this is something that's preventable—"

There was a quick rap on her office door before it swung open. "B, do you have the info on the . . ."

Gavin came to an abrupt halt as he took her in. She fought a cringe when a look she could only describe as seriously pissed off crossed his face.

His hands fisted at his sides, and he hissed, "Who the fuck hit you?"

CHAPTER FOUR

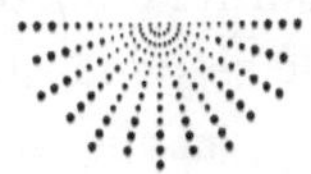

Gavin's breath was lodged in his chest. No matter how hard he tried to inhale, nothing happened. He couldn't even blink. All he could focus on was Bean. On the angry purple-and-black bruise forming around the edge of her right eye.

Their line of work was often physical with both training and fieldwork, and he'd seen almost all his colleagues with various bruises and injuries. But not Bean. She wasn't one of their personal security officers. No. She was a desk jockey. A desk jockey who happened to be one of the most talented hackers in the world. But the woman was sporting a raging black eye.

Bean.

Not. Fucking. Acceptable.

A low growl rumbled through the room. It took a second to realize the growling noise was coming from him. "Who the fuck did this to you, B?" he asked again, his voice like gravel.

Her hands came up as if she were trying to soothe a caged animal. "I'm okay, boss. Really. Everything's okay."

"The fuck it is."

She glanced toward Doc, and Gavin snapped his fingers before crossing his arms over his chest. "Name, B. Now."

She mimicked his posture and shot him a glare that he was sure would have maimed him had he given much thought to it. He didn't.

"Did you just snap your freaking fingers at me, you Neanderthal?" Before he could respond, she was up off the couch and in his personal space, jabbing her finger into his chest. "You do *not* snap at me like some sort of animal. Ever. I will cut your goddamn hand off, shove it up your ass, and absolutely destroy you. Got it?"

He was nodding before she'd finished speaking. He wasn't one to snap at people physically or verbally—*especially* not Bean. But dammit, all he could focus on was that bruise on her face. He swore it was darkening as the seconds ticked by. Whoever had done this—

Another sharp jab of her finger brought his gaze back to her angry blue eyes.

"Are you even freaking listening to me, Frazier?" Each word was punctuated with another stab of her finger. She'd added a second finger to the mix, and he had no doubt she'd be full-on punching him soon.

Exhaling, he gently wrapped his hand around her fist. "I'm sorry, B. And, yes, I'm listening." His attention flickered to the side of her face. Another bruise was forming near her ear. He ground down on his molars and let out another breath. "I'm sorry for snapping at you. That was . . . stupid."

"And rude. And completely uncalled for." She yanked her hand away and recrossed her arms over her chest.

"Agreed. I'm sorry." He shot a glance at Doc and lifted his chin in a belated greeting before focusing back on Bean. She looked normal. Like Hudson Security's very own brunette version of Felicity Smoak in her light-blue blouse, black skirt, and sky-high heels. Even the hints of exhaustion under her eyes were normal. What wasn't normal were the damn bruises on the side of her face. "Who hit you?"

Rolling her eyes, she threw her hands up. Rubbing her temples, she marched to her desk and slapped her hand down on the edge. "Here, boss. You gonna beat up my desk for me?"

Eyes narrowing, he glanced at Doc, hoping for some clarification.

"Uh-uh, buster. He's *my* doctor. Doc doesn't get to talk to you about *my* issues. I fell, hit my face, and called Doc to make sure everything's okay."

Gavin caught Doc's wince at Bean's last statement. Bean was feisty as hell and could verbally spar with the best, but he also knew she was a shitty liar. "So you're fine? Nothing's broken?"

She nodded.

"Just those bruises on your face?"

She remained silent.

"No concussion?"

Again, nothing.

Gavin pursed his lips. So there were more bruises he couldn't see and the possibility of a concussion. Fucking hell. "Well, if you're not going to tell me what's going on, then I'm going to operate under the assumption that you're concussed—"

"I never said that!"

"You didn't have to, B," he said, shaking his head. "Doc's here. The fact that you called him means it's a big deal." He met Doc's stare. "Am I wrong?"

Doc held his hands up. "You know I can't say anything to you either way about my patient."

Frustration tore through him, and he turned back to Bean. She was hurt. He didn't know to what extent, but they'd been friends for a long damn time, and he knew something was wrong. "Bean, please. Let me help you."

She let out a sigh that said he was the most annoying person in the world. And, yes, he knew her well enough to differentiate between her sighs.

"Fine," she huffed as she sank into her plush office chair. "I *may* have a slight concussion. Doc says because I lost conciousn—"

He narrowed his eyes as Bean cut off whatever she was about to say. Then she proceeded to cough the fakest fake cough he'd ever heard.

"Don't look at me like that," she muttered before nodding to Doc. "Anyway, Doc said I need to take twenty-four hours off all this." She waved her hand at her computer setup.

"I actually recommended forty-eight hours, and that we can reevaluate after twenty-four," Doc clarified.

Bean shifted her glare to Doc. "Not helping, Doc. Not helping." The man raised his hands in mock surrender before she turned her ire back to him. "Besides, boss man, we don't even know what's wrong." She gestured to the plastic box of vials on the coffee table. "It'll take like two to three days for the results."

"I can expedite it," Doc said, glancing at his watch. "We use a facility on Port Townsend for our lab tests, and depending on the ferry schedule, I can drop those off to them before they close tonight. If I make it, they should be able to get the results back by end of day tomorrow."

"Oh, that's not necessary, Doc—"

"Great idea," Gavin said. "Better yet, I can have Owen fly you over right now."

Bean's jaw dropped. "Gavin Frazier. We are *not* using a company helicopter to take my blood samples to the lab. That's ridiculous."

Sometimes her haughty tone had him questioning who

was actually in charge. "Are you telling me what I can and can't do with *my* helicopter?" If he had to throw his weight around and remind the stubborn woman it was *his* company, so be it. Asshole move? For sure. But he didn't care. They needed answers. Immediately. "Besides, are you not a part of this team?" He didn't wait for her to respond. "In fact, B, I'd say that you're probably the most important person in this entire company."

Gavin quickly typed a text to Owen and appreciated his pilot's immediate response. "She can have the helo ready to go in fifteen minutes. That work for you, Doc?"

"Wow, uh, yeah. That works fine."

Bean groaned. "A little bit of overkill, don't you think?"

He glanced at Bean. She was relaxed in her chair, her head lying on the rest, her eyes closed, the tiny wrinkle between her eyebrows pronounced. Either she had a headache, or she was annoyed. Probably both. "Nope," he said, making sure to pop the P. The wrinkle deepened, and he didn't bother biting back a smirk.

Doc chuckled as he gathered his things. "Quite the efficient operation you have going here, Frazier."

"Yes, sir." Understatement of the year. But what concerned him was that Bean didn't realize that she was an integral part of their operation. And if he had to fly the damn helo himself, he would. "If you could give me a minute," he said to Doc as he dialed his phone and brought it to his ear, "I need to make this call before I escort you to the hangar."

Hudson Security's Director of Logistics' cool and steady voice answered, "How can I help you, Frazier?"

"B's going dark for twenty-four, Esme. Maybe forty-eight. Let everyone who's need-to-know know."

Esme remained silent, so he was able to hear Bean's muttered, "Kill. Me. Now."

"She okay?" Esme asked.

"She will be. After a shit ton of rest."

"Shit, I knew exhaustion was finally going to catch up to her." Esme tsked like a reprimanding schoolteacher. "You know you'll have to chain B to her bed, right? Her home setup is almost identical to her office."

Damn. That hadn't even crossed his mind. "Good point. And thanks, Esme."

"Of course. Give her my best," she replied before disconnecting.

He shoved his phone into his back pocket. "B, I'm going to take Doc to the hangar and check in with Owen."

"Thanks for coming out, Doc," Bean said, starting to rise.

"Stay seated, dear, and you're welcome. I'll call you with the test results. Take some Tylenol, hydrate with actual water, and get some rest, okay?"

She nodded and sank back into her chair, giving him a tired wave.

"I'll be back in fifteen," Gavin said. "So close up shop, and I'll drive you home." Bean's eyes were closed again, and she didn't reply. Didn't even give a single indication she'd heard him. "Bean?"

She heaved another sigh, and his lips twitched. Yeah, he wasn't her favorite person at the moment. But he didn't care.

"So freaking bossy," she grumbled, her eyes still closed.

Damn right.

CHAPTER FIVE

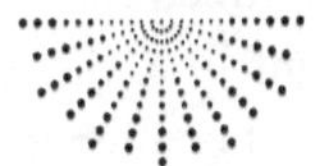

Fine. Maybe Doc had a point. Bean's low, throbbing headache had been steadily growing over the last half hour. From the second she'd stepped out of her office, her bossy-ass boss had been peppering her with questions. How was her vision? Did she need ice for her face? Was she sure there weren't other parts of her that she'd hurt?

Not that she could blame Gavin or anything. She handled almost all the company's technology. There were three others who'd been trained to monitor the cybersecurity systems of their clients, but if any alarms or alerts were triggered, she was the one they notified to handle it. Bean was also the only one who had clearance to do the deeper research into and for their clients. Yes, she'd handed some things off to Tiny, but nothing that was highly sensitive, which encompassed the majority of her work.

So she understood Gavin's concern. He had a company to run, after all. With her temporarily out of commission, a lot of Hudson Security's research work would be at a standstill. Still, she ignored his questions. Not that she wanted to be rude. However, the mere thought of speaking had her head throbbing even harder.

As he followed her out to the parking lot, he took the keys to her white Audi out of her hand and grabbed something from her trunk before steering her toward his Hudson Security-issued armored SUV. She didn't bother questioning him or protesting. She'd recognized that look on his face. The lips pressed together in a tight line, the granite set of his scruffy jaw, the light-gray eyes that challenged her to argue with him.

This wasn't her first rodeo. She knew when to pick her battles with the man. If he wanted to drive her, then fine. They were heading in the same direction—they were neighbors, after all—so what did it matter?

However, getting into Gavin's SUV for the short ride home turned out to be a horrible idea. The moment he started driving, everything tilted to the side. A tidal wave of nausea washed over her. Keeping her eyes slammed shut was the only thing that kept her from puking all over his leather upholstery. That and very slow, very steady, and very shallow breaths.

Gavin was talking, and even though his deep rumble was somewhat soothing, she'd stopped listening the second the vehicle was in motion. To be fair though, her growing headache had probably less to do with her fall and the man's uncharacteristic chatter, and more to do with the budding panic that was building in her chest. The thought of not working for the next day or two? At all? Yeah . . .

Her lungs squeezed tightly, and unease swirled in her gut.

It was no secret that her life revolved around her work. She hadn't been lying to Doc earlier when she said she didn't people well. She didn't. On top of that, she sure as hell wasn't the outdoorsy sort. Living in a small, tight-knit, nature-loving island community meant she mostly kept to herself.

Aside from reading, which she didn't do nearly enough of, Bean didn't have many hobbies that didn't involve some sort of screen. When she wasn't on her computer working, she gamed or decompressed with some mindless coloring or puzzle apps on her tablet.

Super boring? Maybe.

But after digging around people's pasts and online histories, which tended to be bleak, sordid, or vile—often a combination of all three—she wanted to shut her mind off. Coloring a paint-by-number mandala or immersing herself in a matching-tile game often did the trick.

"B, did you hear me?" Gavin asked as the car slowed.

"Maybe," she murmured, peeking an eye open. Instead of feeling the relief of finally getting home and being able to get out of the dizzying car, her eyes widened, and she frowned. Gavin had pulled into a driveway. *His* driveway, not hers. "Why are we at your place?"

"So you didn't hear me," he said with a sigh, placing the car in park. "I'll have one of the guys drop your car off later tonight."

"Fine. But that doesn't answer my question."

His chuckle was low as he shook his head. "You didn't listen to a single thing I said on the way here, did you?"

She opened her mouth but then snapped it shut. Nope. She hadn't heard a damn thing. "Refresh my memory."

Instead of answering, he pushed open his door with a muttered, "Sit tight." Before she could question him, Gavin rounded the front of the SUV and opened her door.

She sucked in a breath as he quickly leaned over her to undo her seat belt. Big mistake. She caught a hint of cedar and pine, and her stomach pitched. Her frown deepened when she realized the stomach flip was *way* different than the earlier nausea-induced ones. Quickly dismissing the thought, she rubbed her aching temples. She must have hit her head harder than she'd thought.

"Come on," he said, gently gripping her elbow to assist her out of her seat.

She wanted to protest his help on principle, but the second she stood up, everything swayed. His arm was immediately around her waist, and once again, that cedar and pine scent she'd never noticed before filled her nose. Taking her weight, he walked her toward his house. It was a home she was familiar with seeing as they'd been friends and neighbors for years.

The Hudson Security property took up a large portion of the northeast corner of Hudson Island, which Gavin leased from the De La Rosa family. The acreage housed not only their office, but also the facilities and training grounds of Hudson Tactical, a new joint venture between Hudson Security and De La Rosa Gym that utilized employees from both companies—security specialists from Hudson Security and martial arts coaches from De La Rosa Gym—to provide hand-to-hand combat and tactical training to law enforcement types.

Gavin had also purchased an eight-acre lot adjacent to the Hudson Security property from the family and built five houses. His was a four-bedroom, three-bathroom, log-style cabin. The other four were various smaller versions of his home that were for employees. She lived in the one closest to him, Xander was in the one farthest away, and the two cabins in the middle were currently unoccupied and generally used as short-term housing for the handful of employees who were based off island.

A ring sounded as he opened the front door, and she winced at the high-pitched noise. Gavin muttered a curse, leaned her against the wall, and rushed to disarm the alarm. He was back beside her within seconds. With his arm once again locked around her waist, he led her into the living room and eased her down onto the couch. "Be right back. Do *not* move."

She wanted to make some sort of smart-ass remark about his bossiness, but her brain was fried. All she could do was sink into the plush leather couch and cringe as her head pounded in time to each of her heartbeats.

After a moment, the cushion beside her sank. "Here, B, take these. If your headache doesn't get a little better in the next half hour, I'm calling Doc."

It was a chore to pry her eyes open, but when she did, concerned gray eyes stared back at her. Gavin held out a glass of water and a couple of pain pills. The cool water was soothing as she swallowed them down.

"Thanks, boss man. I'll be good as new and out of your hair before you know it."

He shook his head. "You're staying here tonight."

She pursed her lips. There was no way she'd heard that correctly. "Sorry. What was that?"

"On the way over here, we talked—"

"*You* talked," she interrupted. "I ignored you." His eyebrow arched, and she rolled her eyes. "In a very polite and respectable way, of course."

"Of course." The edges of his lips twitched. "Well, since you didn't protest what I was saying, I assumed we were in agreement."

She racked her brain for any hints of their conversation in the car and came up blank. "You're going to have to refresh my memory again."

His eyes narrowed as he stared across the room, as if pondering the meaning of life. "Is it really refreshing your memory if you never bothered to hear what I said in the first place? I suppose a bit of what I said must have seeped into your subconscious, right?"

Good. Freaking. God. "Gavin Frazier," she said, putting as much annoyance as she could muster into the two words.

He chuckled. "Damn. Full name. You mean business."

The man wasn't wrong. She rarely called him by his given name. It was always boss man, boss, or Frazier. "That's right, *Gavin*."

He smirked. "Well, *Sabrina*, you're here because I don't trust you. At all."

In the span of a heartbeat, the blood drained from her face. All humor vanished, and her gaze dropped to her lap. Ouch.

"Holy shit, B. I didn't mean it like *that*," he said in a rush, grabbing her hands.

She stilled. Completely. For the life of her, she couldn't take a breath, and her chest squeezed painfully tight. It was as if he'd punched her in the gut.

"Bean, look at me."

She shook her head, gaze fixed on her knees, still unable to breathe. Then his hands were framing her face, and he tilted her head up. Her heart knocked hard in her chest. Physical touch wasn't something she was accustomed to. Especially not from her boss.

"Breathe, B, or you're going to pass out."

Meeting his gaze, she sucked in a breath. Shaking her head, she tried to pull away, but his hands held firm. His gray eyes were intent and imploring. "I trust you with my life, B. I trust you with the lives of every member of our team."

Confusion swirled in her brain. Then what did he mean?

He ran a thumb gently over the edge of her bruised eye before pulling away and raking his hands through his already disheveled hair. "What I meant to say and completely fucked up is that I don't trust that you'll follow Doc's orders. Your place has all your computers. Hell, your home workstation is identical to your office setup."

She shook her head—*Holy. Moly. Overreact much, B?*—and tried to inject some levity into their conversation. "I have one less monitor at home." His eyebrow arched, and that I'm-not-impressed look crossed his face. She cleared her throat. Right. *Hello, awkward.* "You were saying?"

"If you're at your place, I don't think you'll be able to *not* work. You have a concussion—"

"A slight *possible* concussion," she clarified.

He scrubbed his hands over his face as he muttered something she couldn't decipher. Most likely a curse given the frustrated glare he was now shooting at her. "I don't care how slight or possible it is. You have a concussion. You need to rest. And I know you won't do that at your place." He waved a hand at his living room. "Here, I have a laptop. That's it. And you're not getting on it."

There was no use arguing with him. "Fine, but I need to swing by my place to pick up some stuff."

"Like what?" he asked, rising from the couch.

It took everything she had to not roll her eyes. She knew he was trying to help—and, yes, he did have a point since she'd planned to hop on her computer the minute he drove away—but he was being a bit over the top. "Clothes, contact lenses, tampons . . . You know, those kinds of things?"

He crossed the room and picked up a bag. Her eyes narrowed once she recognized it was the emergency bag she kept in the trunk of her car. "I assume this has all the stuff you need for one night?"

This time, her rolling eyes won the battle. Of course he had an answer for everything. "I knew you were bossy," she muttered, "but you have to admit that this is a lot. Even for you."

"Deal with it." He shot her a smile that was more smirk than grin. "Honestly though, I wasn't lying earlier."

Her mind drew yet another blank. "You said a lot of stuff

earlier. Care to be a little more specific?" She could hear the snark in her tone and winced. "Sorry."

"You're fine, B," he said, seemingly paying her attitude no mind.

The thought gave her pause. She wasn't quite sure if that was a good thing or bad.

"When we were talking with Doc in your office earlier today," Gavin continued, "about you being the most important part of Hudson Security."

"Right." She snorted. "Pretty sure that would be you and MacKay. Esme even."

Gavin shook his head. "It's you. And right now, you're injured. So you're going to rest up, because you being hurt is unacceptable."

She studied him. His expression was so serious and intense. Yes, she was used to that, but there was something else she couldn't read. Something that had her wanting to give the guy a hug. Which, holy shit, was *not* something she did. With anyone. Ever. "We're a team, boss man," she said, needing to lighten . . . whatever it was that had settled over them. "We're all equally important. All cogs in an interconnected machine. I may have more tricks up my sleeve than others, but we all have important roles."

Whatever had settled over Gavin lifted, and the corners of his lips tilted up. "Sure, B. If that makes you feel better."

She pursed her lips. "I can't tell if you're being serious or making fun of me."

He shrugged. "I'm going to make us dinner. You can rest here on the couch or in the guest room. Where would you rather be?"

Of course he'd give her an evasive nonanswer.

"Home." She gave him a smile that was all teeth.

"Not happening," he said, snagging a blanket off an accent

chair and tossing it to her. It landed perfectly on her lap. Because of course it did.

Shaking her head, she groaned and swung her legs up onto the couch. "The couch is fine. By any chance, Gavin, do you have some energy drinks?"

"Not a chance in hell, Sabrina," he called over his shoulder as he left the room.

Fighting a smile, she snuggled into the couch cushions. She didn't want to think too hard about why the thought of him not trusting her had hurt so much. Had down right gutted her. Instead, she closed her eyes, let the Tylenol do its magic, and focused on how annoying the man could be.

Well, maybe not *annoying* per se. But irritating.

Yes, she tossed a ton of snark his way on a daily basis, but she'd never really had him toss it right back. Until today. And it was kind of surprising and . . . fun.

CHAPTER SIX

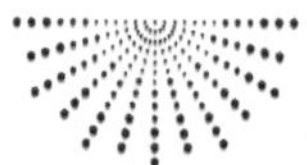

Gavin didn't consider himself a chef by any stretch of the imagination, but he wasn't completely inept. One didn't get to be a single guy knocking on forty without being somewhat capable in the kitchen. At least, they shouldn't.

He frowned when he thought of the woman asleep on his couch. Bean was in her early thirties and lived off energy drinks and frozen dinners. He had no doubt that if she lived in a larger city, she'd add to that a rotation of takeout from all nearby restaurants. He'd been in her house numerous times over the years and knew her kitchen was still basically brand new. The microwave and fridge-freezer were the only things that she used.

The timer dinged, and he pulled the glass dish from the oven and set the baked honey-garlic chicken onto the stovetop to rest. At the same time, the rice cooker chimed, letting him know the last part of their dinner was ready. Chicken and rice. Not the fanciest of meals, but it was a whole lot better than the frozen crap Bean usually had.

After turning off the oven, he made his way back to the living room and stopped short in the entryway. Bean was curled onto her side. Her five foot three looked especially tiny on his oversized couch. The woman was so damn smart and gave him so much shit that he forgot how slight she really was. But seeing her completely at ease on his couch brought it all to reality.

She'd fainted and had been taken out by the corner of her desk. None of that was okay.

A feeling he didn't recognize rushed through him. It wasn't quite worry, and it wasn't quite protectiveness. It was . . . He didn't know what it was, but it made him uneasy. And not in a watch-your-back kind of way. Rather it was . . .

Hell, he couldn't explain it.

Seeing the bruise darkening on her face had his jaw clenching. As much as he hated the idea of her fainting, he was thankful no one had hurt her. Because had that been the case, that person would no longer be walking the earth. However, since her bruised face was due to her passing out, he needed to reevaluate Bean's role at Hudson Security and just how much he put on her plate.

As Gavin had told her, she *was* the most important person at Hudson. Her skills were unmatched. Yes, his various team members—from the personal security specialists and pilots to even him and MacKay—were the best of the best.

However, Bean was next-level. There were very few people in the entire *world* who could do what Bean did, who had the vast innate computer knowledge she possessed.

He knew she enjoyed what she did—everything from the complex research projects to the intricate mission executions —because Bean was a puzzle solver to her core. But she wasn't taking care of herself. She lived off a steady diet of caffeine and processed foods with an unlimited shelf life. It wouldn't do the company or her any good if she worked herself to death.

She looked out for everyone at Hudson Security, but it

wasn't until today—when he saw the utter panic on her face when Doc said she needed to be offline for forty-eight hours —that he realized that no one looked out for her. And that was unacceptable.

He hated to disturb her, but she needed sustenance. No matter how peaceful she looked. Crouching next to the couch, he grimaced as his knees popped. "B, you awake?"

"No," she grumbled, eyes still closed.

He smiled. How had he never realized how damn cute she was when she was crabby?

Wait, what? He froze. *Uh, no. In fact, make that* hell *no.*

Shaking his head, he cleared his throat. "I made chicken and rice. You need to eat something."

Nothing. She gave zero indication she'd heard him.

Part of him was grateful her eyes were still shut. Because that earlier feeling he didn't recognize? It was not only growing, but he also feared his confusion was written all over his face.

"Bean?"

"Go away."

Focus, Frazier. The woman—your friend—*is concussed and needs food.*

Shoving his emotions down, he refused to be deterred. They hadn't been friends for all these years for nothing. He knew the trick with Bean. "Xander said he's going to drop off some ice cream for you later."

Her eyes popped open, and he bit back a smile. Barely. "What flavors?"

"Mint chocolate chip and cookies and cream," he replied with zero hesitation. "But dinner first, B."

"I'm not a child," she said with an exasperated sigh as she moved to sitting. "You don't have to bribe me to eat dinner."

"Would never dream of it," he said, rising. That was *exactly* what he had to do. "You okay eating in the kitchen?"

"Sure," she said as she stretched her arms over her head. After pushing the blanket off, she glanced down at herself and frowned. "Let me change first."

"Take your time," he said as she rose. She grabbed the bag he'd snagged from her trunk and headed down the hallway to the guest room. Once she was out of sight, he pulled his phone from his back pocket.

GAVIN

Are you back on Hudson?

XANDER

Almost. Ferry's just pulling in. I left Team Two with the McClintocks. They're all still at the hospital. What's up?

GAVIN

Can you pick up a gallon of cookies and cream and drop it by my house? Mint chocolate chip too?

When Xander replied with a row of laughing emojis, Gavin silently cursed his friend.

GAVIN

Is that a yes?

XANDER

Sure. I assume it's to bribe Bean?

Gavin snorted. The fact that Bean had the appetite of a teenage boy was no secret to anyone. Frozen food, takeout, chips, ramen, energy drinks, and soda.

GAVIN

You assume correctly.

XANDER

She okay? Heard through the grapevine
she's got a shiner and possible concussion.

GAVIN

She should be fine after some food and rest.

XANDER

Ahhh. Hence the ice cream. Got it. Give me
thirty. Forty-five. Tops.

GAVIN

Thanks.

Pocketing his phone, Gavin made his way back to the kitchen. He grabbed two plates as he heard her footsteps approaching behind him.

"Holy crap, did you actually cook, boss? Like real food? Because it smells great."

Scooping rice onto their plates, he asked, "Do you want one piece of chicken or tw—"

The words died on his lips as he turned toward her. Hell, every damn thought he had evaporated. The only thing his mind could focus on was the woman standing beside him. He'd seen her in her perfectly pressed business attire. He'd seen her in baggy sweats and a T-shirt. But this? Cotton shorts that hit her mid-thigh and an oversized sweatshirt that hung off one shoulder exposing a flesh-colored bra strap?

Holy. Shit.

Seemingly oblivious to his wayward thoughts, she took the plate from his hands and helped herself to the chicken. Thank God, because he wasn't yet able to form words.

"This looks great. Seriously. My idea of cooking is making ramen on the stovetop instead of in the microwave." She glanced at him on her way to the kitchen table, and a frown scrunched her forehead. "You okay, boss man?"

Holy fuck, he was so far from okay it wasn't even funny. "Yeah," he said, fighting a wince at the strangled sound of that one word. "Just hungry, I guess. How's the headache?"

"Mostly gone," she said as she cut her chicken into bite-sized pieces. "I think the catnap and Tylenol helped." She took a bite of the chicken and rice and moaned. Deep and low. "Ohmygod, this is really good."

Holy shit. Kill. Me. Now.

Bean making that noise had his mind spiraling straight into the gutter. He didn't know what the fuck was wrong with him. Because every image that was currently flashing in his mind—images of her making that noise under completely different circumstances—was one thousand percent inappropriate and not okay. He shoveled food into his mouth to buy himself some time to get his head on straight and his thoughts under control.

This was *Bean*, dammit. One of his closest friends. One of his most trusted colleagues. One of his—

She moaned again around another bite of food, closing her eyes in apparent bliss.

Fuck.

<hr>

Bean couldn't remember the last time she'd had a home-cooked meal. Technically, it wasn't a fancy dinner, but considering her usual dinners cooked for four and a half minutes on high, the sweet and savory chicken and rice was downright gourmet.

She took another bite and couldn't help but groan in appreciation. It was *that* good. Maybe she should learn how to cook one of these days?

Gavin cleared his throat. She brought her attention back

to him, and her eyes widened in surprise. She was five bites into her dinner, and he'd already nearly cleared his plate.

After finishing his last bite, he pushed his plate to the side, rested his elbows on the table, and clasped his hands under his chin. "I know it's still pretty early, but I'd like you to get more rest. Even if your headache is gone by the morning, I'd like you to stay offline tomorrow." She opened her mouth, but he held up his hand to ward off her protest. "Call MacKay tonight. Esme let him know you'd be going dark for the next twenty-four and had him line up Tiny to take some things off your plate."

She shoved another bite of food into her mouth to hold off an automatic snarky reply. She knew it was for the best, but damn if she didn't want to throw a temper tantrum.

"Please, B. You passed out."

He looked so earnest, so conflicted that she couldn't help but concede.

"Fine," she said with a sigh. "But there has to be something productive I can do. I can't just sit here all day or I'll go crazy." A little overdramatic? Yes. But not inaccurate. She glanced around his pristine kitchen. "How about I rearrange things here?"

Gavin made a choking noise, and she bit back a smirk. "Uh, how about you not?"

The man was precise. Detailed. Exacting. Hell, he was probably the most anal-retentive person she knew. And she worked with a bunch of nit-picking-alpha types, so that said a *lot*. The idea of her rearranging his kitchen probably had him breaking out in hives. And Bean found *that* idea comical. But she'd throw the guy a bone . . .

"How about this? Instead of rearranging your kitchen and home office tomorrow," she swallowed a chuckle as his face blanched, "I head over to Tactical's training center and meet with Wilson." Gavin was shaking his head before she'd finished speaking. "Hear me out, boss. If I take a look at their programs firsthand, I can give the tech crew a layperson's idea of what should go up on the website. It'll be like free market research."

"You're supposed to be taking it easy."

She waved her hand, dismissing Gavin's concern. "Please. Wilson knows me."

Bennett Wilson was one of their elite security specialists. He also ran the outdoor survival training program for Hudson Tactical.

"Wilson knows I'm indoorsy. It's not like he's going to have me tromping around the forest or anything. Plus, you know there won't be any overstimulation from crowds or anything, because he peoples worse than I do."

Gavin nodded. "That's true. How about a compromise?"

She narrowed her eyes. "Depends on the compromise."

"Fair. You scope out Tactical's programs tomorrow, and in return, when you feel better, you take it."

"Take what?"

"Wilson's outdoor survival course."

"Uh, no." She snorted. "How about a counter proposal? I check out their programs tomorrow, and I *consider* signing up for Wilson's course. Though we both know it would be a complete waste of my and Wilson's time."

"Why would you say that? You never know when you'll be stuck in the woods."

She scoffed. The man had to be kidding. "Uh, yes, I do. Seeing as I don't go into the woods, the answer is never."

He shook his head. "I'm serious, B. It's surprisingly easy to get lost in nature. Even if you stick to the trails, it doesn't take much to get turned around."

For a moment, she studied him. On one hand, she knew what he was doing. God knew Gavin was a be-prepared-for-anything type of man and wanted to extend that to her. It was oddly sweet. However, on the other hand, did he not know her at all?

"Frazier, I don't really like . . . nature."

The wrinkle between his brows popped as if he truly didn't understand her statement. "What exactly about nature don't you like?"

Good God, where to start? Oh, yes . . . "The bugs. The dirt. The lack of flushable toilets. Getting rained on. Getting too hot. Getting too cold. The—"

"Okay, fine." He chuckled. "Counter proposal accepted. However, you have to *seriously* consider taking the course. Don't underestimate the power of nature. It has a way of balancing everything out. Settling you."

"How very Zen of you." She flashed him a wide, toothy smile.

"Smart-ass," he said, shaking his head. "*And* you have to promise not to overexert yourself tomorrow. You know Wilson, he'll want to take you on an 'easy two-mile hike' that will eventually turn into eight miles."

Taking the last bite of her food, she shook her head. "Oh, trust me, that won't be a problem, boss man. Pretty sure Wilson will take one look at my hiking boots and remove any kind of hiking from the agenda."

"You have hiking boots?" he asked, rising from the table as the doorbell chimed.

"Do teal-blue Chucks count?" she asked with a saccharine smile.

"Negative," he called out over his shoulder.

Moments later, Gavin was back with Xander trailing behind him. Bean grinned when she spied the paper bag from the local grocery store in his hands.

She rose and grabbed a bowl and spoon. "Xander, you know you're my favorite, right?"

"What? No bowls for us?" Gavin teased.

Bean snorted as she eyed both him and Xander up and down before grabbing the bag of ice cream from Xander. "Please. Like you two eat this delicious, amazing garbage. You two"—she waved the ice cream spade at them before turning back to the counter to scoop her dessert—"are the my-body-is-my-temple types. So more tasty goodness for me."

"From where I'm standing, B," Xander said, "ice cream seems to be doing you well."

Irritation flooded Gavin's senses as Xander gave Bean a long, leisurely look. Without thought, he punched his friend in the arm. Hard. *The fuck?* he mouthed.

"You're sweet, Xan," Bean said, her back still to them as she placed the two gallons into the freezer. Turning, she walked past, overflowing bowl in hand, and playfully smacked Xander on the cheek. "A liar, but still sweet."

Xander laughed and took the seat next to her at the kitchen table.

Gavin frowned. She should have smacked the fucker harder.

"You know, Bean, in all the years we've known each other," Xander said, his tone deceptively casual with that obnoxious aw-shucks bullshit out in full force, "I don't think I've ever seen you so . . . relaxed."

Taking a bite of her cookies and cream ice cream, she shrugged. "I love my heels and pencil skirts as much as the next girl, but eating a delicious home-cooked dinner and ice cream calls for cozy clothes."

While a part of Gavin preened at her complimenting the dinner he'd made, he also knew the shit she usually ate. The bar was so damn low. Still . . .

"I'm starving. You have any leftovers?" Xander asked as a cell phone rang in the living room.

"Sorry, that's mine," Bean said, rising and wiping her mouth with a napkin. "Be right back."

As she hurried out of the kitchen, Gavin caught the direction of Xander's gaze—Bean's legs and ass—and leaned over the table. "Stop eye-fucking her," he hissed.

Xander's jaw dropped. "What?"

Growing anger had his insides vibrating. "I said," he growled through clenched teeth, "stop. Eye-fuc—"

"I heard what you said, asshole." Xander rolled his eyes. That damn smarmy grin Gavin was too familiar with lifted his friend's lips. "One, I'm not. I was literally just looking at her since she was speaking. You know, that's what normal people do when having a conversation. And two, even if I were, why the fuck is it your concern?"

Gavin's fists clenched. He leaned back in his seat and crossed his arms over his chest. It was either that or strangle his friend. "Because it's fucking disrespectful. This is *Bean* we're talking about, and you don't—"

"That was MacKay," the woman in question said as she reentered the kitchen. "He's going to call you in half an hour, boss, to talk about Tiny coming on full-time."

Gavin nodded but didn't take his gaze off Xander. The fucker's smarmy grin was now a full-on smirk.

Bean cleared her throat. Loudly. "Whoa, boys. I don't know what happened in the thirty seconds I was gone, but knock it off."

Gavin turned his attention to Bean, who continued to eat her ice cream while side-eyeing them.

"Yes, ma'am," Xander said with an easy grin. "And there's nothing to worry about. The boss just got his panties in a twist. For no damn reason. Isn't that right, Frazier?"

Gavin narrowed his eyes at the challenge he saw in his

friend's gaze. However, there was also enough humor staring back at him to make him wonder if he'd read Xander wrong. If he'd jumped to conclusions. If he'd just made a complete ass of himself.

He lifted his chin at Xander and turned to Bean. "We're good. Nothing to worry about." She looked at him like she didn't quite believe him. "Really, B."

While Xander fixed himself a plate of chicken and rice, Bean updated them on Tiny joining the fold. It was a move Gavin was completely on board with, not only because she would be going dark for the next day or two, but in general.

Guilt turned his stomach. She'd passed out. He had no doubt that exhaustion had played a significant role. She'd been burning the candle at both ends, and yet they'd kept piling more shit onto her already full plate. He wasn't sure he'd ever forgive himself for not seeing it sooner.

"That's great you're getting some backup," Xander said, digging into his food. "That'll come in handy, especially this weekend."

She sat up straighter, and that curious sparkle lit her eyes.

Gavin inwardly cringed. *Curious sparkle?* Holy shit, what was wrong with him?

"When I was with the McClintocks earlier, Edward and I briefly talked about the event this Saturday night." Xander glanced at Gavin. "You're going, right?"

"Their family charity thing?" Gavin asked.

Xander nodded. "Edward said he's going to call you about it. He has a colleague who'll be there who's interested in retaining Hudson."

"Pretty sure it's on my calendar," Gavin said. He hated events like these. While he appreciated that these types of events raised money for various charities, they always came across as pretentious. The people who attended and donated heavily had more money than God. Couldn't they just write a check and call it done? Why spend tens of thousands of dollars on a fancy venue and catering? Oh, that's right. Because those same people who donated needed the look-at-me! affirmation of knowing they were better than everyone else.

Jaded and cynical? Absolutely. But was he wrong? Not at all.

"You have to bring a plus-one, though," Xander said.

He frowned. "Why?"

Xander sighed and pushed his empty plate to the side. "Because for obvious reasons, Edward and Rita won't be attending anymore. Edward's sister runs the family's charity and wants you and your guest at the family table in place of Edward and Rita."

Gavin's lips pressed together. "Still not seeing why I need a plus-one."

Xander rolled his eyes. "Because the sister wants even numbers at the tables."

He blinked. Twice. "You're kidding."

"Wish I was, brother. Wish I was." Xander's mouth scrunched as if he'd bitten into something sour. "Constance —the sister—came to the hospital and threw a damn hissy fit when she heard Edward and Rita weren't going."

Bean's jaw dropped. "Their kid's in the *hospital*. Of course they aren't going to a freaking party."

"Right?" Xander shook his head.

Her face scrunched. "Well, I'm not exactly surprised. Even though Constance Whitcomb is Edward's sister, she's also the society trophy wife of old Seattle money Roger Whitcomb who's twice her age. On top of that, she has a reputation of sleeping with her staff, firing them, and then threatening to sue them."

It was Gavin's turn to have his jaw drop. "How do you know that?"

"It's amazing what you can find when you dive deep enough." Bean shrugged. "When Anson was kidnapped, you wanted me to do a deep dive into all of McClintock's associates. Not only is she Edward's sister, but she's the president of the family's foundation and basically the definition of ick."

"Well, she's also batshit nuts," Xander said, tilting back in his chair. "She wouldn't shut the fuck up—and I'm talking screaming in a goddamn pediatric hospital—until Edward agreed to have you and your guest at their table."

Gavin's mouth hung open. "That's the stupidest thing I've ever heard."

"Agreed. However, Constance made sure to tell me to tell you that she is looking forward to seeing you. She specifically wanted me to mention that she's seating you right next to her." Xander shuddered. "Aside from the colleague who wants to meet you, I think Edward's going to offer to pay you to go to the event too. Generally, I'd recommend that it wouldn't be necessary, but . . ." He made a face. "If you're seated next to that woman, I'd ask him for hazard pay."

"I'll take your recommendation under advisement." Gavin chuckled and lifted his chin at Bean. "Want to go on Saturday?"

She snorted. "Negative, boss man. That's Esme's thing. She's much better at playing nice. As an extra bonus, she can also be your personal security for the night and protect you from Constance. Besides"—a look of disgust crossed her face—"I'm liable to dump a glass of wine over that batshit woman's head on principle."

"Good point," Gavin said with a forced smile.

"But you better start sucking up to Esme ASAP, or she'll ditch you and make you fend for yourself with that woman."

"Ha ha," Gavin replied, deadpan.

Damn. What the hell had he been thinking asking B to go with him?

He always took Esme to these types of events. His director of logistics was a former CIA operative and had the uncanny ability to spot a fraud from across a crowded room. She could also schmooze with the best of them. So why the hell did he think bringing B would make the event more enjoyable, more fun?

It's a work *event, Frazier, not a goddamn social hour.*

He shook his head at his lapse, but not before he caught Xander's smirk.

CHAPTER SEVEN

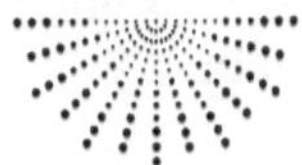

"We have a couple different outdoor tactical survival classes. The one we offer to the general public is pretty straightforward—fire, shelter, food."

"Nope," Bean said, shaking her head at Bennett Wilson. "There's nothing straightforward about any of that. I'm going to need you to expound a little, my friend."

It wasn't a lie. Strolling next to the man, they couldn't have been more different. Wilson looked like the stereotypical former military outdoorsman in his black quick-dry short-sleeve top, shitkickers, and olive-green tactical pants with full pockets. On the opposite side of the spectrum, she donned a slouchy black-and-white striped T-shirt, a pair of teal Converse, and her favorite black Lululemon leggings with her phone and ChapStick in the pocket.

When she'd arrived at the Hudson Tactical facility that morning, Wilson had taken one look at her, shaken his head, and muttered something about the half-mile trail loop. Not that she was complaining. Not at all. The last thing she wanted was to go on any sort of multi-mile nature trek with Rambo.

She walked slowly, knowing Wilson was too much of a nice guy to force her to pick up the pace. It wasn't that her head was hurting or anything, it was that she was—as much as she didn't want to admit it—terribly, terribly out of shape. Her colleagues were all avid outdoorspeople, so she'd heard about this trailhead and how it split. One way circled the base of the hill, the other went up. Straight freaking up with some switchbacks thrown in.

No, thank you.

"Right, forgot who I was talking to for a second," Wilson said with a chuckle. "All right, desk jockey. We focus on making fire without matches, creating shelter—including clothing and blankets, if needed—from available materials, locating water, identifying edible plants, making tools to hunt, along with how to hunt and make traps. Also, using materials"—he waved at the forest surrounding them—"for basic first aid supplies. Splints, tourniquets, bandages . . . That kind of thing."

She blinked. Holy crap. None of that sounded like a good time. "And the *not* straightforward class?"

"It's part of the Hudson Tactical program and geared mostly toward law enforcement types, but we do get a number of search and rescue crews as well. It includes everything I just mentioned, plus more in-depth survival skills."

"That sounds lovely and all, but . . ." She made a circular motion with her hand. "I'd like 'in-depth survival skills' in regular words, please."

"We teach various ways of evading capture, escaping a hostile environment should you find yourself captured, defense, and weapon creation." He glanced around, and a gleam lit his dark eyes. "There are tons of weapons to be had out in nature."

"You're talking about booby traps and stuff."

"Yeah. And stuff." He shot her a wink. "We also work on

firearm safety because this type of environment is different. We do low-light no-light training, but we save that for last."

She frowned. "Why?"

"Because if they don't get everything down first, no way in hell are we trusting people with weapons when it's dark, Simunition rounds or not." When she tilted her head in confusion, he clarified, "Non-lethal bullets that are basically like paintball rounds."

She stared at him for a moment, absorbing all the info he'd spewed. "Not going to lie, Wilson. All of that kind of freaks me out. I mean, aside from all the"—she waved her hands in front of her—"stuff. What if someone gets lost during the training?" Because she'd one hundred percent be that person.

He flashed her a grin. "That's exactly why you should take the class. That way, the *stuff* and the possibility of getting lost won't freak you out. You'd be prepared for whatever happens. Also, this entire area is monitored with game cams. All of Hudson Security's property is fenced in."

She frowned. "I thought the game cams only monitor the property boundary lines?"

"They used to, but we added a shit ton more a couple months ago. Frazier probably didn't mention it to you since cyber already monitors the feeds, and you have bigger shit to deal with. Besides, the perimeter security fence has pass-through points." He chuckled when her frown deepened. "There are areas of the fence that allow wildlife to pass through without injury. With the additional cameras, we no longer have blind spots, and the pass-through points are heavily monitored with giant, obvious cameras. So if anyone ever gets lost on our property or enters without permission, we'd be able to find them. See? Safe. So what do you say? Can I sign you up?"

"Thanks, but desk jockey, remember?" She tapped her

chest with her finger. "As pretty as all this nature stuff is, I have *zero* plans to be hanging out in the great outdoors. I'll be fine."

Wilson began walking back toward the trailhead. "Hey, you never know, Bean. What if the helo you're in goes down?"

She scoffed. "The only chopper I'm in is being driven by Owen—"

"Flown," he cut in.

She rolled her eyes. "Whatever. But if the helicopter I'm in goes down—with *Owen* at the helm—then we've got much bigger problems than the wilderness. Because we'll be in tiny, itty-bitty pieces."

Wilson laughed. "Point to you."

"Exactly. The only way Hadley Owen—one of only three female Night Stalker pilots our country's produced—is going down is if a missile or something equally crazy happens."

"Still, you should try it. It's actually lots of fun. We have a regular survival class this Saturday you could join. Frazier did say you were going to sign up."

She knew she was looking at Wilson like he'd grown a second head. She couldn't help it. "Frazier's delusional. And so are you if you think—"

"Hey, that's just what I was told." He held up his hands in mock innocence.

Bean's cell phone rang, and she'd never been more grateful. "Oh, would you look at that! We're back in cell phone range."

Wilson shook his head and knocked her on the shoulder.

She chuckled as she answered her phone. "What's up, Esme?"

"What are you doing? Well, first, how are you feeling?"

"Fine. Except I've been banned from the office today and

have been relegated to being tortured by Wilson in the forest."

Wilson scoffed beside her. "We're barely on the trail. And it wouldn't be torture if you knew how to navigate the woods properly."

She rolled her eyes as Esme laughed.

"The man does have a point," the other woman said. "Do you even own hiking boots, B?"

"You're breaking up. I can barely hear you," Bean said, deadpan.

Esme laughed harder and then coughed. Horribly.

Bean winced. "You okay, Es?"

"What are you doing hanging with Wilson?"

It didn't escape her notice that her friend had avoided answering. But she'd go with it. For now. "I'm looking at Tactical's outdoor survival classes and giving feedback to the boss from a regular person's point of view. But the more I hear about the classes, the less I'm inclined to actually do one."

"It's a really great class," Esme said. "You should totally do it."

"Yeah, but you know me. I'm strictly an indoorsy sort. There's not much motivation for me to try one out, you know? I mean Wilson's cute and all, but he's not *that* cute."

"Hey!" the man in question protested as she teasingly elbowed him in the side.

"I'm pretty sure my mishap yesterday freaked out the boss man. I think this is his misguided way of trying to help me find my Zen. Something about the healing power of nature . . ." Bean scrunched her forehead. "Or was it balance?" She shrugged. "Whatever, I'm plenty balanced already."

Wilson snorted, and Bean shot him a glare. At the same time, Esme scoffed, "Uh, *right*."

"Neither one of you jerks is at all funny," Bean grumbled.

Esme laughed and broke out into a hacking cough again.

Bean pulled her phone from her ear and held it up, looking at Wilson in concern.

He cringed and called out, "You sound like shit, Esme."

Bean put the phone back to her ear. "You sound terrible. Are you okay?"

"That's why I'm calling," she said, her voice raspy. "I just got off the phone with Frazier and wanted to give you a heads-up. I have a bit of pneumonia and—"

"A *bit* of pneumonia?" Bean's eyes widened. "Holy shit, have you been to the doctor?"

"Yes, Mom." Esme sighed. "I'll be down for at least the next couple days, so I'm not going to be able to join Frazier at the charity event on Saturday."

Tingles of trepidation inched up Bean's spine. "*And?*"

"And I suggested he take you instead. In fact, I have a delivery scheduled to arrive at the office later today for you. There are a few dress options. I included shoes, jewelry, and all the other accessories. Pick an outfit, and you can be my stand-in."

Bean closed her eyes, took a deep breath in, counted to ten, and let it out. "Esme, you know what I dislike more than nature?"

"Crowds. I know. But you'll be fine." Bean could practically see Esme dismissing her concern with a wave of her hand. "It's work, just a run-of-the-mill charity event. You don't even have to go as *you*. Consider it an undercover thing. You and Frazier have plenty of time to come up with some sort of cover identity and a good backstory. Besides, who else is he going to bring?"

"Uh, how about *anyone* else?"

"Sorry, but I talked it over with him, and I think you're the best fit. It'll be fine." Esme paused as another round of coughing overtook her. "Now, the delivery is scheduled for this afternoon. I think the black dress would be best, but the light-gray would work as well. I've also booked you at the resort for Saturday morning for hair, makeup, and all that primping shit. I'll email you the detailed schedule once we get off the phone. Once you get a chance to look everything over, let me know if there are any questions." Bean opened her mouth to protest, but before she could utter a word, Esme started speaking again. "We'll talk more this afternoon, B. In the meantime, make sure you tell Wilson to take it easy on you. Later."

Three beeps indicated Esme had hung up, and for a moment, Bean could only stare at her phone. Holy shit. What just happened?

"Damn." Wilson ran a hand over his jaw. She was pretty sure he was fighting a smile. "Esme's not our director of logistics for nothing, right?"

She met his gaze. "You said there's a survival class starting on Saturday, right?"

With a laugh, Wilson patted her back. "You'll be fine. I'm sure Esme has every contingency covered. And then some."

Nerves took root in her gut. She'd have a fake identity so she wouldn't have to be herself. That was good, right? With the nature of her work, it was safest for her to stay in the shadows. And frankly, she enjoyed it there. Always had. But this? This was *way* out of her comfort zone.

Fancy ballrooms, hobnobbing, and making small talk. It brought back memories she'd rather forget. To a time when she hadn't been allowed to hide in the shadows, but rather had been paraded like a sideshow act, like the oddity she was. To when she'd constantly tried to pretend to be someone she wasn't. And failed. Time and time again.

The nerves in her gut bloomed.

In comparison to the charity event, Wilson's outdoor survival class didn't sound so bad after all . . .

CHAPTER EIGHT

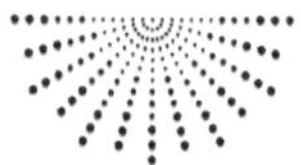

Gavin polished off his second piece of banana bread and leaned back in his chair, stifling a yawn. He didn't usually need much sleep, but today, he was wiped. When he'd first gotten out of the Army, nightmares had plagued him. Over the years, they'd eased—only resurfacing from time to time—but by then, four to five hours of sleep had become a habit. Anson McClintock's rescue had stirred the nightmares back up. Add in having Bean under his roof, and it was no wonder he'd had a nearly sleepless night.

Downing the last of his coffee, he eyed the lone mini-blueberry scone remaining on their table's serving platter, but he figured the ham and Gruyere quiche in the display case was probably a better bet. After the sugar overload, some protein would balance him out. Good thing he'd already logged in a couple of hours at the gym this morning.

"I can see you eyeing something, mister," Roxie Buchanan said, patting him on the shoulder. "What else can I get you?"

Gavin grinned at the owner of Comfort Food, a café in Hudson Island's quaint downtown that was one of his favorite places to eat. The woman was also the very pregnant wife of his good friend and colleague, Joe Buchanan, who ran Hudson Tactical.

"How about a slice of the ham quiche, but to go?" Seeing as it was nearly noon, he'd bet a hundred bucks that Bean was on her third energy drink by now. "Make it two slices but boxed separately." He turned and eyed the case again. "And a couple slices of the blueberry pie."

"You got it," Roxie said with a chipper smile as she made her way back to the counter.

"Thanks, Roxie. And there's no rush," Gavin called after her, concerned that her walk was now more of a waddle.

"Getting extra grub to save for later?" Xander asked from across the table. "Or are you sharing with a certain someone?"

The fuck? He glared at his friend.

When the rest of their table's occupants—Buchanan, Matt Alvarez, and Cade de la Rosa—swung their gazes his way, he groaned. "Fucking hell, Xan. Really?"

His friend shot him a shit-eating grin and waggled his eyebrows.

"And who the hell is this certain someone?" Buchanan asked before turning to Alvarez, another colleague at Hudson Security, and Cade, Gavin's business partner at Hudson Tactical, who was also the co-owner of De La Rosa Gym. "You guys know anything about this?"

"No, but I can make an educated guess," Alvarez answered. A small smile played on his face before he turned somber. "How is Bean? She doing okay?"

"Wait," Cade interjected. "What happened to Bean?"

"Rumor is that she fainted and knocked her face on the edge of her desk," Alvarez replied, grimacing.

Gavin frowned. "How the hell do you know that?"

Alvarez stared at him like he was a moron. "We have a small office, dude. And it's not like you guys are quiet talkers.

Besides, when Doc showed up yesterday, it got everyone's attention. When you took Bean home early, Mel was at the front desk and was worried. Said B had quite the bruise on her face. Not to mention you had Owen fly Doc to Port Townsend to drop off B's blood work." Alvarez snagged the last remaining scone, broke it in half, and popped one of the pieces into his mouth. "See, this is why you pay me the big bucks," he said around his bite of food. "For my top-notch investigative skills."

Gavin shook his head. Alvarez had been a detective with the Seattle Police Department before recently joining their team at Hudson Security. While Alvarez did indeed have top-notch investigative skills, the current scenario was due to Gavin, in fact, being a moron. His actions yesterday hadn't been subtle. At all. But he didn't regret any of it as the worry and panic he'd felt at seeing Bean's bruised face was still fresh in his mind.

"Fine," Gavin said. "I'm bringing food back for Bean, because God knows what shit she's eaten today. She claimed she didn't have a headache this morning, but she's still banned from working in her office today." He glanced at Buchanan. "Your dad's swinging by later this afternoon to check her out to make sure there's no concussion and go over the results of her blood work."

"That's sweet of you," Xander said, that stupid grin still on his face.

"It's the least I can do for her, you fucker," Gavin grumbled. "We pile so much shit on her plate, and she *always* gets everything done without complaint. I can at least bring her some goddamn food. Don't read more into it."

Xander leaned back in his chair with a furrowed brow. "What the hell's that quote, you guys? The Shakespeare one? Something about protesting too much?"

A chorus of chuckles sounded around the table. He flipped them all off. Fuckers.

"All right," Cade said, rising. Along with running De La Rosa Gym with his brother, he was also a former MMA world champion and now one of the top MMA trainers in the world. "I have to head over to the Seattle gym for the weekend, but I have three of my coaches on Tactical's schedule for the hand-to-hand training for the group coming in tomorrow. Is three good, or do you need another?"

"Thanks, man," Buchanan said. "It's a group of about twenty from a few different sheriff's offices in Eastern Washington, so your three guys should be fine."

"Cool. Thanks for the food, Frazier," Cade said with a chin lift. "I'll see you guys next week."

As everyone said their goodbyes, Gavin reveled in the competency of the men around him. When he stepped away from the Army, he'd been at a loss about what to do. The skills he was adept in, things he had been trained for, didn't translate to the civilian world. Hudson Security had been born out of still wanting to make a difference, but without the bureaucratic bullshit. At first, it had just been him. He was a control freak to his very core, but he'd added trustworthy people slowly. One at a time. Now, here he was. Immensely proud of not only how far Hudson Security had come, but how Hudson Tactical was standing on its own.

With just Alvarez and Xander left at the table with him—Buchanan had wandered to the Comfort Food offices to check in with his wife—Gavin said, "So there's been a change of plans with the McClintock charity event this Saturday."

"Everything okay?" Xander asked.

"Esme's sick. Pneumonia. She's arranged for Bean to go with me to the event. And before you say anything"—he gave Xander a pointed stare—"I haven't run any of this by B yet."

"Are you sure that's a good idea?" Alvarez asked, concern evident on his expression. "We keep her under wraps."

That was one hundred percent true. Bean's technical title was IT Specialist. However, they made no mention of her on the company website, nor did they mention any of her skills to clients. Ever. She was completely behind the scenes. Not only for her own safety, but for Hudson Security's safety as well.

In fact, Gavin was pretty sure her legal name was under wraps too. He and MacKay knew. Esme knew since hiring fell under her umbrella. But he was pretty sure their colleagues didn't know B's first name was actually Sabrina. To everyone both inside and outside of their organization, she was simply Bean.

"We still will. That's where I need your help." Gavin wouldn't do anything to risk Bean's anonymity. "We need a cover—a plausible and simple identity for her. A legit reason for her to be there with me last minute instead of Esme."

"Well, why exactly are you going?" Alvarez asked. "You usually push off the charity event things."

Gavin nodded. He sure as shit did. "I was initially invited by Edward McClintock. At the time, he was considering us for some cybersecurity at one of his start-ups. Then the shit with his kid went down. I was going to bail on the entire thing since Edward and Rita aren't going anymore, but I spoke with him yesterday, and he wants me to meet one of his business partners. Esme was going to scope things out as well, get a feel for the partner."

"I'd say Bean's a good judge of character," Alvarez said. "Maybe not as savvy as Esme, but with what she does, she can definitely see through bullshit pretty well."

"True," Xander chimed in. "But she's always observing over cameras. Never in person. You think she'll agree to go? I mean, she's not exactly a fan of . . . people."

Gavin shrugged. "We're keeping Esme's name on the RSVP info. That way, if Bean doesn't go, it's no big deal."

Alvarez ran a hand over his chin. "Then why bother bringing her in the first place? Like Xander said, she's not exactly what anyone would call a people person."

"I'm supposed to bring a plus-one to keep the table numbers even." The second the words left Gavin's mouth, he fought a cringe. And failed. The words sounded even dumber out loud than in his head.

"Bullshit. More like you're afraid of Constance Whitcomb." Xander snorted and turned to Alvarez. "She's the head of the McClintock Family Foundation. You were in Seattle for forever. Do you know her?"

"Oh, *everyone* at the Seattle PD knows who she is." Alvarez chuckled with a grimace. "When I was there, she was a big supporter of the department. She was a fan of the younger detectives, and I had a few colleagues who knew her *quite* well."

"Not you?" Xander asked.

Alvarez shook his head. "Not that it mattered to Constance, but I was married to my ex back then. And frankly, the woman was always a little too . . . predatory. Not my thing."

"I just met her the other day, and I get you," Xander said. "I wouldn't touch her with a ten-foot pole. Hell, *Carmichael* wouldn't touch her—and believe me, she sure as shit tried with him—and that guy will bang any woman with a pulse." He nodded at Gavin. "Pretty sure Constance has her sights set on this one. Purposely seated him next to her."

Alvarez let out a low whistle. "Good luck, brother. Too bad about Esme. She would have held that woman at bay for you. As for Bean, just say she's your girlfriend—not that that alone will deter Constance—but it will give you a good excuse to reject her advances."

"Yeah," Xander said, that smarmy fucking smirk on his face. "Have B act as your girlfriend."

Gavin shook his head. That's the *last* thing he wanted to do. After spending the last evening with her, after having her in his home, things were . . . off between them.

Correction: things were off with *him*.

Bean treated him like she'd always treated him. Like a friend and colleague who she could give shit to without any worries he'd get offended. But now, when he looked at her—hell, when he *thought* of her—he pictured her seated at his kitchen table, dressed in little cotton sleep shorts and her sweatshirt hanging off her shoulder looking so . . .

He didn't even know what. But whatever it was, it was so damn alluring and tempting and completely fucking inappropriate.

"No," Gavin finally said, shaking his head, trying to dislodge that fascinating image of Bean. No luck. "That would be uncomfortable for her." Not to mention him.

"*Right*." Xander rolled his eyes.

Gavin was tempted to flip his friend off, but before he could, Alvarez pointed between him and Xander. "I don't know what the fuck this is about. Nor do I want to know. So let's focus." Alvarez leaned on the table with his elbows. "Since Frazier's determined to make this more complicated than necessary, let's come up with a simple backstory that Bean will actually agree to. Shall we?"

Gavin was grateful for Alvarez's redirect.

More specifically, he was grateful to get Xander's attention off him. His friend was perceptive and had uncanny instincts. It was one of the things that had kept Xan in one piece when he'd been a Special Forces operative, and what made him an elite security specialist and invaluable member of the Hudson Security team.

Gavin prided himself on keeping everything close to the

vest. But Xander had been there last night when Bean had had him completely out of sorts. For all the shit his friend was throwing his way, Gavin had no doubt Xander had seen every second of it.

As much as he didn't want to admit it, something had happened yesterday. Bean getting hurt had him seeing her—his longtime friend, trusted colleague, and employee—in a completely new light. A bright and intriguing new light . . .

Not good. This was not good at all.

CHAPTER NINE

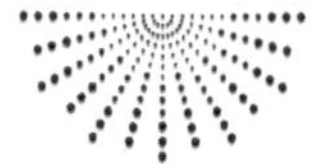

Bean glanced up at the quick rap on her door. A split second later, it opened, and Gavin walked in. He came to an abrupt halt, a frown growing on his face.

"Why are you at your computer?"

She swiveled in her chair to face him and held back an eye roll. Barely. "Because Doc just left and gave me the all clear." She waved at her monitors. "I'm catching up on some additional background checks for the McClintock security candidates."

He stepped into her office and closed the door behind him. Leaning back against the closed door, he crossed his arms over his chest. His frown deepened.

She waited for him to say something.

Anything.

But nothing. *Okay . . .*

"Did you need something, boss? Because"—she tilted her head toward her workstation—"I have stuff piled up."

He straightened and shifted on his feet. She arched an eyebrow. *What is his deal?*

"I need you to come with me to a fundraising event on

Saturday night. It's over in Seattle. Owen's flying us over so we can be down and back that evening."

"Why?" From her earlier conversation with Esme, she knew her friend was sick, but Bean was still unsure why she needed to go. When she'd tried to call Esme back for clarification, the call had been pushed to voicemail.

"It's a long, stupid story, but I need to bring someone. Esme's sick. She and I talked and think you're the best person to bring."

Again, she waited for him to clarify.

And again, nothing.

"You didn't answer my question, boss man." Suspicion tickled her spine, and she tilted her head to the side. "Why?"

He raked a hand through his dark hair. "To meet a potential client. To get your opinion on the situation."

She frowned. Esme had made no mention of meeting a potential client. That was *not* her area of expertise. At all. Taking a deep breath, she forced her expression to relax. She turned back to her monitors, dismissing him. "No."

For a few heartbeats, there was blessed silence.

"No?" Gavin sputtered. "But, B, I—"

"But nothing, Frazier," she said, opening an encrypted search engine. "Meeting clients isn't my thing. Take someone else."

"There is no one else."

The desperation in his voice had her turning to him. "Sure there is. Xander, Wilson, Tash, any of the Tactical guys. Hell, bring Mel."

He gave her a get-real look. "Be serious. Besides, Tash is on assignment, and even if she weren't, she sticks out like a sore thumb. And Mel . . ." He shook his head. "That would just be weird."

This time, her eyes rolled. "We've known each other a long time, right, boss?" She didn't give him a chance to answer. "In all that time, have I ever volunteered to go to any social function that included clients?" She waited a split second before she rushed on. "The answer is no. I don't people well. You know this about me."

The look on his face spoke volumes. He thought she was being dramatic. "You people just fine, Bean."

She shook her head.

"Please, B?" he asked, meeting her gaze. "I'd like you there because this client doesn't know you, doesn't know you're a part of Hudson Security." He held up a hand to stall the question on the tip of her tongue. "We can come up with a cover for you, but I'd really value your opinion on this potential client."

She leaned back in her chair and crossed her arms over her chest. "Who's the potential client?"

He shrugged. "Not sure. All I know is it's a colleague and possible business partner of McClintock's. He was vague on their exact connection and didn't give me their name, said they want anonymity until we meet."

She arched her eyebrow. Seriously? "That sounds a bit dramatic, don't you think?"

He nodded, and she pursed her lips in thought, recalling the info she'd pulled up earlier on Edward McClintock. "He has a few start-ups going and a couple in the pipeline. There's a handful of different business partners I know he's working with. I can run them all for you if that would be helpful."

"It would. Thank you." He settled at the edge of her desk. "But I'd really appreciate you coming with me so you can see this person face-to-face. You have a good bullshit detector, and I'd really like your help. Please."

She stared at him for a moment. Gavin Frazier rarely asked for help. The man just belted out orders and delegated.

Everything else, he took care of himself. This asking-for-help business . . .

Bean let out an exasperated sigh. "Fine. You owe me, though. Big-time."

The corners of his lips twitched as he rose. "Thank you."

"Wait," she called out as he made his way to her office door. "Esme said she's sending me dresses and stuff. I assume this is a formal event?"

Gavin nodded. "I'll be in a tux. I talked with her earlier this morning, and she was confident you'd agree to go."

"Obviously." She chuckled. "I talked to her this morning too, and she'd already sent the packages here."

He shook his head, humor lighting his face. "Of course she did. Sick and all, she said she's working on our itineraries and will send them to us by end of day." He opened his mouth to say something else but immediately slammed it shut. The wrinkle between his brows popped.

Her eyes narrowed. He was usually calm, steady, and to the point, but he was being . . . weird now.

Clearing his throat, he ran his hand over his jaw. "Thanks, B." Before she could acknowledge his comment, he was out the door, closing it softly behind him.

If she didn't know better, she'd say the man had been uncomfortable, borderline awkward. But this was *Gavin Frazier* she was talking about. The man was never uncomfortable. He was scary efficient, beyond intense, and a super alpha control freak.

Turning back to her monitors, she shook her head. It must have been her imagination.

CHAPTER TEN

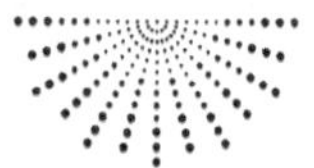

Bean was trying to hold on to her irritation, but it was slipping away.

She usually spent her Saturdays working in the comfort of her own home in sweatpants or leggings with zero need to dress professionally. There were no colleagues dropping in with last-minute requests, and she was able to work at her own pace, at her own leisure.

But no.

Esme had booked her Saturday solid. Down to fifteen-minute increments. Being a control freak herself, it was annoying simply because it wasn't a schedule of her own making. And she hated being on other people's schedules. But Bean went with it because she was too afraid to get on Esme's bad side, and it meant she didn't have to deal with Gavin.

Yesterday had been a Friday from hell. Quite possibly the longest day of her life. The guy had taken grumpy to a whole new stratosphere, and he'd been blowing up her phone with message after message about the charity event tonight ever since four this morning. This was *exactly* why she left this kind of stuff to Esme.

But now her phone was on silent, tucked away in the women's locker room at the Pacific View Resort, a world-renowned luxury wellness resort located on the north-western tip of Hudson Island. A guy named Sergio was adding pressure to her right trapezius muscle. Letting out a breath, she sank her face deeper into the head cradle. He'd been massaging her upper back for the last thirty minutes, and she was having a hard time remembering why she was so annoyed.

"You should really make massages a regular thing," Sergio murmured. "You carry an incredible amount of tension in your shoulders. And since you sit at a desk all day, your lower back is extremely tight as well."

"Talk to my boss," she said with a sigh.

Oh, yes. *That* was why she was annoyed. Her boss.

After her outdoor excursion with Wilson Thursday morning, she had met with Doc at her office. With the headaches gone and no signs of a concussion, he'd given Bean the all clear to go back to work. However, he'd informed her that her blood work showed that she was anemic. He'd given her an iron supplement, a not-so-gentle lecture on her diet, and orders to take regular breaks so she didn't work herself into more fainting episodes. Seeing as she didn't want to smack her face on the corner of her desk again, she'd readily agreed.

Then, after she'd spoken with Gavin about the charity event, the infuriating man had somehow gotten wind of the anemia thing, and the bossy man had made it his personal mission to not only be her hydration monitor, but to feed her seemingly on the hour.

The man was ridiculous.

All day Friday, every time she'd finished an energy drink,

Gavin had knocked on her door with a bottle of water and a healthy snack. But not in a nice, concerned way. No. He'd been a growly beast. A borderline jackass. Like he'd rather be doing anything else.

Every time he'd stepped into her office, he'd had some lame excuse of checking in with her on whatever project she was working on. The man wasn't a micromanager, and he sure as hell didn't micromanage *her*. She'd even double-checked the office's video feeds to make sure he wasn't spying on her, because his timing had been uncanny. Seconds after her empty energy drink hit the recycle bin, he was there. Bottle of water and snack in hand. And questions. So many damn questions about what she was working on, what was this, what was that.

Holy hell.

By late afternoon, she'd put her foot down and let him know she was done with his constant interruptions. Yes, the food had helped, and she'd actually felt better, but enough was enough. In hindsight, she supposed it was kind of him to make sure she was okay. It was sweet in a still-very-annoying kind of way.

"Whatever you're thinking, sweetie, please think of something else. Preferably something relaxing," Sergio said, his deep, melodic voice pulling her from her thoughts. "I can literally feel the tension returning to your back. We only have another hour or so before you're whisked off for more pampering, hair, and makeup."

"Sorry," she murmured, consciously relaxing her shoulders. After a few minutes, she asked, "You know Esme, right?"

"I do. She's a regular of mine."

Bean's eyes popped open, and she lifted her head from the cradle. "Esme gets regular massages?"

"She sure does. Every other Saturday." Sergio chuckled

and gently pressed her face back down into the cradle. "She called me earlier this week to let me know she's sick and sending you in her place."

It was a little presumptuous of her friend, but Bean mentally shrugged. It's not like Esme had been wrong. However, presumptuous or not, her brain had a hard time wrapping around the fact that not only did Esme—who was just as much of a workaholic as she was—get regular massages, but that she was also on the island more than Bean had realized. Her friend lived in the Seattle area and only came to the Hudson office every few weeks. Or so she'd thought.

Frowning, Bean supposed it wasn't all that much of a surprise that she was in the dark. Not really. She didn't get out of her work bubble all that often. In fact, this was the most unusual Saturday morning she'd had in a long, long time. Maybe ever.

Per Esme's detailed schedule, Bean had arrived at the Pacific View Resort's world-class spa at nine. She'd been treated to a fancy breakfast in a private room that had a spectacular panoramic view of the Puget Sound. After she'd eaten, she was taken to yet another private room, this time a Himalayan salt chamber to relax. It had taken her a few minutes for her mind to settle, but there was something about the cool, salty air combined with the heated, plush recliner that had her nearly falling asleep.

After who knows how long—there wasn't a clock in sight —she'd been brought to the eucalyptus-scented massage room she was currently in. As Sergio had said, she was scheduled for a mani-pedi, hair, makeup, and lunch. In what order? She couldn't remember. She would be done by four, which would give her enough time to get home and change before Gavin picked her up at five to take her to the company's aircraft hangar, where they had a fleet of four helicopters and three airplanes of various sizes.

Simply put, the Saturday schedule Esme had arranged for her was bananas. Because Bean's Saturdays were usually like every other day. Work. Which she was more than okay with. In fact, it's what she preferred. It's what she did. Who she was.

This? The massage, the made-to-order crepes with fresh fruit? The Himalayan freaking salt room? *Not* what she did. Ever.

A moan escaped her as Sergio dug into an especially tender spot along her side. Holy crap, maybe she needed to reevaluate adding this into her packed schedule.

She sighed under Sergio's ministrations, and her mind drifted to the conversation she'd had with Gavin about her joining him at the McClintock charity event. Her lips twitched at the recollection. He'd been surprisingly awkward. But looking back on it, she found it kind of endearing.

Awkward. Endearing. Up until this exact moment, those were two words that she'd never associated with the man. It was nice to know that beneath that intense surface, he was actually human.

Forty-five minutes later, Bean was lying on her back, letting out a deep sigh.

"How do you feel?" Sergio asked, humor lacing his words.

"Jell-O. I feel like human Jell-O." She smiled as she stretched her arms over her head. "Thank you so much. I may have to take Esme's lead and make this a regular thing."

"You absolutely should. Now, take your time. When you're ready, get up slowly. You can redress in your robe, and I'll be waiting for you outside." He gestured to the side table. "There's a bottle of water for you. Make sure you stay hydrated today."

The door closed behind Sergio, and she relaxed for a few more minutes before rising. Back in her robe and after chugging half the bottle of water, she joined her massage therapist in the hallway. He escorted her back to the private dining room she'd been in earlier.

"A light lunch will be brought in," he said. "You'll have an hour to eat and relax—or check your messages if you're anything like Esme—then the girls will be in to get you."

"Thank you again," she said before he left her alone in the room.

Moments later, two uniformed staff members brought in an amazing-looking lunch. While they set her up at a small table near the floor-to-ceiling windows, Bean excused herself and rushed to the locker room to retrieve her phone. With it tucked into the pocket of her robe, she approached her private room, and the door opened.

"Everything's set up, ma'am," the man said, holding the door open for her. "If you need anything, there's a button next to the phone. Just press it, and one of us will be right with you."

"Thank you," she said, noting the call button next to the room's landline.

"Of course. Enjoy your lunch," he said before closing the door behind him.

Bean's stomach grumbled as she looked at the spread laid out for her on the table. A BLT on thick, crusty bread and a side salad with what looked like crumbled feta. She wasn't a salad fan, but it actually looked good. Then again, cheese made everything better. Next to the glass of ice water was a dessert plate holding three small fruit tarts, with strawberries, peaches, kiwis, and blueberries creating a delicious-looking rainbow.

She settled onto the cushioned chair, not sure where to

start. A small smile lifted her lips. *Bacon. Always start with the bacon.*

Taking a bite of her sandwich, she groaned as the thick-cut bacon's salty goodness and the sweet, fresh tomatoes tickled her taste buds. As she licked the breadcrumbs from her lips, she wanted to go home and toss all her frozen meals in the trash. This simple sandwich was so, so good. After another bite, she chuckled. Yeah, right. Though she wished she could eat like this every day, the reality was that if it were left to her to prepare meals like this for herself—as simple as the food seemed—she'd starve.

Munching on her lunch, Bean did what she did best. Multitasked. She grabbed her phone and replied to countless emails and texts as she ate. Maybe one day she'd come back to the spa and do the full relaxation thing, but today was not that day.

After popping the final bite of the last fruit tart into her mouth, she sent Esme a text.

BEAN

Thank you for this.

ESME

Tell me the truth—you were kinda pissed at first, weren't you?

Bean grinned.

BEAN

Well, yeah! But Sergio made me forget to be annoyed with you. Holy shit, the man has magic freaking hands.

ESME

That he does.

ESME

I figured you'd be nervous about the charity event. May as well get you as relaxed as possible before you start to freak out again about tonight.

Oh, her friend knew her well.

After a moment, Bean frowned.

BEAN

I'm overthinking all of this, right? I mean, the cover story we settled on is solid and I'm just making this thing tonight a bigger deal than it really is, right?

ESME

Absolutely. I've been to so many of those types of events with Frazier that I've lost count. You smile. Nod. Shake hands. Since no one knows you're with the company, it'll be a breeze. What dress did you decide to go with?

She huffed out an exhale. Smile. Nod. Shake hands. No problem.

BEAN

They were all gorgeous, but I picked the black one.

ESME

It was the shoes, wasn't it?

Yup. Her friend knew her well.

BEAN

Uh, you paired the dress with red Ferragamo T-strap pumps. You bet your ass it was the shoes!

ESME

> Technically they're "flame red" and you're welcome. Actually, you can thank Frazier since he's footing the bill.

Chuckling, Bean's thumbs flew over her phone.

BEAN

> Even better. But seriously, thank you for arranging this.

ESME

> Of course. Now, if my schedule is being correctly followed, the resort's staff should be moving you to the next part of the itinerary soon.

A quiet knock sounded, and the door opened. Two women who looked a little bit younger than her stepped into the room. Giving them a warm smile, she shot off another text.

BEAN

> They just walked in. You're kinda scary, you know that?

ESME

> Ha! Enjoy.

BEAN

> Thanks again!

"Come on in," Bean said, silencing her ringer and tucking the phone into her robe's pocket.

"Good afternoon, Ms. Ventura. I'm Freya," the woman with shiny black hair said. "I'll be styling your hair." She gestured to the woman next to her. "This is Brynn."

"It's nice to meet you, Ms. Ventura. I'll be doing your makeup for the evening." Brynn had the most spectacular eye makeup—a shimmering shadow in an ombre of pale purple to dark plum with a perfectly winged liner.

Looking between the two, Bean nodded. She was in good hands. "It's nice to meet you both, and please just call me Bean." She wrinkled her nose. "Ms. Ventura is a bit too formal when I'm dressed in a robe."

"You got it, Bean," Freya said with a laugh as she approached. "Esme just texted us a photo of the dress you'll be wearing this evening. I have a few hair options for you to consider. Whenever you're ready, we can take a look at the different hairstyles and Brynn's makeup options to see what kind of vibe you're going for tonight. While we do our thing, the mani-pedi girls will take care of you as well."

Bean's eyes widened as she processed everything Freya had said. Esme really had thought of everything. After the last few hours at the spa, Bean had been impressed with Esme's planning. But this? This was next-level.

As nervous as she was about the event tonight, she had to admit she was excited to see what kind of glow-up Freya and Brynn could do. Taking a breath for courage, Bean stood. "Great. Let's do this."

Three hours later, her nails were done, and her hair had been trimmed, washed, dried, and styled. Makeup had been artfully applied and set. She'd even been given a small clutch of products so she could touch up her makeup throughout the evening.

Bean stared slack-jawed at herself in the mirror. Letting out an astonished exhale, she turned to the left and then to the right, studying her face and hair from every angle.

Yes, she dressed professionally pretty much every day. She knew she could rock a pencil skirt and heels with the best of them. But this? This was one thousand percent ridiculous. Her hair fell around her in loose, soft waves, and her makeup was immaculate. There were no traces of the lingering bruises on her face. Her eyes had a subtle smoky look that wasn't too overdone but also had just the right amount of oomph. If she were being honest . . . she looked fantastic.

Yup. Forget the title of Director of Logistics. Esme was an absolute magician.

CHAPTER ELEVEN

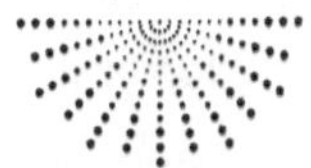

Gavin climbed the steps to Bean's front door and scowled. Her front door was ajar, and he could hear some bass-heavy pop song blaring. After ringing the doorbell —not that it would do any good since the music was so damn loud—he let himself in.

"Bean!" he shouted, hoping she'd hear him. Doubtful, since he could barely hear himself.

Her house had a similar layout to his. It opened into a great room with an open kitchen to the left and a living area to the right. The stark difference was that where his television was set up, she had a seven-screen workstation that was nearly identical to her office setup. Spotting her portable speaker on the coffee table, he made his way to it and lowered the volume. How the hell she listened to this crappy music, he had no clue.

"Oh, hey!"

He spun at her voice, and his mind went blank.

Gone were the thoughts of giving her shit for her taste in music. Gone were the thoughts of lecturing her on leaving her door not only unlocked, but open. Gone were the thoughts of their plan for the evening. Hell, he wasn't even sure what the hell his own name was.

Because holy shit . . .

She looked fucking amazing.

When his brain finally became unscrambled—well, less scrambled—he took her in one more time. Seeing her dressed up shouldn't be a surprise. He'd seen her dressed in her fitted skirts, silk blouses, and sky-high heels countless times. As much as he hated to admit it, she had the hot librarian thing down pat.

This was different.

The front of her black dress had a high neckline and long sleeves, but with each step she took, it showed off a surprisingly high slit that damn near went up to her right hip. Not to mention her bright-red heels did amazing things to her already fabulous legs and—

Wait. No. Shit.

"You know, you shouldn't leave your front door unlocked or hanging wide open." He inwardly cringed. As far as segues went, that was shit. So was his tone. He probably should have started with a simple hello, but the synapses in his brain weren't firing.

Her eyes rolled as she waved him off. "Calm down, caveman. I didn't open it until I got the notification that you were coming up the driveway."

Turning her back to him, she made her way toward her workstation on the opposite side of the living room. And he nearly swallowed his tongue.

Her dress.

Fucking hell.

While the front had a high neckline and fully covered her, the back of her dress was nonexistent. Her dark-brown hair was the only thing covering her. Every inch of her creamy skin was exposed in a V that showed off where her tiny waist nipped in and dipped low into the small of her back.

Holy. Fuck.

He needed to rein in all his damn thoughts. Immediately. No more thinking of her legs. No more thinking of her dressed as a sexy librarian. And definitely no more thinking of her creamy skin and wondering if it was as soft as he thought it would be.

His dick twitched.

Shit. Focus, dammit!

She turned once again and made her way back to him carrying a slim burgundy briefcase, while that leg played peekaboo with her dress's mile-long slit.

He swallowed. Audibly.

Desperately needing a distraction, he shoved his hands into the pockets of his pants and nodded to the briefcase. "What's that?"

"Oh, just the usual." She shrugged, set it on the table next to him, and flipped the top open. "Laptop. Tablet. Comms. You know, just in case."

The intelligence shining brightly in her eyes was just as hot as her outfit. Damn. "Are you anticipating problems tonight?"

The smile she flashed him was that smart-ass and slightly condescending one he oddly enjoyed. "I never know with you, boss. I never know."

He nodded, conceding her point. It never hurt to be prepared for anything. "Are you bringing a phone?"

She scoffed. "Is that a real question?" She gestured to the table where a small, red purse sat. "My phone links to my laptop, and I have a few other small tech goodies in there. Nothing that will set off a metal detector, of course."

Of course she did. She was a badass like that.

Gorgeous and kick-ass. It was a potent combo.

He wanted to slap himself upside the head, but he couldn't focus on anything except her. Clearing his throat, he asked, "Did you eat lunch today?"

Her hands moved to her hips, and she made a growling sound. "Holy crap. Stop with that already."

"With what?" His eyes narrowed in confusion.

She dropped her head back and stared at the ceiling. She muttered something he couldn't decipher and then let out a breath as she met his gaze. "At least you seem to be done being a grumpy ass. That's a plus, I suppose."

This woman had him off-fucking-kilter. "How have I been grumpy? I'm just making sure you're fed and watered."

She glared at him as he cringed. "Like livestock?"

Yeah . . . The second the words had left his mouth, he'd known he'd fucked up. But the way her cheeks flushed pink with irritation was mesmerizing.

He couldn't help himself. Like the immature dumbass he was, he had to poke at her a little more. "I don't know why you're being so sensitive, B."

Slapping the lid of the briefcase shut, she stomped toward him. "Keep talking, bud, and I'm going to bash you. Over. Your. Damn. Head."

Each of her final words were punctuated by a jab of her finger. He was itching to grab hold of that finger and pull her closer. See what she'd do then. "I'd like to see you try."

She leaned closer and narrowed her eyes. "Don't tempt me, boss man."

His lips kicked up in a smirk. Why the hell he found that so hot, he had no clue. But damn . . .

Mischief twinkled in her blue eyes as she took a step back.

The evening was young. He may just have to rile her up some more. See what she'd actually do to him.

Realizing where his thoughts were going, he shook his head. *Nope. Bad idea, Frazier. Bad fucking idea.*

CHAPTER TWELVE

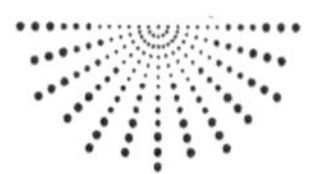

"Where did Esme arrange for you to land?" Bean heard Gavin ask Owen through her headset.

The Bell 505 they were flying in was the smallest helicopter of the Hudson Security fleet. It only held five, including the pilot. Gavin sat up front next to Owen, while Bean sat behind them.

"Esme received clearance for the Safeco Plaza helipad," Owen replied. "So you'll be right downtown. Carmichael is meeting us there and will be your driver for the evening."

As they continued to talk logistics, Bean hoped the headphones didn't mess up her hair. Not that she really cared. She wasn't the biggest fan of flying in helicopters to start with and throw in the growing nerves that were swirling in her stomach, her hair wasn't something she was truly worried about, but it was a good distraction. Puking all over the interior of the helicopter? Now that was the growing worry.

Taking in a deep breath, Bean took in the view as they approached downtown Seattle. Having spent the majority of her life in San Francisco and now living on quaint and quiet Hudson Island, she appreciated Seattle's beautiful skyline.

Her stomach dropped as Owen approached their landing spot that was smack-dab in the middle of downtown atop one of its many skyscrapers. Once they landed, Bean removed her headset and hung it on its hook. And froze. Her mind whirled as she second-guessed herself. It had been eons since she'd played any sort of smile-and-nod part. Once she'd been old enough, she'd made a life for herself that didn't include small talk and mingling.

Why the hell had she agreed to do this again?

"You got this," Owen said. "If you get nervous, just know you look better than everyone else. I mean, those shoes alone, girlfriend."

Meeting Owen's steady gaze, she smiled, grateful for the support. She shoved her nerves down and held her foot out, rotating her ankle and showing off the flame-red beauty. "They are pretty fantastic." She leaned forward and slapped Gavin on the shoulder. "Thanks for the new kicks, boss man."

"I officially volunteer the next time you need a plus-one, Frazier," Owen said, elbowing him in the side. She gestured to the door on the opposite side of the rooftop. "Carmichael should be inside waiting for you guys. Text me when you're about ready to leave, and I'll be here waiting."

"Thanks for the lift," Gavin said as he slid open the door. He quickly got out and turned back. With one hand holding her briefcase, he held his other out to her. "I don't plan on us being at the event too long, Owen. I'm thinking a couple hours max."

"No problem. Just let me know when you're ready." Owen grinned and waggled her eyebrows. "It took us twenty minutes to get here, but you know I can make it in half the time if you need."

"No, thank you," Bean said, placing her hand in Gavin's as she carefully stepped out. "That was plenty fast enough. I don't think my stomach could handle you doing all your fancy flying stuff." She grinned at the other woman. "Thanks for not making me airsick. It'd be a shame to puke on this dress."

Even though the helo's blades had slowed, Gavin kept a firm grip on her hand as they quickly made their way to the building's entrance. As they approached, the door opened, and Carmichael held it open for them.

"Daaamn, B," Carmichael drawled. "You look crazy fuckin' hot."

Her face heated, and she rolled her eyes as they stepped into the elevator. The guy was always joking around with her.

Carmichael pressed the button to the parking garage. "When are you gonna agree to finally go out with me?"

"Uh, that would be never, my friend." She chuckled, knowing the guy wasn't serious. "But thanks, I think."

Gavin made a grumbly noise, and she glanced up at him. His jaw was clenched tightly, and he was glaring at Carmichael, who was making a production of eyeing her up and down, which she didn't mind since she knew he was a harmless flirt.

"Carmichael," Gavin snapped.

Their friend's eyes widened, and he held up his hands. "Sorry, Fraz." He turned to her. "No disrespect intended, B."

"I know. None taken." She made a face and inclined her head at their boss, shrugging. She patted Gavin on the chest, and he tensed further. "Ease up, boss man."

The elevator dinged, and the doors opened. She waited while both men stepped out, their heads on a swivel. She didn't move until Gavin held his arm out for her to take. This wasn't her first rodeo, but their alertness was a good reminder that they were on a mission.

She inwardly winced. Okay "mission" may be laying it on a bit thick, but this definitely wasn't a fun, social evening out.

And just like that, nerves bloomed anew in her belly.

Looping her arm with Gavin's, she let out a breath that was intended to be steadying but was more holy-crap-what-did-I-get-myself-into.

She was a hacker, *not* a field operative.

Trying to remember Owen's words of encouragement, she glanced at her fabulous new shoes. Yes, they were beautiful. But, no, they did nothing to soothe her nervousness.

You've got this. It's just a routine work assignment.

She repeated the words in her head as she settled herself in the black SUV. Carmichael hopped into the driver's seat while Gavin sat next to her in the back for the short ride to the Four Seasons Hotel. With another deep breath, she did her best to ignore the trepidation inching up her spine.

CHAPTER THIRTEEN

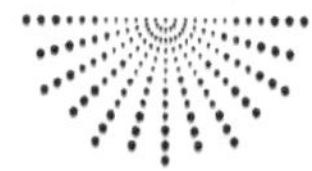

"Good evening, Mr. Frazier. You and your guest are seated at table one, sir."

"Thank you," Gavin said to the woman at the entry table.

Bean waited for the woman to acknowledge her—the "guest"—but nope. The other woman didn't bother to look her way. Not even a glance. The lady only had eyes for Gavin.

Not that Bean could really blame her. The man did fill out a tux stupidly well. If Henry Cavill had a love child with *Fight Club* Brad Pitt, it would be Gavin. He exuded a confidence and an intensity that was breathtaking.

She pressed her lips together.

Whoa. Not that *she* thought of him that way, of course. She was simply stating a fact. It was unfair how good the man looked all prettied up. Not that he didn't look just as good in jeans and a T-shirt, because he did. It's just that—

Stop.

She flinched when his hand settled at the small of her back and wanted to clobber herself.

Holy shit, focus!

"You good?" he asked, his voice low for only her to hear.

Clearing her throat, she nodded and straightened her shoulders. "Of course. Let's do this."

With his hand warm against her skin, they stepped into the ballroom. And she came to a halt.

"Holy wow," she muttered on a sigh, taking in the opulence of the room. "This is ridiculous."

Understatement. She'd been to a handful of charity events in her lifetime, but none like this. She'd only ever seen event decor like this in the society pages, usually linked to the uber *uber* wealthy, which she supposed these people were. Gold and crystal accents shimmered throughout the large ballroom. Instead of looking tacky, it was astonishing. Stunning. Like a freaking fancy fairy tale come to life.

"Stop messing with your sleeve," Gavin said under his breath. "You look perfectly fine."

She bit the inside of her cheek. She hadn't realized she'd been fidgeting. Her left hand had a death grip on her red clutch, and the fingers of her right hand had been twisting the hem of her sleeve. Clearing her throat, she strove for a carefree and confident tone, though both were a lie. She was never carefree. And confident? Only when she was seated at a computer doing what she did best.

She put on a pleasant smile and glanced around at the other attendees. "I look perfectly fine? Yikes. Just what every woman wants to hear. You've got to work on your compliments, Frazier," she said, her voice low and teasing.

Bean didn't recognize anyone, which was a positive. Still, the event had "bad idea" written all over it. When it came down to it, she was a hacker. As pretty as her outfit was, she was way out of her depth.

Gavin dipped his head and spoke quietly into her ear.

"You know what I mean, B. Stop fidgeting. You're high society tonight, remember?"

Right. She could do this, dammit.

With each step she took into the glitzy Four Seasons ballroom, the impeccably dressed women around her—with their opulent jewels, designer labels, and Botox—made her feel like a country bumpkin. Oh, wait . . .

Although reclusive former-big-city girl turned small-town bumpkin was probably a more apt description for her.

But not tonight.

Tonight, she was Sabrina Darcy. A high society friend of Gavin Frazier who was originally from San Francisco but now living the high life in London. And, yes, she'd gotten a crash course on the swanky who's who of London from both MacKay and Esme.

Gavin squeezed her hip. "You good?"

She nodded. The smile on her face was both familiar and foreign. Growing up, she'd been stuck at numerous events like this during the few times she'd been allowed to come home from boarding school. She'd been decades younger than everyone in attendance, but she'd learned how to play the small-talk-with-fancy-people game. She'd hated every moment of it and wanted more than anything to be back in her dorm room, curled up on the couch watching movies or playing video games. But it wasn't like she'd had a choice back then.

Gavin popped his elbow out, and she gladly clutched onto him. His solid arm grounded her, let her know that unlike when she was growing up, she wasn't alone now.

Smile, nod, make polite conversation. *It's like riding a bike, Bean.*

It had to be. Or else it was going to be a long, long night.

They made their way around the perimeter of the ballroom, nodding and smiling but not stopping. The plan was to do one full loop to assess the room, then stop for a drink to reevaluate. They were nearing the bar, and the tension in her shoulders was finally easing. Forget the fact that her grip on Gavin's arm would probably leave a bruise. Thankfully, the man hadn't made one single comment about it.

As they stepped into the line for the bar, a woman in Bean's peripheral vision had her nearly stumbling.

No.

Her pulse kicked as the woman continued to make a beeline toward her.

It couldn't be.

"Sabrina?" Gavin murmured, glancing down at her.

Turning toward the woman, Bean's stomach dropped. The blood drained from her face, and she couldn't stifle her gasp.

Holy. Shit.

Before she could process anything, Gavin's solid body blocked the incoming woman. "B?" he whispered, leaning over her, his hands squeezing hers. "Talk to me. What's—"

"Florence Sabrina. I thought that was you."

Bean turned to the woman who was now standing beside her and Gavin. She fought a shiver while goosebumps tore across her skin. Inhaling, she allowed that long-forgotten feeling of detachment to settle over her.

Straightening her spine, she donned a smile—not too big as to appear gauche, but not too small to appear rude—and air-kissed the other woman.

"Good evening," Bean said, proud of how her voice was serene and steady. "It's so lovely to see you."

Huh. Would you look at that? It is like riding a damn bike.

Gavin wasn't sure what the hell was going on, but the tension pulsing from Bean was at complete odds with the pleasant smile on her face.

He didn't like it. Not one bit.

The fake smile. The air-kissing. Hell, even Bean's tone had changed. It was one he'd never heard from her before. Like she was indeed some socialite.

And *Florence Sabrina*?

What. The. Fuck?

"We haven't been in Seattle in eons, so imagine my surprise when I saw you walking by. And *here* of all places." The other woman's laugh was grating. And fake as fuck. "What are the chances of running into you?"

His eyes narrowed. The woman looked to be anywhere from her early fifties to late sixties. She was slim and slightly taller than Bean—even though B wore sky-high heels—and had straight, shoulder-length salt-and-pepper hair. There was something familiar about the older woman, but . . . he couldn't quite put his finger on it.

"I'm equally shocked as well," Bean said, stepping to the side and moving them all out of the drink line. "What brings you to Seattle?"

"Oh, well, your—" The woman glanced at him and laughed that shrill laugh again. "Pardon me. Where are my manners?" She shot Bean a disapproving look—one he would have missed if he hadn't been studying the other woman so intently—before holding out her hand to him. "I'm Dr. Flora Buena Ventura."

He shook her extended hand, and trepidation crawled up his spine. "Gavin Frazier."

"Gavin's my partner," Bean said, linking her arm with his. She leaned into him in a way that made no mistake that their supposed partnership was of the intimate sort.

Interesting.

He'd play along.

"That's lovely," Dr. Buena Ventura said, eyeing him up and down before meeting his gaze. "And what is it you do for work, Mr. Frazier?"

Gavin immediately sized her up. Though, truthfully, it wasn't difficult. The woman thought she was *far* superior to him. "Corporate security, ma'am." He had zero desire to provide any further information.

"That's nice," she said, her nose scrunching as if she'd smelled something foul. She gestured toward the general area of the tables. "My husband, Dr. Leonardo Buena Ventura, is a guest speaker at the University of Washington this week. We were invited by Herbert and Julia Croft to attend this evening as they're very large donors to the McClintock Family Foundation. We're heading off to London on Tuesday as I'm a guest lecturer at the University of Oxford."

He was surprised she didn't pat herself on the back.

"Well, it was fortuitous we were able to run into each other," Bean said with that smile he was beginning to hate still on her face.

"Fortuitous, indeed." The woman glanced around before waving at someone across the room. "The Crofts are waiting for me. They're enthralled with my latest research. If we don't see each other the rest of the evening, it was lovely seeing you again." She turned to Gavin with her hand extended. For Bean's sake, he shook it. "It was a pleasure to meet you, Mr. Frazier." When she released his hand, she turned back to Bean and air-kissed her. "Shall I give your regards to your father?"

"Please," Bean replied. "Be well, Mother."

As the other woman pranced away, Gavin's mouth fell open. He prided himself on his poker face, on masking his emotions, on always being professional. But holy fuck. Had he heard that right? That was Bean's *mother*?

He steered Bean toward the edge of the room until they stood next to a giant eight-foot vase that would give them some privacy. "B, what was—"

"Change of plans," she said in a low voice, looking out at the ballroom. "I'm no longer Sabrina Darcy, your high society friend from London. It's Florence Sabrina Buena Ventura now. Daughter of Drs. Leonardo and Flora Buena Ventura." Continuing to watch the various guests milling about, her lips pursed. "They're kind of a big deal in academic circles. Six years ago, he won the Nobel Prize in Physics. The following year, she won the Nobel Prize in Chemistry."

He frowned. That was fucking great and all, but . . . "B, what's—"

"I promise I'll explain. But later." She finally met his gaze, and the turmoil swirling in her blue eyes stopped his heart. "Please, Gavin."

His chest squeezed as it resumed beating. "Of course, honey." His lips quirked immediately after the endearment slipped out.

Bean's right eyebrow arched, and when she smiled, it reached her eyes, easing some of that turmoil. "*Honey*? That's a new one."

He chuckled and popped out his elbow for her to take. "Well, apparently, we're *together* together now. Honey is fitting, right?"

Letting out a shaky breath, she linked her arm with his. "That's right."

Covering her hand with his, he squeezed. "I've got you, B."

"I'm counting on it." She glanced up at him and flashed him a smile that was both sweet and shy and nailed him directly in the chest.

Without thinking, he leaned down and pressed a kiss to her forehead, taking a moment to drink in her familiar soft floral scent. "Ready to do this?"

Her gaze held a hint of surprise, but she nodded. "Lead the way, Mr. Frazier."

"It's Gavin, honey," he said with a wink.

CHAPTER FOURTEEN

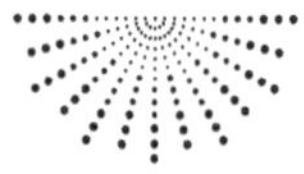

They'd been seated at their table for an hour, and Gavin was ten seconds away from pulling out his phone and texting Edward McClintock to demand he tell him who this supposed business partner was. Gavin was ready to meet with the person and get the hell out of here. He was so done with this entire event.

Correction: he was so done with Constance Whitcomb.

As the woman had promised, she'd seated him beside her at their round table of eight with Bean on his opposite side. Next to Constance was her husband, Roger, a multimillionaire in his late eighties who came from old Seattle money and looked like he'd rather be anywhere but here. The man wasn't rude, but after greeting the table, he remained mostly silent except for occasionally reprimanding his son who sat beside him. Branson Whitcomb was a thirty-something-year-old douchebag who reeked of privilege and entitlement and was scrolling on his phone like a teenager while throwing back glass after glass of whiskey.

Yeah . . . Gavin was ready to be done.

During dinner, Gavin and everyone else at their table

barely spoke as Constance prattled on with tales of her own amazingness. He figured the woman was oddly similar to Bean's mother in that way. The two women sure did like the sounds of their own voices.

Eventually, their dinner plates were cleared away, and post-dinner drinks were served. Copious amounts of wine and spirits flowed, though he and Bean stuck with coffee. Their tablemates broke off into separate conversations—though Roger seemed content to simply observe those around him and Branson focused on his phone. Constance was now keen on having Gavin's undivided attention. Playing his part, Gavin made the obligatory small talk with her. Thank you for having us, your foundation does wonderful work in Seattle, the food and program this evening were lovely . . . That kind of thing. However, with each word he uttered, she scooted closer and closer toward him.

At first, he thought she simply had a few too many glasses of champagne, but the closer Constance got, the more he could see the clarity and shrewdness in her gaze. Initially, it was a simple touch on his hand, then a lingering hand to his arm. Now, she cozied up so much that her breast rested against him.

He peeked over at Bean to catch her attention, but she was deep in conversation with the woman on the opposite side of her. Something about whether Ibiza or the Maldives were the better vacation destination. Bean was using that polished voice she'd used with her mother, so he knew she didn't really give a shit about what she was saying. If he could only get Bean to look his way . . .

"So, Mr. Frazier," Constance said, trailing her finger over his forearm. Thank God for the material of his tuxedo separating them. He was certain he would have recoiled at her touch without it. "Can I call you Gavin?"

More than anything, he wanted to snatch his arm off the table and scoot away, but he wasn't about to cause a scene. Besides, he was already at the edge of his seat as it was. Hell, if he moved any farther away from the woman, he'd be in Bean's lap.

Schooling his features, he nodded. "Gavin is fine."

"As you know, Edward has his hands in all sorts of pies these days. As I'm sure he's mentioned, my baby brother and I are starting a new business venture together."

It took everything he had to not cringe. *Please don't say what I think you're about to say.*

"It's taken some time, but I've developed a new social payment app that's similar to Venmo and PayPal but with fewer fees."

Shit. Of course she would have to be Edward's mysterious business partner.

"Edward will be joining on as an investor and silent part-ner," Constance continued. "I'm looking for a company that can set up additional cybersecurity measures, and he mentioned you and your company. After what happened with his son, I thought it prudent for me to enlist personal security for myself. Again, when Edward mentioned that area of expertise was also in your company's bag of tricks, I just had to meet you."

She punctuated "had to meet you" by running her long fingernail over the back of his hand.

Fisting both hands, he crossed his arms over his chest. He leaned away and turned in his seat, hoping to make it appear as if he were simply turning to better face her. In the process, he bumped into Bean with his back.

"Your business venture sounds intriguing, Constance." It didn't.

"If you're amenable, Gavin, I'd love to discuss our start-up's needs in more detail." She sat back in her seat and dropped her hands to her lap. "Perhaps we can meet up later this week and talk more *in depth* about it."

He realized his mistake in turning to face her. Before he could blink, her hand was on his knee, gently squeezing. *Holy. Fucking. Shit.*

"That won't be necessary. Our cybersecurity division isn't taking on new clients at the moment. As far as personal security goes, our teams are booked out through the end of next year." Neither of the statements were true.

"I'd be more than happy to pay double your fee for both the cyber and personal security. Happy and willing."

The hand on his knee began to slowly climb higher, and he arched an eyebrow at her. Goddamn, the woman was bold. Her husband was right there. Gavin hadn't missed her double entendre and was sure her husband hadn't either. After all, the woman wasn't being subtle in the slightest. But no, thank you.

No. Make that hell no.

"Gavin, sweetie?" Bean said, pressing her front to his back. One of her hands settled against his neck, and she trailed her fingers over the skin below his ear. Unlike with Constance, the feel of Bean's fingernails on him had his heart hammering in his chest.

The hand climbing his thigh stilled. Uncrossing his arms, he dislodged Constance's hand.

"Yes, honey," he said, turning his head so he nuzzled the side of Bean's face.

"Can we dance?"

"Of course," he said, standing.

"Constance, I wish my company could be of help, but as I said, we're maxed out for the foreseeable future."

"Even for double your fee?" Incredulous disbelief colored her features.

"As wonderful as the double fee sounds, we're loyal to our

current clients. I'll let you know if anything opens up in either division, but it most likely won't change until late next year."

As he spoke, Bean molded herself to his side. He gladly put his arm around her, pulling her even closer. So what if his hand dropped low on her hip so he was borderline grabbing her ass? It was absolutely fine, because he caught Constance's glance at his hand and the resulting press of her lips.

"If you'll excuse me, Constance. My lady wants to dance, and God knows, I can't ever say no to her."

CHAPTER FIFTEEN

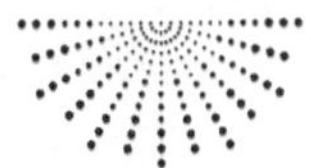

"You doing all right there, boss man?" Bean whispered.

She tried to convince herself that the reason she kept her voice low was to protect their cover. Not that her brain was off-kilter because she was dancing with Gavin—her boss. That his arms being wrapped around her were short-circuiting her brain. That the hand she had resting on his solid chest made her want to see how strong the rest of him was.

No.

That was *not* the cause of her whisper. Not at all.

Right.

Not wanting to think about how comfortable and thrilling dancing with him felt, she focused on the job at hand. On their purpose for being at the event in the first place. She glanced up at him. Even though her three-and-a-half-inch heels brought her closer to Gavin's six-two, she still had to crane her neck to look up at the man, and her lips tipped up at the dour expression on his face.

She had to tease him. How could she not?

"What? You're telling me you're not interested in

discussing Constance's start-up's *needs* in more detail?" She grinned when he let out a low grumble.

He took a moment to glare at her before letting out a sigh. "Did you hear that woman? I know you couldn't see it, but she was getting handsy under the damn table."

He shuddered, and she couldn't hold back a chuckle.

"It's not funny," he muttered.

"Oh, I beg to differ." She patted his chest and did *not* think about how muscular he was. "You know, I've never seen you this frazzled before."

"Frazzled?"

It was stupidly cute how his eyebrows pulled down into a sharp frown, as if she'd just insulted the very core of his being. She may be the only person in the world who'd describe a man with this much intensity as *cute*. But whatever. "Don't worry. On the outside, you looked like your regular James Bond self. All cool and collected. But I know you, Frazier. I know when you're freaking out and, yes, frazzled."

"Gavin."

She tilted her head. "What?"

"I like when you call me Gavin." His eyes widened, as if he'd surprised himself by saying that. "I mean"—he cleared his throat—"since we're acting like we're together and all, I figured you should call me Gavin."

"Of course." She smirked at him. There it was, that awkwardness that was so endearing. "So you can't say no to me, eh? Is that what I heard you say to Constance?" She playfully tapped her finger to her lips. "Maybe I should ask you for a couple new monitors? Or another pair of Ferragamos?"

He shook his head and turned her toward the edge of the dance floor. "Please. If you want new monitors, you just order them yourself. As for more shoes—"

He quickly dipped her, and her leg unconsciously kicked

out before he effortlessly righted her. She may have squeaked, and her stomach definitely did a somersault, but holy shit, who knew he was so freaking smooth?

No one had ever slow danced with her before, let alone dipped her. So she knew she was looking at him slack-jawed, but she couldn't bring herself to care.

"Those red shoes are growing on me." He winked. *Winked!* Who the hell was this guy? "It wouldn't break the bank to see you sporting more like those at the office."

Heat washed over her face, but she managed to find her wits. "You are something else, you know that? And how did I not know you could dance?"

"There's still a lot we don't know about each other." He shrugged. "We have time though."

As he turned them again, she wasn't quite sure what he'd meant by that. For now, it was definitely something she was adding to her mental list of things to think about later. Glancing around the room, she caught Constance's gaze and flinched. The woman did not look happy. At all. Shifting in Gavin's arms, she dropped her voice. "Yikes, that woman has a mean death glare."

He let out a low rumble that she felt more than heard. "Pretty sure you aren't her favorite person, honey. Oh, well."

Grinning, she tsked and met his gaze. "She must be jealous of that dip. After all, it showed off my amazing outfit perfectly *and* with dramatic style. After all, you did say I looked okay, right?"

He shook his head and pulled her closer. "I said you looked perfectly fine."

Her heart tripped at the growl in his voice. Good Lord, this man was lethal. She peeked at Constance again and bit back a chuckle. Killer laser beams had nothing on the woman.

"Ah yes, that's right. How could I have forgotten?"

Because she could since they were playing a part, she moved her hand that was resting on Gavin's torso to the back of his neck. She traced the bottom edge of his hairline with her fingernails, and he grumbled something she didn't quite catch. "What was that?"

He pulled her tighter so there was no space between them. "You look fucking gorgeous, and you know it." His gray eyes flared with heat, and butterflies took flight in her stomach.

After audibly swallowing, she aimed for a confident and flirty smile. Usually, that would be something she'd be abysmal at, but with Gavin it was . . . easy. Though it was no less nerve-racking. "Look at you. Your compliments have gotten so much better."

"You're a smart-ass, you know that, right?"

She shrugged one shoulder. "Who knew?"

He scoffed. "Everyone, honey. Every damn one."

Grinning, she scanned the crowded dance floor to gather her wits. Because yeah, the verbal whatever-they-were-doing was taking every ounce of brainpower she had left.

Sarcasm and snark? Check. That came naturally. Flirty and teasing banter? Nope. Not in her regular repertoire.

Her gaze landed on a familiar couple at the opposite end of the room, and she tensed. Her parents, who she hadn't seen in person for over a decade, were in deep conversation with another older couple. Just like that, all the humor and lightness of the past few minutes fled. In their place was a giant sour ball in her gut.

"Talk to me, B," Gavin said, squeezing her hips. "What just happened?"

The last thing she wanted to do was talk about her parents with Gavin. Simply put, her entire familial situation was depressing.

Shaking her head, she met his gaze. The concern in his

gray eyes warmed her heart and made that heavy ball in her gut a little less sour. "We'll talk about it later. Now that you've nixed the potential client, can we get out of here?"

He studied her for a few moments, and she fought to not squirm under his gaze. She knew the man was shrewd and would see more than she wanted him to.

"Do you promise?" he asked.

"Promise what?"

"That you'll talk to me about it later?"

That warmth in her heart grew. He really was one of the good ones. "I promise. And if I forget to say it later, thank you. You've been pretty great tonight. Curveballs and all."

"Right back at you, honey." His gaze never left hers as he ran a thumb along her jaw, and her heart thumped hard in her chest. Letting his hand drop from her face, he took hold of her hand that was around his neck and laced their fingers together. "Let's say our goodbyes to Constance and get the hell out of here." He squeezed her hand. "Ready to play nice one last time?"

It took a couple of heartbeats for her to regain her senses, and all she could do was nod.

Good God, when had this man become so potent?

CHAPTER SIXTEEN

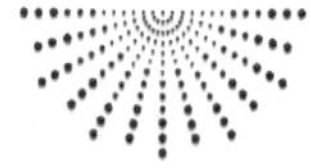

While Carmichael held the SUV's back door open for Bean, Gavin quickly rounded the vehicle and climbed in the opposite side so Bean wouldn't have to slide over. If she did, it would likely hike the slit on her dress even higher, and the damn thing was distracting enough.

She was distracting enough.

A part of him wanted to be irritated that he'd had to come to the event tonight. That Constance Whitcomb had ended up being their prospective client. It seemed like a waste. But as they sat there waiting for the valet to give Carmichael the okay to exit, he glanced at the woman next to him and realized he had zero regrets.

He had a ton of questions about that interaction with her mother. Because frankly, it had been completely fucked up. But if Bean said she'd explain later, she'd explain. She was a woman of her word. A damn beautiful woman of her word. Unlike Constance, who was a piece of work.

Physically, the other woman was attractive, though it was mostly due to genetics, facial symmetry, and fillers. That was it. She checked off the boxes on what society deemed to be the stereotypical "beautiful woman." It was horseshit though, because the woman was atrocious. Not only had she shamelessly flirted with him while Bean sat right next to him, but with her own husband beside her as well. Then she'd had the gall to throw her brother's money around, expecting Gavin to drop his current clients for her.

It didn't matter that he'd lied to the woman. Their cyber division, which Bean oversaw, absolutely had the capacity to take on another client. They could probably add on another five and not bat an eye, but there was no way in hell he'd work with the woman. He respected Edward and would continue to work with him, but if Constance was in any way involved, it was a hard no-go.

"How'd the shindig go, guys? The food any good?" Carmichael asked as he slowly pulled their SUV out of the valet circle and took a left onto First Avenue.

"It was," Bean replied, a tired smile gracing her lips. "They had this salmon that was fantastic. It was—"

Carmichael took a hard right, and Gavin's arm shot out to steady Bean even though she was buckled in.

"What is it, Carmichael?" Gavin asked, immediately on alert.

"Shit," the other man muttered, taking another abrupt right. "Picked up a tail."

"Where'd you put my briefcase?" Bean asked.

"Under the seat in front of you," Carmichael replied.

As she leaned forward to retrieve it, Gavin opened the hidden compartment in the middle seat between them. He pulled out a Glock and two magazines. He racked the slide a couple times, confirming it was clear. After loading the mag, he slid the extra into his suit pocket. "Talk to me, Carmichael."

"Black Audi. Two cars back." He took another hard turn. "There."

Gavin turned, and sure enough, a black Audi sedan with heavily tinted windows turned in behind them.

"It was following me after I dropped you guys off earlier. Thought I lost him on the freeway." Gavin saw his friend's frown in the rearview mirror. "Apparently not."

"You sure it's the same car?" He trusted Carmichael but had to ask.

"Yup. There's a dent off the driver's side hood, right by the side mirror."

"What do you want to do, Gavin?" Bean asked, laptop fired up and perched across her lap.

He frowned. As Carmichael darted in and out of traffic, the other car did nothing to hide the fact they were following them. "It's too risky to get to the helipad here . . ."

"We can go to the one at Boeing Field." Bean's fingers flew over the keyboard as she gnawed on her lower lip. "If you give me a couple minutes, I can get us cleared and get Owen in the air."

"Shit, gun!" Carmichael swerved to the left, and a ping sounded.

Reacting on instinct, Gavin reached over. His hand went to the back of Bean's head and tried to press her forward. "Get down, B!"

Instead of complying, she swatted him away, her focus never wavering from her laptop even when two more pings rang out. For a moment, he could only stare at her dumbfounded.

"Bean. Get the fuck down," he seethed.

Again, she waved him off. Literally. Her left hand stopped typing long enough to shoo him away. Like he was a damn fly.

A growl left his chest before he could stop it.

"Stop growling, boss. This is an armored freaking vehicle. Unless they're shooting an RPG at us, we have nothing to worry about."

There was no way she could be for real right now. "And how the hell do you know they aren't?"

Gavin could have sworn she rolled her eyes, but he couldn't be a hundred percent certain since she was still typing away.

"Because Carmichael said *gun*." She glanced at him, and he caught that familiar gleam in her blue eyes. She had an idea, had come up with a plan of some sort.

Yes, they were being shot at and chased through the streets of downtown Seattle but seeing that sparkle back in Bean's eyes made him feel a little better. He hadn't realized how much he'd appreciated it until it had been snuffed out both times she'd seen her mother tonight.

Before he could ask what she'd figured out, she turned to Carmichael, who was zigging and zagging them between cars. "I've overridden the lights. Take the next right and then make a left on Alaskan Way. Traffic's lighter that way. I'll make it all green for you and figure out a way to lose this asshole."

"Hang on," Carmichael said as he turned, the screech of tires insanely loud in the vehicle.

As they rounded the corner, Gavin lowered his window halfway. When the other car came into view, he fired two rounds into the open passenger window, aiming at the shadow shooting at them. When the person's gun retreated, he quickly rolled his window back up.

"Did you get 'em?" Carmichael asked.

"Not sure," Gavin muttered, keeping his eye on the car behind them.

"Turning onto Alaska," Carmichael said. "Work your damn magic, B, and I'll get this fucker off our ass."

For the next few minutes, Carmichael flew through the streets of Seattle as Bean hijacked the traffic lights, turning them red immediately after their car passed through. It got hairy as they approached the ferry terminal. A wall of red taillights was in front of them since there was a line of cars disembarking.

"Where am I going, Bean?" Carmichael asked.

"Get into the far right lane." She glanced over her shoulder, furiously typing. "When I say go, hop into the bike lane." Three long seconds ticked by. "Go!"

Gavin grabbed the back of the driver's seat and braced as the SUV jumped the dividing curb into the bike lane. Swerving past the line of stopped cars, they followed the narrow pathway, which was lit green for them.

"All the lights will be red at the ferry terminal, but keep going," Bean said. "When you pass the terminal, get back onto Alaskan Way. Immediately."

Carmichael followed her instructions, and the second he passed the terminal, she turned all the traffic lights green. Horns blared, and cars blocked the intersection. The black Audi was nowhere in sight.

"Fuck yeah!" Carmichael whooped as he sped down the street. "That was fucking awesome!"

Gavin let out a breath and looked at the woman next to him. *Holy shit.* He was probably going to hell for finding that insanely hot. "Good job, you guys."

Ten minutes later, and after more instructions from Bean, Carmichael pulled to a stop at a nondescript hangar at Boeing Field. Roughly seventy yards away was their Bell 505 with Owen at the helm. Bean must have let her know the urgency was gone since Owen didn't have the main rotor going.

By the time Gavin had rounded the SUV, Bean stood next to her open door clutching her skirt with both hands—the tarmac was surprisingly windy—and Carmichael had her briefcase and purse. They hurried toward the helo.

Once Bean was situated, Gavin got in next to her and turned back to Carmichael. "Stay alert. Check in when you get back to the hospital—let me know how Anson's doing—and keep your tracker on."

"Got it. And thanks for those evasive driving lessons, man. That was kinda fun. And B was right, you know. If they'd had more than a gun, I'd have yelled RPG, missile, or some other shit." He lifted his chin at Bean. "Thanks for all the green lights, lady."

"Any time." Bean frowned while putting her headset on. "Well, maybe not when I'm actually in the car with you."

"Damn straight," Gavin muttered.

"Later, guys," Carmichael said with a salute before he slid the door shut.

"Holy shit," Owen said, beginning her start sequence. "Do I even want to ask about his 'RPG or missile' comment?"

"The car following us fired at us, and Frazier was being paranoid. I was in the process of taking over the lights, and he wanted me to duck for cover." Bean shook her head.

He stared at her, his mouth agape. "They *fired* at us."

"Were you in a Hudson Security vehicle?" Owen asked.

"Yeah, one of the armored Rovers," Bean replied, her tone very much can-you-believe-this-guy?

Owen chuckled as they took off. "Yeah, don't start getting all paranoid on us, Frazier."

He shook his head but kept silent. He knew he couldn't win an argument when these two teamed up.

Moments later, the helo's nose dipped, and Bean grabbed his forearm and squeezed it in a death grip. Even in the limited light, he could see that she'd paled. He glanced at the flight display system. They were going much faster than on their inbound flight.

"Hang in there, honey," he said, covering her hand with his. "Owen will have us back on land in no time."

She pressed a hand to her stomach. "That's kind of what I'm afraid of."

CHAPTER SEVENTEEN

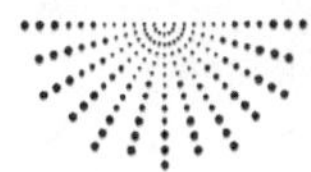

"Thanks again for the lift, Owen," Bean said as she walked with the other woman and Gavin toward the hangar where his SUV was parked.

"One of these days you'll agree to let me take you up and do a scenic tour. You'll be over your fear of helicopters in no time."

"What's with everyone trying to get me out of my comfort zone? First Wilson and this guy with the great outdoors, and now you." She groaned, setting her hands on her hips. "For the record, it isn't the helicopter I have an issue with."

Owen shot her a smirk. "Oh, no?"

"No. It's the height from the chopper to the ground that I have a problem with. And the stupid fast speeds you go."

"How about a hot-air balloon?" Gavin asked with a sly grin. "Those go pretty slow."

"*Boring,*" Owen said in a singsong voice.

As far as Bean was concerned, a hot-air balloon was hell on earth personified. The two jokers in front of her knew what her feelings on those death traps were. Hell, everyone at Hudson Security knew it.

She took a moment to give each of them her best glare. "I hate you both."

Gavin smothered his laugh with a cough, while Owen cackled. "You love us!"

"On that note," Gavin said, taking Bean by the elbow, "we're out, Owen. Thanks again."

Walking backward toward her small office, Owen waved at them. "Have a good night, you two."

The drive to Bean's place was short and passed in comfortable silence. She was mentally rehashing the events of the last hour, and she assumed Gavin was doing the same. When he pulled up to the front of her house, it was nearing ten o'clock. She didn't question him as he cut the engine and followed her to her front door.

They had work to do.

Dropping her keys, briefcase, and clutch onto the entryway table, she slipped off her heels.

"Let me change real quick, and we can get to work figuring out what the hell is going on." She made her way toward her bedroom but turned back. Her mind went blank.

Gavin had taken off his tux jacket and draped it over the back of one of her dining room chairs. His bow tie was undone, and he was in the process of rolling up the sleeves of his still-crisp white shirt.

Well, hello, arm porn.

Dragging her gaze from his arms up his chest to his face, her cheeks heated when she met his mischievous gaze.

Knowing she'd been caught checking him out, she held up a finger. "Not one word, buster."

The corner of his lips kicked up in that smirky smile. "Wouldn't dream of it, honey."

Shaking her head, she turned and headed to her room, calling out, "Make yourself useful, please, and get MacKay and Tiny on the line. Xander too."

After changing into leggings and her favorite red 49ers sweatshirt, which she knew needled Gavin since he was a lifelong Seahawks fan, she quickly washed her face, slapped on some moisturizer, and pulled her hair back into a high ponytail with a matching red-and-gold scrunchie. Yes, she generally tried to keep up the professional appearance when she worked, but she'd just spent the last few hours being super fancy. Enough was enough.

She returned to the main room, and Gavin turned toward her. He grimaced as he took her in from head to toe. "You're wearing that shit on purpose, aren't you?"

She shrugged as she made a detour to the kitchen and grabbed a bottle of water and an energy drink. "I don't know what you're talking about."

"Damn, you even have a matching hair thing." He made a face and took the bottle of water from her as she passed him on her way to her workstation.

"I have an extra Niners sweatshirt if you want to get more comfortable." She shot him an overly sweet grin as she cracked the can of her energy drink. She gestured to her dark monitors. "Are the guys unavailable?"

Gavin took a drink of his water and shook his head. "I called them, and they're ready whenever you are." He grabbed a dining chair and pulled it up beside her plush office chair. "I didn't want to touch your computer."

The corners of her lips twitched. "Smart man."

She settled into her chair and tapped her keyboard. After she typed in her fifteen-digit passcode, her monitors came to life. Another four clicks, and MacKay's, Tiny's, and Xander's faces were on her center screen.

"What's up, gentlemen?"

"We should be asking you two that," MacKay said. "Car chase through downtown Seattle? Seriously?"

"Frazier's always gotta keep things interesting, right?" Bean said with a chuckle.

Gavin shook his head. "We can't be certain I was the target."

Bean rolled her eyes. "Please. No one knows who I am, and if they were after Carmichael, they had hours to take their shot while he was waiting for us."

Gavin muttered under his breath as he moved his chair closer to hers so they were in the same shot for the rest of the team. They were nearly shoulder to shoulder.

"Well, thank God Bean was there," Xander said. "Carmichael said she was able to do her thing and create a route for him to get out of there."

"All true," she said as she shot off an email to her cyber division team.

"Xander," Gavin began, "why don't you update everyone on what Carmichael reported."

While Xander gave everyone Carmichael's play-by-play, Bean sent a company-wide notification to all their employees. Within seconds, everyone's phones sounded with the alert. Even though they didn't have a grasp of what was going on, when their head boss was targeted, the entire team needed to be extra cautious.

Once he concluded his brief recount of Carmichael's statement, Xander asked, "Do you want me to head back to Seattle?"

"We just have Team Two keeping watch over Anson and Rita at the hospital, right?" Gavin asked.

"Correct," Xander replied. "Riviera is currently stationed

outside of Anson's room, and both Carmichael and Bonson are on-site."

Gavin frowned and rose, pacing behind her. Having worked with him for so long, she knew it was his way of ordering his thoughts while releasing his pent-up energy. She often joked that pacing back and forth brought out his best thinking.

He stopped behind her and leaned down so he was in the video-call frame. "Those three should be good. Where's Tash at?"

"LA," Xander said. "After the McClintock mission, she went down there to meet up with Hanniger and the rest of Team Three. They're meeting with some record label minions about a possible security detail for one of their people."

Bean noticed a look of confusion crossing Tiny's face. "Tiny, I'll explain the team breakdown to you later." She glanced up at Gavin. "Do you want to call everyone in?"

"I don't know yet," Gavin murmured before he resumed pacing.

Bean frowned. It was safe to say that when Gavin got a bad feeling, it was *not* a good thing.

"What do we know, B?" MacKay asked.

She glanced at her bottom right monitor and saw an incoming email. "I've pulled the cyber division in. Abbot just confirmed that she'll get the team on identifying the car that was following us. She and her crew are going to go through whatever video footage they can find. I'm going to assume the vehicle's plates won't match up, but if they can get me anything, I'll run it through my programs. I'm hoping they can get facial rec—even a partial—on either the driver or passenger who shot at us."

"How can I help?" Tiny asked.

For a moment, she hesitated. *This isn't about your ego,*

dammit. Letting out a breath, she addressed the man. "I'd like you to look into Constance Whitcomb."

"She was the potential client that Edward McClintock mentioned," Gavin added.

Xander let out a low whistle. "No shit?"

"Exactly," Bean said. "As much as the woman rubbed me the wrong way—"

"I'm sure she wished she could've rubbed Frazier in more ways than one," Xander cut in with a chuckle.

Bean laughed. "Oh, dude, you have no idea. The poor guy kept inching farther and farther away from her until he was practically sitting in my lap. He was doing that thing where he keeps his expression neutral, but it ends up making him all broody, which had the woman practically salivating. It was too much!"

"Jesus." Gavin groaned, scrubbing his hands over his face. "I'm right here."

"I know, boss." She shot him a cheeky grin that had everyone but him laughing. "Anyway, there's something that doesn't feel right about her. She had a story about needing cybersecurity for a new pay app that she said she'd developed. She said Edward's a silent partner, but it doesn't make sense."

"How so?" MacKay asked.

She grabbed her energy drink and brought it to her mouth for a sip. It was plucked from her hand and replaced with a bottle of water.

Mustering her best glare, she threw it at Gavin with an arched eyebrow. "You're kidding me, right?"

He met her glare with an arched brow of his own. "Humor me. We're going to have a long day tomorrow. I need you in top form."

Grumbling, she took a sip of water and scrunched her face as she turned back to the three faces on her screen. Two were snickering, while the other looked confused. "Zip it, you two," she snapped, pointing at Xander and MacKay. "You're being a bad influence on Tiny."

MacKay snorted. "Whatever. It's not like Tiny's going to give you shit. You're technically his new boss."

"There is that," she said and then glanced at the bottle of water and frowned. "This crap's disgusting."

"Wait, are you talking about actual water?" Tiny asked.

She stared the man down. "I'm sorry, Tiny. Did you say something?"

His eyes widened, and he cleared his throat and shook his head. "No, ma'am."

"That's what I thought. Now, as I was saying, Constance Whitcomb is *not* a tech person. She has zero history of any involvement in app development. Not in her work history, not in her education, nothing. Tiny, I need you to peek into her search history and emails to see how this is even on her radar. As far as I saw on my initial pass, her professional history includes charity events, fundraising, and community outreach. Her personal history didn't include anything tech related either."

"I'm curious," Xander said. "What did her personal history reveal?"

"An affinity for med-spa visits, high-end shopping, and banging younger men—her staff and fitness instructors included. So her claiming she's developed any sort of app doesn't ring true." Bean leaned back in her chair. "Also, run her husband, Tiny. The man's a very fit and spry eighty-seven, but he barely spoke a word the entire evening. My gut says he isn't his wife's biggest fan."

"On it, Bean," Tiny said. "And thanks for giving me something fun and not that CCTV footage shit."

She shrugged. "Well, as much as I hate delegating—"

MacKay, Xander, and Gavin broke into laughter. Loud, obnoxious guffaws.

Crossing her arms over her chest, she waited a few seconds. "Are you hyenas through?"

MacKay made a production of wiping away a tear. "Sorry, but that was rich. You're the biggest control freak out of all of us."

"And that says a fucking lot," Gavin chimed in.

"No shit," Xander added.

Rolling her eyes, she spoke over them. "As I was saying, Tiny, you're a damn good hacker, and it would be a waste of your talent to have you scouring through video footage looking for a partial plate or facial rec."

"Holy shit," MacKay said, a world of disbelief in those two words. "Did she just compliment someone else's hacking skills?"

Ridiculous. These guys were ridiculous.

"I said he was good, MacKay. Which he is." She leaned back in her chair. "Though he's still not as good as me."

"Aaand there's the cocky-ass Bean we all know and love!" Xander laughed.

"All right, guys," Gavin said, retaking his seat beside her. "All we currently know is that Carmichael spotted the tail after he dropped us off at the Four Seasons. Lost him. Then picked him back up the moment we left the hotel. Cyber's running their programs, so until we know more, we're in a holding pattern. Reconvene at zero eight hundred tomorrow?"

Xander groaned. "Fine."

"What?" Gavin asked. "You had plans?"

Xander rolled his eyes. "No, but I was going to spend my Sunday watching football like normal people."

"Please," Bean said. "Like we won't have the games on in

the corner. Besides, Gavin's bringing in breakfast for everyone."

"I am?" His eyes went wide with surprise.

She simply stared at him until he cleared his throat.

"Right. I'll get breakfast for everyone from Ray's Diner."

She smiled at the screens. "See, Tiny. You and MacKay should consider moving here. We get perks for working on a Sunday."

Everyone said their goodbyes, and Bean cut their connection. Pushing back from her workstation, she rose and stretched with her hands high above her head. Glancing behind her, she cleared her throat.

Gavin's eyes darted up from her legs. A blush tore over his cheeks as he ran a hand over the scruff on his jaw. "Sorry about that."

The teasing glint in his eyes said he wasn't really sorry.

She chuckled, then cleared her throat again as a flurry of nerves sprouted in her belly. "I know I promised I'd talk to you about that awkward meeting-my-mother thing, but I'm beat. Can I get a rain check?"

His teasing expression turned soft. Sweet. "Of course. I'll head out."

After he grabbed his tuxedo jacket, she followed him to the front door. Hopefully she could put off explaining her family dynamics to him for . . . Would forever be too much to ask for?

"Get some rest tonight, B. Like I said. It'll be a long day tomorrow. And thanks again for coming with me tonight."

She toed the red heels she'd left by the front door. They sure were pretty, not to mention much nicer to think about than her parents. "Well, thanks again for the shoes." Glancing back at him, she sucked in a breath.

Gavin was standing close. Very close.

Her heart galloped when he brought his hand to her face.

Cupping her jaw, he softly skimmed his thumb over the bruise near her eye that makeup no longer hid. "Still hurt?"

With her words lodged in her throat, she shook her head.

"Good." She remained silent as he continued to study the bruise on her face, his thumb moving in a slow, hypnotic motion. "Aside from the car chase, getting shot at, and Constance's wandering hands, I had fun with you tonight."

A smile lifted her lips, and she finally found her voice. "I saved you from that woman, you know. You owe me. Big-time."

He met her gaze. Lightness and heat warred in his steel-gray eyes. "Oh, I know."

She held her breath as he leaned down and pressed a kiss to her forehead. "Night, B."

Straightening, he turned and let himself out.

The door closed softly behind him, and she finally remembered to breathe. Her forehead still tingled where his lips had pressed, had lingered.

She wasn't quite sure what was going on, but something had definitely changed between them. She couldn't define it, but what she did know was that despite everything that happened tonight, she'd enjoyed being with Gavin too.

Probably more than she should have.

CHAPTER EIGHTEEN

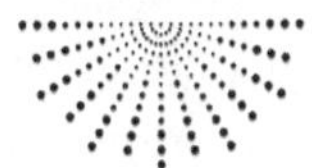

After a restless night plagued by dreams of car chases, intense helicopter rides, and some not quite appropriate moments with her boss, Bean arrived at the office at seven. She'd already guzzled four cups of coffee and was beginning to feel somewhat human. Her first objective was to avoid Gavin at all costs. She didn't have the greatest poker face and knew if he took one look at her, he'd know something was up. The seriously filthy dreams she'd had about the man were the last things she wanted revealed this morning.

Her face heated as she entered their building's empty lobby. Since it was Sunday, their receptionist, Mel, was most likely lounging at home unlike Bean and her fellow workaholic coworkers, whose cars she'd passed in the parking lot. After using her security card and typing in her personal code, the door made a quiet buzzing noise and slid open to allow her to enter the secure part of their building. Well, the entire building was secure, but this part was like Fort Knox. As the door slid closed behind her, she paused a moment to take it all in.

The main area was basically one giant room with

numerous workstations. Each of the security teams were grouped together with the cyber division's group being the largest cluster of workstations in the center.

Off to the right side were four conference rooms of various sizes, the restrooms, and the kitchen, which included a break room with couches, televisions, and numerous video game consoles. Along the left were private offices for Gavin, herself, Alvarez, and Esme, along with a utility and storage room that also housed a secure weapons cache. They were a security company, after all.

The far wall was floor-to-ceiling windows—one way and bulletproof, of course—so the place didn't feel claustrophobic. Gavin had spared no expense when building the place. All in all, it was a gorgeous place to work.

As she made her way to her office, she noticed the cyber division team—Samantha Abbot, Slade Witherspoon, Isaiah Torres, and Jace Oliphant—were busy at their workstations, plates of pancakes, eggs, and other breakfast goodies in front of them. They waved at her as she passed.

"You better hit the kitchen ASAP," Abbot called out. "Xander, Wilson, and Alvarez just showed up, so there may not be any food left once they're through."

"Thanks for the heads-up," she replied. "Give me thirty minutes and then come on in and we'll do a quick catch-up."

"Sure thing, Bean," Abbot said. "The good news is we actually have some intel to share."

That's what she loved about working at Hudson Security. Even though it was a Sunday, no one complained about coming in to figure out what the hell was going on. She was sure it helped that everyone was very well compensated for their time, but the entire team's attitude was top-notch. She was also certain everyone was taking this latest incident personally. After all, she sure as hell was.

No one was messing with their boss. Not on her watch.

Entering her office, Bean flipped on the light and dropped her purse onto the coffee table. She sat at her workstation, but as she was about to boot up her computer, she froze. Next to her keyboard was a paper plate with a maple bar and a chocolate glazed donut with rainbow sprinkles. Her two favorites.

She glanced at the note next to the plate and sucked in a breath. Even if she'd tried, she couldn't have stopped the grin from spreading over her face.

Bean,
Snagged these for you before the heathens
descended.
I'll find you later and we'll touch base.
Gavin

Taking a bite of the maple bar, she smiled. She wasn't quite sure what was happening between them, but things certainly felt . . . different. If her dreams last night were any indication, she was definitely thinking about the man in a very non-boss, non-platonic way. She'd always acknowledged that he was ridiculously good-looking. She wasn't blind. Added to that, she'd known Gavin for so long that she knew him to be a genuinely good human. Intelligent, empathetic, fair, and loyal.

As the maple sugary goodness melted in her mouth, she let out a sigh.

No, she didn't know what was going on between them, but the more she thought about it—the more she thought about *him*—she wasn't opposed to finding out.

However, first things first.

She had work to do.

An hour later, Bean had been briefed by the cyber team.

As she'd expected, the license plate they'd pulled was from a stolen vehicle. Regardless, she ran it through one of her programs that would triangulate the original car's location and backtrack it for the last forty-eight-hours. Perhaps if they could figure out where the last known spotting of that original vehicle was, they'd be able to get footage of whoever had taken the license plate off the vehicle.

However, as Abbot had said, there was good news. Because the cyber team were absolute badasses, they'd been able to get a partial facial image of the shooter by way of a reflection off a nearby building. Complete badasses. The image was currently being run through Bean's facial-rec software, and she was cautiously optimistic they'd be able to narrow it down to a manageable number of possibilities.

Satisfied her programs were doing their thing, she sent a video-call request to Tiny. Seconds later, his face appeared on her center screen.

"Morning," she said.

"Hey, Bean."

"It is morning wherever you are, right?"

The corners of his lips twitched. "Yeah."

"And where exactly are you?" She saw him hesitate, so she added, "You know I could figure it out in like a minute, so you may as well just tell me."

He grinned. "Denver."

"See, that wasn't so hard, was it?" She popped the tab on her energy drink and took a sip. "If you ever want to work on-site, even temporarily, we do have extra workstations here. Secure lodging too."

"I'll keep it in mind."

"So you and I have worked together over the years, but it's always been contractor work. With the incident last night, I feel like you're kind of getting thrown into the deep end here."

He was nodding before she'd finished speaking. "Tell me about it."

"Have you even had a chance to meet with Esme to get all your paperwork sorted?"

"Yeah, we had a video call Thursday afternoon. She had all my employment stuff squared away within a couple hours."

Bean chuckled. "I don't doubt it."

"If you don't mind me saying so, the woman's intense."

Her chuckle turned into a laugh. "Oh, my friend, you have no idea. Let's start with the basics. I know you've worked a lot with MacKay over the last few months. What has he told you about Hudson Security?"

"Not much," Tiny said. "Basically, he said that I'll most likely continue to work with him on his projects, but I'll report to you, and all my assignments will be dictated by you as well."

"That sounds about right." With her elbows resting on her desk, she laced her fingers together. Not quite sure where to begin, she tapped her hand to her lips. She'd been flying solo for so long . . .

"Let me give you a quick structure rundown first. Head and founder of Hudson Security is Gavin. Next in line is MacKay. Esme is our director of logistics. As you've witnessed, she coordinates everything. And I mean everything. All the company's logistics from HR to individual rescue missions."

"MacKay mentioned she was with the CIA."

Bean nodded. "If you thought she was intense over a video call, be prepared if you ever meet her in person. She looks all demure, but—"

"She's a badass who can kill me in nine different ways."

"And no one would ever find your body." Bean shrugged, grinning.

Tiny chuckled. "Good to know. Don't fuck with Esme. Got it."

Okay, fine. The guy wasn't half bad.

"As far as the rest of the team goes," Bean continued, "we have three security teams of three operatives each. We're looking at adding at least one more team, maybe two, but it's slow going to find the right fit. Frazier and MacKay are particular."

"Understandable. Hudson Security's reputation is renowned."

"It's something we all take pride in." Meeting Tiny's gaze, she was reassured by the sincerity she saw. "So Team One is obviously our lead team. Those three are Xander, Tash Silver, and Bennett Wilson. Xander also oversees all the personal security operatives. They're also the only ones authorized to do solo assignments. Team Two is Carmichael, Riviera, and Bonson. You're probably most familiar with Team Three since Hanniger, Rizzo, and Schreiber are the ones that tend to get teamed up with MacKay."

Tiny's eyes narrowed. "I'm familiar with Team Three, though I've seen them take on solo work."

Bean shook her head. "They're always either in pairs or as a trio. There may be one individual assigned to a client, but the others are lurking around somewhere."

"Gotcha."

"Then there's me. My position isn't public information, but it's technically *IT Specialist*." She finger-quoted the title, and when they both chuckled, some of the hesitation she'd felt about letting go of her work eased. "Aside from doing information retrieval, which, as you know, is project by project, I oversee our cyber division. We have four people on the team—Abbot, Witherspoon, Torres, and Oliphant—with Abbot being the lead. They handle the majority of installation and monitoring of the various security systems, both physical and online. They're an extremely talented group, but I test their systems regularly." Bean couldn't help her grimace. "I hate to give this up since it's one of my favorite things to do, but aside from project-specific stuff, this is something I'd like you to take over."

"By test, you mean hack into the systems they install?" Even through the online feed, Bean could see the twinkle in the man's eyes.

"Yup," she said, deliberately popping the P. "See where it's weak. Suggest code to shore it up, and then hack it again until you're satisfied with it."

A giant grin grew over Tiny's face. "Nice."

"When we have specific missions—the kidnapping and ransom types—you and I, along with the cyber division, will get pulled to track and provide intel. We have to be fast and accurate. As you've just experienced, weekends and off-hours don't matter."

"Understood," he said, nodding. "MacKay gave me the basics of the last mission with the McClintock child. Good work."

"Thank you." Though it had technically been a success, her heart still hurt for what that little boy and his family had gone through. "So now that's all squared away, have you found anything on Constance or Roger Whitcomb?"

CHAPTER NINETEEN

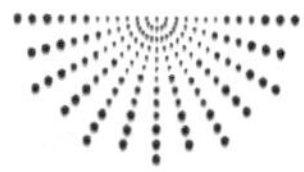

It was almost noon, and Gavin leaned back in his chair, twisting his neck from side to side. As he'd been ordered to do, he'd made sure breakfast was brought in for everyone, and lunch was scheduled to be delivered within the next thirty minutes.

He'd arrived at the ass crack of dawn, and it had been a long morning checking in with MacKay and each of the security team leads, not to mention contacting a few high-maintenance clients who needed extra hand-holding. All the while, he'd been in a shit mood.

Generally, he was a fairly even-keeled guy, but today . . .

Not so much.

He was restless and out of sorts. And he didn't know why.

Closing his eyes, he slouched in his chair and rested his head on the back. That was a lie. He knew exactly why.

He wasn't a spur-of-the-moment kind of person. Everything he did was well thought out. Planned. Methodical. Every contingency was taken into account. But yesterday, he'd fucked up. He hadn't thought of the possibility of someone targeting him, let alone firing at him. His lack of foresight could have gotten Bean hurt. And that was unacceptable.

On top of all that, he'd done something uncharacteristic—he'd acted before thinking. Last night, not only had he gotten more physical with Bean than was appropriate, but he'd bought her a gift . . .

His gaze landed on the two boxes sitting at the edge of his desk. They'd been delivered to the office an hour earlier via special courier. As requested, both were plain, nondescript, brown-lidded boxes.

Nervous energy coursed through him as he stood and peeked into both of the boxes. It wasn't like he hadn't checked them three times already.

It's no big deal, Frazier. It's just a friendly gift.

Bullshit.

It wasn't just a damn gift. And as much as he could try to convince himself it was friendly, it wasn't.

Standing, he grabbed the boxes and headed for his office door. His hand froze on the doorknob.

Holy shit. What the hell was he doing?

Part of him yelled to drop the boxes, turn around, and sit his ass back down at his desk. But the other part of him? It begged him to get his ass in gear. To stop being a pussy, open the damn door, and give Bean her presents.

Gripping the doorknob, he thunked his forehead against the door. Once. Twice. Three times. Then an image of Bean popped into his mind from late last night as he'd said goodbye to her. How her eyes had heated as he'd caressed her face. How damn soft her skin had been. How he'd caught her floral scent as he'd leaned down to kiss her forehead.

Yeah . . .

Decision made, he straightened and opened the door. Knowing their colleagues were milling about, he walked the few steps to her neighboring office as nonchalantly as he could, knocked on her door, and waited.

"Come in," her muffled voice called out.

Closing the door behind him, he approached her workstation. Finding a clear spot at the corner of her desk, he set the boxes down with the larger of the two on top.

Her eyes ping-ponged between him and the boxes. "What's this?"

"Open it." He wanted to pat himself on the back for how casual the two words had sounded, considering his heart was threatening to beat right out of his damn chest.

With a suspicious look, she rolled her chair closer to the boxes. "What are you up to?" she muttered, lifting the lid of the top box. Then her jaw dropped. "Hiking boots?"

Jaw dropping was a positive thing, right? "Yeah. Wilson said you went out with him in a pair of Converse sneakers. I figured, this way you'd be prepared for next time." He bit back a grin as she pulled one of the boots from the box, analyzing it like it was a foreign specimen.

"You know, when we'd talked about you owing me another pair of shoes, this isn't exactly what I had in mind." She swiveled in her chair to fully face him and kicked out her feet to show off the flame-red heels she'd worn last night. Today, she'd paired them with a black flowy skirt that hit right above her knees and a white sleeveless blouse. He knew she had a white cardigan floating around somewhere because he'd noticed every damn detail about her the second he'd seen her walk by his office this morning.

He schooled his features and shrugged. "Hey, you never know when you'll take my advice and decide to go hiking. Remember, the great outdoors can do a lot to reset the brain."

"Fine, Smokey the Bear, I'll give it a shot one day." Her nose scrunched. "Maybe."

Damn, she was cute. Then her words penetrated his brain. Before he could tell himself to shut the hell up, he blurted, "Did you know his name's actually Smokey Bear and not Smokey the Bear?"

For a second, she simply stared at him, and he wanted the floor to open up and swallow him whole.

Shaking her head, she chuckled. "The fact you know that says a lot about you. But either way, that's the only famous outdoorsy name I know. It was either that or Yogi Bear." She gave him a sheepish smile and replaced the lid on the box. "Thanks, boss."

"Gavin." He shrugged when she tilted her head to the side. "I like it when you call me Gavin."

She opened her mouth to say something, but he held up a hand, stepped toward her desk, and swapped the boxes, placing the smaller one on top of the hiking boot box.

Suspicion colored her face, but this time, there was a hint of a smile that warmed his insides.

He tapped the top of the box, winking at her. "Hope you like these."

She lifted the lid and pushed the tissue paper aside. Her mouth fell open, and she let out a small gasp. She sat frozen for the longest three seconds of his life. Shit, had he overdone it?

"Gavin, holy crap," she finally said, her voice a reverent whisper. "These are the Louboutin Follis Strass stilettos. They're like honest-to-God glass slippers." She carefully pulled one of the shoes from the box, held it in her hands, and stared at it in wonder, gently caressing its side.

He'd never wished to be a shoe before, but here he was . . .

Seeing her fawn over the shoe filled him with pride and eased the embarrassment he'd harbored over how long he'd spent researching fancy heels. In the early morning hours, he'd gone down the rabbit hole of high-end footwear. Some of the things he'd seen were god-awful. There were heels that were basically plumes of feathers—like a giant purple bird had exploded and died on the model's foot. Did women actually wear that shit in real life? Then he'd come across the ones she was holding in her hands. They'd screamed Bean. The heels had the designer's signature red sole and were tan and glittery but not too much.

They were simple and classy and had just the right amount of sparkle. Just like Bean.

She could wear them at the office in her sexy librarian clothes. Or, if she got all dolled up in the dress from last night again, the heels were fancy enough to go with that. What truly sold him was he could easily picture her in those sky-high, twinkling heels . . . and nothing else.

"Gavin, I can't accept these. They're like over a thousand dollars and—"

"What am I going to do with a pair of stilettos? Besides, like I said last night, it's not going to break the bank."

"But—"

"Do you like them?"

Her eyes remained fixed on the shoe as she placed it back into its box. She let out a sigh before she met his gaze. "I love them, but still—"

"Still nothing, B. They're yours. No strings."

She stared at him, and he worried she could see right through him. Then she stood, and he sucked in a breath when she stepped close and hugged him.

Without thinking, he wrapped his arms around her and brought his lips to the top of her head.

"Thank you, Gavin. No one's ever . . ."

He waited for her to finish her thought, but she remained silent. Squeezing her tighter, he inhaled, letting her soft floral scent fill every pore in his body. "You're welcome."

This. He could get used to this . . .

The thought had him tensing.

With her arms still around his waist, she glanced up, resting her chin on his chest. "You okay?"

He was certain she could hear the beating of his racing heart. "Yeah." *Shit.* That sounded more like a croak than an actual word. He cleared his throat and loosened his arms but kept them looped around her. He motioned to the door with his head. "I have some calls I should probably go make."

She stepped away, but not before giving his chest a pat.

Wait, was that a friendly pat? Or something else? *Fuck.* He needed to get out of here.

It looked like she was trying not to smile, but he couldn't be sure. Hell, he wasn't sure of anything right now. One breath of this woman's intoxicating scent had obliterated every coherent thought in his brain.

Clearing his throat yet again, Gavin gave her a chin lift and made his way to her door. As he opened it, he peeked back at her. Yup, there was definite humor in her gaze. Fuck if he knew if that was a good thing or a bad thing at this point. "Come find me before you take off today, okay?"

Before she could answer, he turned and quietly shut the door behind him. Glancing around, he was grateful that no one seemed to be paying any attention to him. He scrubbed his hands over his face, biting back a groan.

Smooth, Frazier.

Real. Fucking. Smooth.

CHAPTER TWENTY

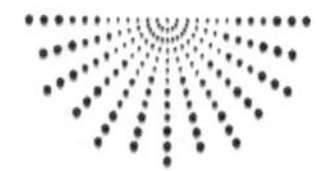

After Gavin left Bean's office, he immediately went to the gym. He cringed at recalling how damn awkward he'd been as he'd scurried out of her office like a terrified schoolboy standing in front of his crush. There was nothing like pounding on a heavy bag to make the mortification go away.

Or so he thought.

Twenty minutes of bag work did nothing to clear his head, so he laced up his running shoes and spent an hour sprinting through the trails of Jackson Cove State Park that abutted the Hudson Security property. Since it had taken all his focus to not face-plant on the trails, his mind was a little clearer now, and that antsy feeling had been replaced with exhaustion. However, he was no closer to figuring out what he was going to do with these newfound . . . feelings.

Damn. Feelings were something he'd purposely avoided for the last decade.

He quickly showered at the gym and headed back to his office. Now that he was spent, he could lose himself in work. Not exactly the healthiest way to handle things, but it was what he did. And so what if he harbored hope of seeing Bean again today?

He frowned as he strode into his office. "Fucking pathetic," he muttered.

"Who's pathetic?"

The voice had him startling.

Gavin's frown deepened. His situational awareness was fucked. He'd like to blame it on exhaustion but knew that would be a lie. As he'd walked through the office, he'd been trying to slyly look for Bean, oblivious to everything else. *Fucking hell.*

Flopping down into his office chair, he lifted his chin at Xander, who stood in his doorway. "Don't worry about it. What's up?"

"Just wanted to check in." Xander pointed to the chair on the opposite side of Gavin's desk with a questioning look.

"Of course," Gavin said as Xander closed the door behind him. "Everything okay?"

"I checked in with all the teams today and all is well. Nothing exciting to report, which is good."

When Xander didn't say anything else, Gavin waved his hand in a circular motion. "And?"

"And I got a call from TJ at the gym. He's concerned."

TJ was one of the head trainers at the De La Rosa Gym. Nice guy, excellent striking coach, and a badass Muay Thai specialist.

"About what?" His eyes narrowed in confusion when Xander looked at him in disbelief. "Seriously, what's he concerned about?"

Xander shook his head. "You, fucker."

"What?" No way had he heard that right.

"TJ said you basically took off the new check-in girl's head when you showed up. Then you were an asshole to a couple of the fighters who were working out near you. And when TJ went to talk to you, you nearly bit off his head before storming out of the damn place."

He could only stare at his friend dumbfounded. "Xan, I have no fucking clue what you're talking about." He racked his brain, thinking about the short time he'd spent at the gym.

He frowned as he vaguely recalled being irritated at the new kid at the front desk when she'd asked him to check in. He'd never had to check in before and hadn't seen why the hell he had to start today.

He cringed. Okay, fine . . .

And now that Xander mentioned it, he did recall the two fighters at nearby heavy bags. They'd approached him, but he'd ignored them. And yeah . . . he may have also told them to fuck off.

Heaving out a sigh, he scrubbed his hands over his face and slouched deeper into his chair. "Fuuuck, fine. I may not have been in the greatest mood earlier. There's been . . . a lot going on."

"I get it, man. Someone took a shot at you. That's gotta piss you off." Xander stared him down, and Gavin was certain he wasn't going to like what his friend was going to say next. "But I also think your pissy attitude isn't just about that."

Yup. He wasn't quite sure where Xander was going with this, but he wanted no part of it.

"You've been out of sorts since we wrapped up the McClintock rescue. More short-tempered."

Gavin arched a brow. "Short-tempered?"

"Yeah," Xander said. The look in his eyes dared Gavin to disagree. "Things usually roll off your back, and you keep calm. But you've been . . . the opposite of calm. Snappy. A borderline asshole. We all expect that from MacKay. Not from you. And to top it all off, you're micromanaging, which you usually don't do."

Gavin stifled a groan. "Look, the last week has been more hectic than usual."

"I'm sure the McClintock rescue stirred up some shit for you—because it sure as hell did for me—but I also think you've been in a shit mood because of what happened with Bean."

He jerked. "Nothing's happened between me and Bean."

"I meant her passing out last week." Xander smirked. "But it's interesting that you thought I was referring to something else."

Christ. He blew out a breath. "Bean's a friend. What she does here is vital. She's so damn good at what she does, and she's so driven, but it makes me crazy when she forgets basic things like fucking eating or drinking water. Then she passes out and gives herself a fucking black eye." His stomach rolled at the recollection, and because he was partially to blame. "I think I push her too hard."

"She wouldn't have it any other way, man."

"Yeah, but it doesn't help that I keep piling more shit onto her already overflowing plate."

"She's an adult. An adult who has serious control issues." Xander shrugged. "But she agreed to take on Tiny, which is fucking huge, right? You and MacKay have been talking to her for years about adding on another hacker, and she basically gave you both the middle finger the entire time."

"Yeah." Gavin sighed again, but then he smiled. "She's so fucking stubborn."

"That she is. And you're attracted to her."

He froze but tried to hide it with a shrug. "She's attractive. As are all the women who work here."

Xander rolled his eyes. "Cut the bullshit, man. Me and you? We go back. Aside from that, I was there last week when she stayed at your house, remember? I was a firsthand witness to you going completely stupid around her."

"Fine." He paused, unsure how to vocalize what he was feeling, unsure if he even wanted to. But apparently, keeping everything bottled up was turning him into an asshole.

Xander was one of his best friends, and he trusted the other man with his life. He supposed he could use all the advice he could get. Still, when he tried to put it into words . . . "I really can't explain it."

"Try."

He met Xander's gaze and didn't see judgement, just concern.

Gavin took a deep breath in and let it out. Unfortunately, the nerves swirling in his gut were still there, so he settled for bouncing his leg. "I've always found Bean attractive. All the women who work here are pretty in their own way. It's just a fact. An observation. Nothing more, nothing less."

"But?" Xander prodded when Gavin remained silent.

Fuck, here goes nothing. "After Bean got hurt . . . When I saw that black eye on her face, I don't know. Something changed. One second, we were just friends and colleagues, then just like that"—he snapped his fingers—"I started seeing her differently. I've always felt protective of her, but now it's so much more intense. And it's not just about keeping her safe. It's more than that. She and I have been friends for so long, but there's so much I don't know about her. And I want to get to know her better." He wanted to know every little detail about her—from her favorite childhood memory to her best vacation to what she tasted like. Every. Damn. Thing. "I don't know, man. I guess, I can't really explain it."

Xander grinned at him. "You explained it just fine. You should ask her out. Who knows, maybe she feels the same way."

"There's chemistry there for sure, but . . . I don't know.

I'm not really cut out for relationships." He'd seen too much. Done too much.

"Is that what you want with Bean? A relationship?"

"I think she deserves a relationship."

Xander shook his head. "That's not what I asked. Do *you* want a relationship with her?"

He was quiet for a moment as he thought about his friend's question, then he answered honestly. "If I was capable of having a relationship, I'd want it to be with her."

"Then ask the woman out already. Shoot your damn shot. You never know, man."

Easier said than done. Gavin knew a relationship wasn't in the cards for him. Especially not with someone as good as Bean. Because he'd inevitably fuck things up, and it would make things awkward—with their friendship, with work, with . . . everything.

She deserved so much more than what he could give her. He just had to keep reminding himself of that.

CHAPTER TWENTY-ONE

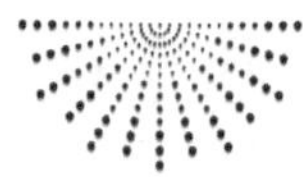

Bean stood and stretched, her stomach grumbling loudly. Hours had passed since she'd eaten those delicious donuts, she'd worked through lunch, and her frustration was at its boiling point. It was nearly seven in the evening, and she'd sent the cyber team home two hours earlier. She scanned her far monitor, impatience gnawing at her as the various programs—hers, the cyber team's, and Tiny's—were running at a snail's pace. They were no closer to finding out who had gone after Gavin.

She thought about heading to the staff kitchen to see if there were any leftovers remaining from the lunch Gavin had delivered, but her attention snagged on the two brown boxes sitting at the edge of her desk. Despite her hunger and growing irritation, they brought a smile to her lips. She chuckled as she peeked at the boots and set them aside. Hiking boots. The man had bought her *hiking boots*.

She slipped off her beautiful Ferragamos, opened the smaller box, and carefully removed the Louboutins. After putting them on, she walked the length of her office and couldn't help but stare at her feet in wonder. She still wasn't quite able to wrap her brain around the fact that Gavin bought these for her. Not only because of the hefty cost of the beauties—they were even more expensive than the Ferragamos—but because the moment she'd seen them online months ago, she'd practically salivated. She'd really, really wanted them, but they were way out of her price range. Yes, she pulled in a fantastic salary at Hudson Security and could technically afford them, but she hadn't been able to justify the price.

She kicked a foot out and bit back a swoony sigh, because they were *that* freaking gorgeous. They gave the illusion of real-life glass slippers with just enough sparkle to catch the eye, but not too much so that she'd look ridiculous wearing them to work.

Having spent her entire childhood in boarding schools, she'd been a sucker for fairy tales and Disney princesses. The magical and fanciful stories had been so different from her own life that they'd captivated her.

By the age of four, she'd been considered a gifted child prodigy in both math and science, so she knew fairy tales weren't based in reality. By the time she'd hit her teens, she'd still harbored a secret love of those stories, but all she'd had to do was look at her own life to know those happily ever afters didn't exist. At least, not for her.

Facts. Hard work. Persistence.

For as long as she could remember, those were her three pillars.

But one look at the pretty shoes had those old, fanciful longings stirring. And *Gavin* gifting them to her had her wishing for things she had no business wishing for.

With a sigh, she slouched into her chair. They were friends. Good friends. Good friends who were attracted to each other. She may not be the best when it came to inter-acting with people, but she'd stood on the sidelines and in the shadows observing others her entire life. She knew people, could read them. Yes, she'd made mistakes here and there, but she was almost certain that her newfound attraction to Gavin wasn't one-sided.

Just thinking about him had those butterflies in her belly launching. Partly from excitement, and partly from nerves. After all, she hadn't been with a man in far too long. Years, in fact.

She winced. Nearly seven years if she wanted to be exact.

Her last and only adult relationship had ended in disaster. Geoffrey, the man she'd thought she'd loved—the man she'd thought loved her back—had been a liar. He'd not only lied to her, but to everyone, including their country. Knowing he had deceived and used her for over two years to gain access to classified information had been humiliating. The man had played the long game with her and had nearly succeeded since she'd been too inexperienced, too naïve . . . too stupid to figure it out. Until it had almost been too late.

Shortly after joining Hudson Security, she'd attempted to do a casual, one-night thing with some guy she'd met at a bar over on neighboring Whidbey Island. She was no stranger to casual—the two experiences she'd had before Geoffrey had been the epitome of casual friends-with-benefits situations—but the sex-with-a-complete-stranger thing, the him-not-remembering-her-name-two-minutes-after-he'd-pulled-out thing hadn't been for her. Between the embarrassment and shame of what had happened with Geoffrey, and the cheapness she'd felt after that one-night stand, it was safe to say she was wary of ever getting involved with anyone again.

But Gavin was different. She knew him.

You thought you knew Geoffrey, too, and look how that turned out.

Her stomach twisted. No, dammit. The two men were nothing alike.

Geoffrey had been arrested for treason. God knows what had happened to him after he was convicted and sentenced. She'd tried to find out, but whoever was in charge of him had buried his info deep. Too deep to be worth the risk of finding out more.

It wasn't the same with Gavin. Not at all. If Gavin was deceitful, he was conning a whole hell of a lot of people. Granted, that's exactly what Geoffrey had done, but she had learned her lesson and had done extensive research on both Gavin and MacKay before joining Hudson Security. So it was apples and oranges, right?

Stifling a groan, she stared at her ceiling tiles. It was times like these that Bean wished she had a close girlfriend. Someone she could talk to and hash everything out with. Yes, she was friends with Esme and even Owen, but not like that. She occasionally got together for drinks with her coworkers, but she mostly kept to herself. It was a habit. Years of virtual solitude tended to do that to a person. Combine that with her workaholic tendencies, and she was lucky she even knew her colleagues on any sort of personal level.

The Hudson Security crew were an odd bunch. The men were a tighter group than the women. Granted, aside from her, there were only six other women on payroll out of the twenty-odd employees, but still. In her humble opinion, the entire crew were a ragtag bunch of emotionally unavailable people. Well, maybe not Xander. He seemed pretty well-adjusted. And not Alvarez either, since the man was basically married—but he was fairly new to the team, so she wasn't really sure he counted. However, everyone else was a bit closed off. Whether it was due to their time in the service or whatever alphabet agency they'd been a part of prior to joining the Hudson Security team, it didn't seem like any of them were in the market for any sort of long-term or meaningful relationship.

Tired of her back-and-forth questioning thoughts, Bean rose from her chair and crossed her office. Opening her storage closet, she looked at herself in the full-length mirror that hung on the back of the door. Really looked at herself. Dark-brown hair, blue eyes. Average in both looks and build. At five-three, she was shorter than she'd like, but she made up for it with her shoe collection.

She glanced down again at the beauties Gavin had given her, and her stomach did that fluttering thing again. If she was reading things right—and she was pretty sure she was—Gavin liked her, looked at her as more than just a friend, was attracted to her. It wasn't quite a fact, more of a theory at this point, but she'd never heard of him gifting anyone else anything. Let alone shoes that cost over twelve hundred dollars. Still, it was only a theory.

However, there was one certain fact she was sure of. She was one thousand percent attracted to Gavin Frazier. He stirred a want in her that she hadn't felt in a long, long time.

They were both adults, and it was okay for them to see what happened, right? She didn't want to jeopardize her position at Hudson Security, but if they went into it with their eyes wide open and with ground rules, everything would be fine. However, she could also be jumping the gun, and her theory could be totally off base.

She glanced again at her shoes, and the corners of her lips ticked up. *Doubtful. Highly doubtful.*

Mind made up, she fluffed her hair, adjusted her blouse, and smoothed her skirt. Though a slew of nerves remained, she closed the closet door.

First things first. She needed to thank him for the gorgeous shoes. There was nothing wrong with that. Besides, she knew that it was unlikely Gavin would make a move on her. One, he was her boss. Two, he was her friend. Those two facts alone would most likely keep her in the friend zone forever. Which . . . would be a damn shame.

It's not like she was going to try to give him a nudge or anything. Or to see if her theory had any merit. She was simply going to thank the man for his gift. It was the polite and kind thing to do.

She made her way to his office and stood in front of his closed door. As she raised her fist to knock, a smirk grew over her lips.

Right.

CHAPTER TWENTY-TWO

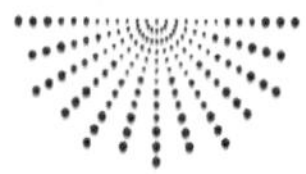

"Come in," Gavin called out in response to the knock on his door.

As the door opened, he glanced up, and his chest did that squeezing thing when Bean walked in.

She came to a halt just inside the doorway with her hip cocked like she was at the front of a fashion runway. "Well?" she asked, shutting the door behind her.

All he could do was stare. He wasn't sure exactly what he was supposed to notice, because he noticed every damn thing about her. And every part of her looked amazing.

Her eyebrows rose, and she gestured to her feet.

He jerked. Ah, yes. The shoes. The corners of his lips kicked up. "Very pretty." He wasn't lying. Nor was he just talking about her shoes.

He rose, rounded his desk, and leaned back against it, making a swirling motion with his finger.

She rolled her eyes but complied. As she spun, he allowed himself to take her in from head to toe. Yeah. She was so damn gorgeous.

"I take it you like them?" he asked when she faced him again.

"I do. I love them. They're beautiful and surprisingly comfortable. Thank you."

"You're welcome," he said, loving how her smile had her eyes twinkling. "Did you try on the hiking boots too?"

"Uh, no." She chuckled. "These kind of took priority."

"You're not going to get any complaints from me, B. They do look amazing on you." Tilting his head to the side, he eyed her legs appreciatively, not bothering to hide the fact he was doing so. "Though they do look a little higher than the red ones, don't you think?"

His pulse picked up speed as he straightened and stepped toward her with his hand held out. He had to be closer, was desperate for her touch.

That suspicious smirk lifted her lips, but she placed her hand in his.

Electricity shot through him at her touch, and he didn't miss how her blue eyes darkened. All his blood rushed south, and his heart thudded hard in his chest. She felt this too.

Pulling her close, he wrapped an arm around her waist and began to sway. There was no music playing, only the quiet hum of his electronics, but it didn't matter.

"See, I was right," he said as a blush stole over her cheeks. "These make you a little bit taller than the red ones."

She leaned closer, and for a split second, fear surged through him. There was no way she could miss the effect she had on him. But then heat and humor colored her expression as she stepped fully into him, pressing herself against his straining erection. "That's quite observant of you, boss."

"Well, it *is* my job to be observant." With one arm still holding her close, he traced his thumb over her jaw. "And it's Gavin. You have no idea how much I like hearing you say my name." God, what he'd do to hear her moaning his name, screaming it . . .

"Oh, I have a pretty good idea, Gavin," she whispered, pressing even closer.

Her gaze darted to his mouth, and when the tip of her tongue licked the center of her lower lip, he sucked in a breath.

The smirk she sent him had his blood heating. He needed to taste her.

Lowering his head to hers, he stilled, savoring the warmth of her body pressed tightly against his. She exhaled, and he felt her breath over his lips. Goosebumps tore over his skin.

He'd never wanted another woman as much as he wanted Bean. He physically ached for her. But he had to be sure. She was too damn important . . .

"Tell me this is a bad idea," he growled. "Tell me to back off."

"Shut up and kiss me."

He wasn't sure if he moved first or she did. It didn't matter. His lips were on hers and it was fucking glorious. She was soft and sweet and intoxicating. Then she nipped his lower lip, and an inferno engulfed him. Her lips parted, and he sought her tongue with his. Every nerve in his body tingled, and he was hard as steel.

He needed more.

Her fingers snaked into his hair, tugging him closer. The slight sting had him moaning. His hands cruised down her body and hiked up her skirt. Slipping his hands beneath the material, he cupped her ass, squeezing. "Hold on," he muttered against her lips.

Holy shit, he couldn't get enough.

She gasped and wrapped her legs around his waist as he lifted her. With his mouth still fused to hers, he walked her backward until they bumped into his desk. Setting her on the edge, he hiked her thighs higher against his sides, pressing his straining erection into the V of her legs. One hand gripped the back of her neck, while the other clutched her hip, rocking her against him.

"More, Gavin," she moaned, her head dropping back.

Holy fuck. Yes. His name moaned from her mouth had him growing impossibly harder. Her exposed neck was like a red flag to a bull, and he had to taste her. He licked, nibbled, and feasted on her delicate skin. The sharp tug of her fingers in his hair had him meeting her gaze. Lust, desire, and want stared back at him.

His need for her nearly brought him to his knees. "Holy shit, woman—"

Her mouth crashed against his and there was only her. Only Bean.

"Less talking," she muttered when they came up for air. "More—"

A quick rap on the door was the only warning they had before it swung open. "Hey, man. I have something you need to— Fucking hell!"

Bean yelped and scrambled out from under him, nearly kneeing him in the balls. She was hastily smoothing out her clothes and about to step away from the desk, but Gavin spun and gripped her hips, holding her still. Glancing down at his tented slacks, he positioned her so she stood directly in front of him. Since his hard-on was the very last thing Xander needed to see, Gavin racked his brain for every repulsive thought he could muster.

"Oh, no, you're fine, Xan," Bean stammered. "We were just, um, going over some notes and stuff." She cleared her throat, and her spine straightened as she gestured to the tablet Xander was carrying. "What's that?"

"Um . . ." Xander glanced at the device in his hand and

cringed when he looked back at them. "It's kind of important. I was going to call you in too, B."

With his hands still on Bean's hips, Gavin dropped his forehead to the back of her head and chuckled. He couldn't help it. How fucked up was this? He'd acted on impulse—again. And of course they had to get interrupted.

Perhaps it was a good thing, though. Despite how mind-blowing their brief make-out session had been, this wasn't the time and it most definitely wasn't the place.

"Sorry, man," Gavin said, meeting his friend's gaze. "Give us a couple minutes, would you?"

Xander nodded. "Yeah. Sorry to interrupt that . . ." He gestured to them and shuddered. "I'll be back in five. I'll be sure to knock *loudly* this time."

The moment the door closed behind Xander, Gavin turned Bean in his arms. Yeah, it may not be the ideal time and place, but he had to taste her. One more time.

Her mouth parted in question, but before she could say anything, he was kissing her. Her body was tense for a couple seconds before she melted into him. Deeping their kiss, he framed her face in his hands before he pulled away. "We're not done, okay?"

The corners of her lips twitched. "We better not be done, mister."

Damn, she was hot. "Yes, ma'am."

He dropped a quick kiss to her lips, and as much as he didn't want to, he untangled himself from her arms. Taking her hand, he led them to the couch in his office's seating area. "I feel like I should apologize for mauling you at work," he said as he sat and pulled her down next to him.

"Pretty sure it was a mutual mauling. But, yeah, I should have probably locked the door when I first came in to distract you."

His eyebrows kicked up. "Distract me?"

She held her leg out and wiggled her foot. "When I came in to thank you for the shoes, I was curious if this was one-sided."

"This?"

She waved a hand between them. "I'm glad to know it's not. Who knew you'd be such a great kisser, boss?"

He let out a breath that was more like a growl. "Shit," he muttered, adjusting his growing erection. "You're killing me, B."

There was a loud knock on the door, and she grinned at him and patted his knee as she glanced at his crotch. She handed him a throw pillow and winked. "You should probably keep that on your lap." Then she called out, "Come in."

Xander peeked around the door. "Is it safe?"

"You're fine," Bean said, rolling her eyes.

"You may be fine, Bean, but Frazier sure as hell isn't." Xander smirked at him. "Nice pillow."

Kill. Me. Now.

"Can we get this over with?" Holy shit, the very last thing Gavin wanted to do was have a conversation with Xander while he was still sporting an uncomfortable boner. The entire situation was so fucking awkward. "What is it you wanted to show us?"

Xander held up a tablet and stepped toward them, then he hesitated.

"Oh, good freaking God," Bean muttered. "Just sit down already and show us whatever it is you have."

Taking the seat across from them, he placed the large tablet onto the coffee table that separated them. "As you know, after the kidnapping, Edward McClintock shook up his security teams. While he fired everyone working on the personal security detail for Rita and Anson, he kept Polanski and a small group as his own personal security and to watch their house." Xander pulled up a collage of photos. "These are stills taken from the exterior security footage along the northern edge of the McClintock property. It's the public street that leads to their main gate. Cyber went back two full weeks, and there are a number of people who walk this route regularly."

Gavin glanced at the photos. The majority of the people were dressed in exercise wear. Most were walking dogs, though there were a handful of runners in the mix.

Scrolling through the photos, Xander stopped on one and enlarged it. "This guy started going by on Thursday morning."

"Thursday," Bean murmured. "That's two days after Anson was rescued."

"And the day after the McClintocks let the majority of their security staff go," Xander added.

As they spoke, Gavin analyzed the photo. It was of a white male jogging. He was dressed in trackpants and a hooded sweatshirt with a baseball hat pulled down low to shield his face. Gavin estimated the man to be in his late twenties to mid-thirties, probably around one-eighty, and fit.

Shaking his head, he gestured to the photo. "That guy could be anyone. Maybe he's just starting a new running route. After all, it's a popular area since there's not a lot of traffic."

Xander tapped the screen, and multiple photos populated the display. They all showed the same man mid-jog. "He ran by three times Thursday, three times Friday, once Saturday morning, and again Saturday afternoon. He's wearing a different outfit each time, even on the same days."

Part of Gavin wanted to ask Xander if he was certain it was the same man since none of the photos had a clear shot of his face. But when Xander rearranged the photos so they were displayed side by side, there was no doubt it was the same person.

Tapping the screen again, Xander brought up a video and pressed play. "This footage is from this morning. Notice anything different?"

"He's walking and not running." Gavin frowned. "But his arms aren't swaying. He's favoriting his right arm, like his right shoulder hurts."

Bean's eyes narrowed as she leaned closer to the screen. Suddenly, she gasped and turned to him. "You said you got a shot into the car that was chasing us, right? Do you think this could be the shooter?" Before he could respond, she turned to Xander. "Please tell me you were able to get a clear shot of his face. At least a partial."

Xander winced and pulled up a photo onto the screen. "Kind of."

Gavin's frown deepened. It was obviously enlarged from the video feed and was grainy as fuck.

"This was the only shot. Tiny's doing his thing on it and wanted me to tell you he's running it through a number of facial-rec programs, yours included."

Bean glanced up with hopeful eyes. "Any luck?"

Xander shook his head. "He thinks it'll take a while since the image is shit."

Raking her fingers through her hair, Bean groaned.

Gavin froze and inappropriate thoughts flooded his mind. Like Bean making that noise under different circumstances. His fingers running through her hair while she was under him and—

Motherfucking shit! Focus, Frazier! Fucking focus!

He cleared his throat. "Unfortunately, it's still a waiting game. This is good info, Xan."

"But we don't know exactly what the info is," Bean grumbled.

"True." Gavin nodded and couldn't help but smile at her

scrunched-up nose. She was so damn cute. "But it's still more than we had earlier."

"Maybe I can take this new partial photo and the partial from the car chase and create a different program that will—"

Gavin reached over and covered her hands with his. "Let's let the current programs do their thing first, B."

As much as he wanted to find answers, it was late. The last thing he wanted was Bean to get wrapped up in work. He had other plans for her. For them. Plans that had nothing to do with surveillance footage, Xander, or identifying shooters.

Knowing Xander wasn't an idiot, and that their friend had seen them making out earlier, Gavin slung his arm around Bean's slim waist and pulled until she was snug against his side. "We'll look at this more tomorrow, Xan. By then, maybe Tiny will have generated some matches. Thanks for coming by, but you can leave now. Have a good night." He gave his friend a pointed look. "And get the door on your way out."

Xander chuckled as he grabbed the tablet and stood. "Got ya loud and clear, Frazier. Loud and fucking clear. See you guys."

He waited until Xander left and then locked his office door. Settling back onto the couch, he turned his attention to Bean, who stared at him in disbelief.

"Gavin. Frazier. That was extremely rude. Xander was bringing us informa—"

His mouth claimed hers and satisfaction surged through him when he swallowed her moan. When they came up for air, they were both breathing hard. "You were saying?"

The dazed look in her eyes had him wanting to pump his fist in the air. "I have no clue."

He dropped a kiss on her lips. "No more work tonight."

"Oh yeah?" Her lips lifted into a mischievous grin.

"Yeah. I have plans for you." Grabbing her by the hips, he hauled her toward him so she straddled his lap.

"Wait! Xander will know—"

"Don't care," he murmured, nibbling on that perfect spot where her neck and shoulder met. He ran his hands up the smooth skin of her legs, grabbed her ass, and squeezed, grinding her against his rock-hard cock.

Her eyes drifted to half-mast, and she gripped his shoulders for balance. Her mouth opened on a gasp. Yeah, this may not be the most appropriate time or place, but he had to have her. At least a little taste.

Rocking her harder, his fingers traced the edge of her panties.

"Touch me, Gavin," she moaned, her hips picking up their rhythm.

He grazed the damp material with the pads of his fingers, and she groaned. With one hand, he pulled the material to the side so his fingers could explore her slick folds. His cock twitched violently. She was so fucking wet.

"Gavin, please." Her breaths came in pants as she writhed atop him.

"Tell me what you want, baby."

She glared at him, and he chuckled, his fingers still playing between her legs.

"Gavin," she said, her voice stern.

"You want this?" He dipped his finger between her folds, taking her moisture and rubbing it against her clit.

She threw her head back and groaned. "Yes!"

"You like that?" he growled.

Meeting his gaze, her face was flushed with desire. "More, Gavin. Please."

Rubbing her clit with his thumb, he slipped two fingers into her, groaning when she squeezed his fingers tight. "That's it, B. Your pussy's so fucking wet for me." She whimpered as she clenched around his fingers again. He grinned. *Someone likes a little dirty talk.* Satisfaction and need surged through him. She was so damn sexy. "You like when I finger-fuck you, baby?"

She slammed her mouth to his, shoving her tongue into his mouth. He thrust his fingers in and out of her, the wet noise of her excitement making him painfully hard.

"Yes, yes, yes," she chanted.

"Look at me," he demanded as he pinched her clit while fucking her hard with his hand. "Let me see you come all over me."

A second later, she tensed, her pussy milking his fingers, and she slumped against him.

For a few moments, the only sounds were their heavy breaths.

"Holy shit, that was amazing," she murmured into his chest.

His fingers were still inside her, and he softly stroked her. His lips lifted into a smile when her body trembled.

"Oh my God, Gavin," she said on a sigh, pushing up onto his chest to see him. All the while, he continued to lazily finger her, enjoying the renewed flush spreading over her face.

"Bean, honey, I'm so not done with you." Pulling his hand from her, he held her gaze as he licked his fingers clean. Her tangy and musky taste had his mouth watering.

More.

He was desperate for more.

Her pupils were blown, and before she could take her next breath, he flipped her onto her back. He tossed her skirt up, yanked off her panties, and threw them to the ground. He pushed her thighs wide. Her smooth pussy lips were shiny with her excitement. He licked her from ass to clit, savoring every delectable inch. Her delicious flavor consumed him, and he buried his face between her legs until she was screaming his name.

"Holy crap, Gavin."

Pride surged through him at the satisfied smile on Bean's face. He was kneeling on the floor between her spread legs, not giving a shit about the bite of the hardwood on his knees. Her chest was still heaving, and her arms were sprawled out bonelessly beside her, which he was grateful for since she'd grabbed onto his hair so hard he'd been afraid he'd end up with bald patches.

She let out a blissed-out sigh, and he immediately changed his mind. He'd be fine with her grabbing onto his hair any day of the damn week. Eating her out may be his new favorite thing, because, holy shit, when she'd come all over his tongue . . . His dick pulsed, aching for release.

Sitting up onto her elbows, she crooked a finger at him. "Since you just tried to kill me with two orgasms, I think it's only fair that I return the favor."

Not needing a second invitation, he rose and sat beside her on the couch, leaning back into the cushions with his tented slacks on full display. She tossed a throw pillow onto the ground between his spread feet, and his cock throbbed. When she dropped to her knees between his legs, he nearly came in his pants.

"Oh yeah?" He should have been embarrassed by the way his voice cracked, but he didn't fucking care.

All he could focus on was Bean. On her knees. About to suck him off. It was like his wildest fantasy come to life.

Reaching for his belt buckle, her hands rubbed against his

straining cock, and he couldn't help the groan that escaped. "Holy fuck, B."

She grinned, licking her lips. "Pretty sure you're gonna enjoy what I have in mind—"

They both froze when their phones rang, their ringtones obnoxiously loud in the quiet room.

He groaned, dropping his head to the back of the couch. So damn close . . .

She chuckled, sitting back on her heels. "You know, I feel like the universe is conspiring against us."

"Yeah." Blowing out a breath, he sat up and held a hand out to her. She placed her smaller hand in his, and he helped her onto the couch. As much as he wanted to be with her, be inside her, he needed to slow things down. Needed to remember he was in his damn office.

He wrapped an arm over her shoulders and pulled her to his side. "We have time though. There's no rush, right?"

"Well . . ." Giving him a sly grin, she gestured to his erection. "Maybe not a *rush* rush, but I'd say there's some urgency. Wouldn't you?" Before he could respond, she yanked him close for a scorching kiss and then pushed him away. Rising, she grabbed her panties off the floor, shimmied them on, and then smoothed out her skirt and adjusted her blouse. Grabbing her phone from his desk, she glanced at it and her nose scrunched. "MacKay wants a call. Give me five, and we can call him from my office."

Nodding, he sighed, not wanting his time with her to end. "Go hiking with me tomorrow?" When a look of disbelief crossed her face, he rushed on, hoping to appeal to Bean's logical side. "We can head over to Jackson Cove State Park around lunchtime, and it'll have a two-fold purpose. First, you can try out your new hiking boots."

She snorted, and her blue eyes danced with amusement. "Please tell me your second reason is better."

God, he loved her sass. "It'll give us both a break from work. I'll pack a lunch for us, and we can get out and stretch our legs. Plus, I want to see you away from all this." He waved his hand at his office. "I don't want to wait until after work tomorrow to spend more time with you."

The humor in her eyes softened, and she nodded. "Next time lead with that."

As she reached for the doorknob, she glanced back at him —well, at his cock—and licked her lips. Holy shit, if his cock didn't have a mind of its own. The damn thing strained toward her.

"To be continued, boss man," she said with a grin before walking out of his office, leaving the door open behind her.

Grabbing the throw pillow that was still on the ground by his feet, he placed it over his lap. The last thing he wanted was someone to walk by and see him in his current condition. Holy fuck. His breath was still ragged, and he could only stare at his empty doorway.

Bean had damn near blown his mind. How had it taken him so long to notice her? Yes, he'd always found her attractive, but now? Now that he'd tasted her, had her explode on his fingers, on his tongue . . . He wasn't sure he'd ever get enough of her.

He sure as hell wasn't going to rub one out before they had to be on a call with MacKay, so he needed to calm the fuck down. Hell, he needed to slow things down between him and Bean. They'd seemingly gone from zero to ninety out of nowhere. As much as he desired her, the last thing he wanted was for their first time to be a quick and frantic fuck in his office. Yeah, he'd hoped they'd do that at some point, but not for their first time.

He had no idea where Bean stood on things, if she even wanted to pursue anything beyond a physical relationship with him. He hoped to hell she did, but he had a feeling her walls were even higher than his.

He was a patient man. Determined. He may not be the best bet, and God knew, she deserved more than him, but he was dead set on making her his. For as long as she'd have him, he'd give her everything he had.

CHAPTER TWENTY-THREE

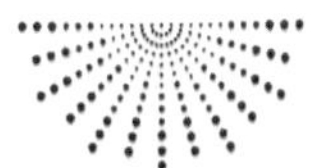

"Ready?" Gavin asked, releasing a deep breath. It was as if he were trying to clear his head, which considering the hectic morning Bean knew he'd had, wouldn't be a surprise.

Following his lead, she took in the crisp air, and the forest's earthy scents filled her nose. Was she ready?

Before they'd left the office, she'd changed out of her pencil skirt and sweater set and into leggings, a half-zip fleece top, and a down vest. She wiggled her toes, glanced down at her new hiking boots, and then up at Gavin. Seeing the tension he carried in his posture and the dark circles shadowing his eyes, she aimed for light. "The boots are comfy."

He grinned as he took her hand and led them toward the trailhead. "Nice nonanswer."

She snickered, surprised by how things weren't awkward between them after they'd crossed a huge line the night before. Granted, she'd done everything she could to play things casually, like her mind hadn't been completely blown by being with Gavin that way. Once she'd gotten home, she'd stayed up half the night overanalyzing every minute detail and trying to figure out what it all meant. Obviously, he was attracted to her. But did he want more? Did it mean more? Or was it casual? Were they fuck buddies?

In the wee hours of the morning, she'd finally admitted to herself that she hoped things between them could maybe possibly hopefully—no, not *hopefully*, just maybe and possibly—be more than something casual. Not that she expected any kind of forever. Not at all. She just thought that given their history as friends and all, it could mean . . . more.

Clearing her throat, she aimed to focus on the now. The last thing she needed was to spiral down the overanalyzing rabbit hole while the man was literally holding her hand. "You know I'm not much of a hiker, right?"

"Uh, yeah." He chuckled. "Pretty sure everyone who knows you knows that."

"Does that mean you'll take it easy on me?"

"Oh come on, B. Where's your sense of adventure?"

She rolled her eyes. "I do have to be back by two, so with travel time, we have just under two hours."

"I know, honey." He pointed to a trail to the left. "That's an easy trail too. More of a gradual elevation change. It has some nice streams and a waterfall farther in. A few difficult trails branch off it, but the main trail is a five-mile loop."

"We should do that one, then." She frowned when he tugged her past it.

"Next time." He led her toward a narrow trail to the right. "This one is also fairly moderate, but it has great views of the water."

The trail narrowed, and she released his hand, gesturing ahead of her. "Lead the way." Her eyebrow arched when the trail grew steeper within seconds. "Hate to break it to you, boss man, but I think your definition of 'fairly moderate' is different from mine."

Her breaths came in huffs as she focused on the uneven path before her.

"This is the hardest part. I promise."

She couldn't even appreciate his firm backside. All she could focus on was the trail that continued to go up. She yelped as her footing gave way and she landed on her right knee. But seeing as the trail was ridiculously sloped, it wasn't too bad. "Aren't there supposed to be switchbacks and stuff."

He coughed over a laugh and glanced back at her. "You doing okay?"

She scowled. "Peachy."

He waited for her to reach him and then moved behind her. His hands went to her hips, steadying her. "It flattens out after this," he said, nudging her forward.

After a few more minutes of hiking basically straight up, they crested the hill, and Bean came to a halt.

"Oh, thank God," she muttered.

Relief washed through her as her heart pounded with exertion. She hadn't realized just how out of shape she was, and holy shit, the lungs-burning thing was not okay. Thankfully, the trail immediately widened and was indeed flat. At least as far as she could see. But who the hell knew with Gavin and his stupid "fairly moderate" trails.

"You did great," Gavin said, retaking her hand. "Easy sailing from here." She shot him her best glare, and he laughed. "I promise."

They continued in comfortable silence for a few more minutes. As the fire in her lungs died down, she kept sneaking glances at him, relieved how some of the earlier tension she'd noticed had eased. Though the dark circles beneath his eyes remained.

Gavin shook his head and let out an exaggerated sigh. "What? I know you're itching to ask me something."

Her mouth opened and then closed. She wasn't crossing

any lines, right? They were friends. She internally cringed. Considering he'd had his mouth between her legs less than twenty-four hours ago, she wasn't sure "friends" was the correct word. But whatever.

"Out with it, B."

"You look a little tired and I was just wondering if you're sleeping okay." Her words came out in a jumbled rush, and she took in a deep breath. Exhaling, she aimed for a more normal tone. "I remember you saying a while back that you used to have nightmares from your military days."

It was close to three years ago that he'd shared that with her, but their conversation had stuck with her. He'd been vague about what the nightmares entailed, but she knew they'd revolved around a mission with children that had gone horribly wrong. He hadn't shared the mission details, and she wasn't sure she wanted to know. All she knew was that whatever had happened had left a scar in his heart.

"I know the whole mission with Anson was awful, and it hit everyone hard. What that poor kid was put through . . . I just want to make sure you're okay."

He squeezed her hand, and some of the nervousness fled. A hand squeeze was a positive sign, right?

"I'm good, Bean. I'm not going to lie to you and say the nightmares haven't resurfaced with the McClintock mission, because they have. But last night?" A small smile ghosted his lips. "My lack of sleep last night had nothing to do with nightmares this time. In fact, I'd welcome that kind of lack of sleep any day. Or night. Hell, even afternoon." He shot her a wink.

Heat washed over her face, but she managed to muster up a smirk. "Well, I figured since things were left a little . . . *unsatisfying* for you last night, 'hiking' might be a euphemism."

He barked out a laugh. "Trust me, honey, there was

nothing unsatisfying about what happened between us. You're the best thing I've ever tasted. Would I have liked to come inside you? Absolutely. Thinking about doing just that definitely kept me up last night." He wagged his eyebrows at her and grinned. "There's no rush, though. We'll get there."

Shaking her head, she slapped both hands over her flaming cheeks. "I thought I could do this sexy-banter thing with you, but holy shit, I can't."

He slung an arm over her shoulder and pulled her into his side. "I think making you blush may be my new favorite thing." He dropped a kiss to the top of her head before retaking her hand and leading her down the trail.

"So aside from a restless night, how did your morning go?"

He shook his head. "It was going fine until I got stuck on the phone with Constance Whitcomb. The woman is determined to have us do her personal security."

"You mean, she's determined to have *you* be her personal security."

He cringed. "She's relentless."

"Are you going to do it?"

"Hell no. I told her we didn't have anyone available."

She bit the inside of her cheek to keep from laughing. "Uh, Team Three just got back from California."

He eyed her. "Whose side are you on?"

"Just messing with you, boss." She chuckled and jabbed him in the side with her elbow. "The woman's a vulture."

He made a face, shaking his head. "We're here to relax. Let's not talk about her."

She smothered a snort. He was adorable when he was all irritated and bothered. Though she did prefer him getting bothered for completely different reasons. In fact, maybe she could distract him—

She came to a halt and gasped.

The trail had cut abruptly to the right, and the Pacific Ocean was laid out in front of her, its waters calm with an occasional whitecap dotting the expanse. The gray, overcast skies met the water at the horizon. "Holy crap, Gavin. It's gorgeous."

"Sure is," he said. "Absolutely breathtaking."

She glanced at him, and her face heated when she saw his focus was entirely on her. Biting her lower lip to keep from grinning like a loon, she nudged him with her hip. "Aren't you a charmer?"

"Nah, honey, just being honest." He dropped a kiss to the top of her head again and then tugged on her hand and continued down the trail. Gesturing to the view, he said, "It stays like this for about a half-mile, then it snakes back into the forest and there are some switchbacks to the trailhead."

They walked a little longer, and she was mesmerized by the view. And by the man beside her holding her hand.

After a few minutes, Gavin cleared his throat. "So . . . how did you come up with Sabrina Marie?"

She stilled. A chill ran through her body that had nothing to do with the crisp temperatures. She'd secretly hoped that in all the mayhem of the past few days, he'd forget about that whole you-have-an-entirely-different-name thing. Apparently, she was wrong.

"Well, as I'm sure you gathered, Sabrina was my original middle name. It wasn't like I had a problem with the name Florence. It was my grandmother's name, and from what I recall of her, she was nice. But I was never just Florence. My parents insisted on calling me Florence Sabrina, and it was . . ." She wrinkled her nose. "A lot. Especially when you added in Buena Ventura as the last name."

"It's quite the mouthful." He winked at her, squeezing her hand. "Was Bean a nickname for Sabrina?"

She nodded. "I was sent to this fancy boarding school for

the gifted when I was four. When I was around eight, there was this one cook that started calling me Flo Bean. After a while, it was just Bean. Marie was really nice too. She made cookies with me on the weekends and holidays I didn't go home."

"You didn't go home for the holidays?"

She shook her head. "Not usually. My parents traveled a lot. They did host a few big Thanksgiving events, and I went home for those. They liked to parade me around at those parties."

"Why would they do that?"

She scoffed. "You met my mother. It's safe to say they aren't exactly the humble sort. So if they could show me off to their colleagues, they did. After all, their colleagues' kids didn't graduate from high school at twelve. They didn't get a double bachelor's degree at fifteen from Cal Poly or two master's degrees from Stanford at eighteen."

He let out a low whistle. "Damn, Bean. I knew you were crazy smart, but I didn't realize you were a bona fide genius."

"Child prodigy," she clarified with a wink. "Not genius."

He chuckled. "Well, I beg to differ. The fact you know there's a difference between the two means you're a million times smarter than me."

"Only when it comes to computers, Gavin." She waited for the party trick request. Or for him to ask her questions that would prove her intelligence. When they continued to walk in silence, she glanced up at him.

"That's pretty cool." He met her gaze and smiled. "So when did you decide to change your name?"

"After I graduated. My parents wanted me to continue to get my doctorate, but I was done. At that point, I had some pretty big companies trying to recruit me. All that sounded so much more exciting than continuing on with school. So, for once, I told my parents no. Suffice it to say, they were not pleased, so I walked away and didn't look back. Changing my name was my little act of rebellion."

"Good for you. I can't imagine it was easy."

She shrugged. "I'd been on my own for so long already that it didn't really matter. I got scholarships for all my schooling, and it included boarding. And the private firms threw big money at me."

"You worked for Orion, right? Digital security?"

She smiled and nodded. "That was a lot of fun." She'd dabbled in hacking before, but once she started working at Orion, one of the world's trillion-dollar online retail companies, to hack into their various systems, there had been no stopping her. "I was really good, and it wasn't long until I was on the FBI's and CIA's radar."

"They recruited you hard."

"They sure did."

"But you said no."

"I didn't like the idea of working for one agency. Especially for the paltry amount of money they were offering." She shot him a cocky grin. "Since I was better than anyone either agency had on staff, they really didn't have a choice but to let me do contract work."

"How was it working for the alphabets?"

"Boring, mostly. But I managed to keep it entertaining. When I got access to their systems, I was able to peek into a lot of interesting information. Of course, I covered my tracks well, because with those alphabet agencies—boring assignments or not—you can never be too careful with them."

He squeezed her hand. "See, a freaking genius."

Bumping her shoulder against his, she returned the squeeze. "What about you? What's your family like?"

He gave a slight shake of his head and a look she couldn't decipher flashed over his face. "My mom took off when I was a baby, so growing up it was just me and my dad. Just a boring, regular childhood." Gavin's jaw tensed, then he let out a chuckle that held no humor. "That's a lie. I mean, I suppose he did the best he could, but honestly? He was a drunk. He'd get sober for a little bit and things were good. Then he'd fall off the wagon and things were . . . not so good. He struggled."

Her stomach dropped, and her heart broke for him, for the child he'd been. She knew it hadn't been just a struggle for Gavin's father, but for him too. From the little he'd said—and hadn't said—she imagined his upbringing had been tough, chaotic.

It explained a lot though. Made her see the man beside her a little clearer. Her admiration for him grew because the Gavin Frazier she knew was the epitome of dedicated and determined. He had a drive and focus that was unmatched. And that was all his own doing.

Unsure if she was overstepping, she asked, "What happened to him?"

"A couple weeks after I graduated from basic training, he was driving drunk and hit a tree. They told me he died instantly."

Gavin's flat, lifeless tone had her pulling them to a stop. Before she could second-guess herself, she wrapped her arms around his waist and hugged him. "I'm sorry," she murmured with her cheek pressed against his chest.

For a moment, he was tense in her arms. Then he let out a deep exhale and embraced her back, the rigidness in his frame easing. "Thanks, B," he said, pressing a kiss to the top of her head. "My dad was an only child and was estranged from his parents long before I came along. So there's no extended family or anything. It's just me now."

With her arms still around him, she tilted her torso slightly away to meet his somber gaze. "You're wrong." His eyes narrowed in obvious confusion, and she rushed on, "It's not just you. You may not have any family by blood anymore, but the family you've built, that you've created at Hudson Security? *We* are your family, and we'll always have your back."

The edges of his lips kicked up, and some of the heaviness around them lifted. "That's kind of you to say."

She wagged her finger at him, tsking. "Not kind. Just facts." Stepping away, she retook his hand and continued walking. "And since we've established that I'm the genius here—those were your exact words, yes?"

He shook his head. "*Freaking* genius, B."

"That's right." She shot him a smug grin. "I'm a 'freaking genius' so you can't argue with me on this one. Got it?"

He brought their joined hands to his lips and pressed a kiss to the back of her hand. "Wouldn't dream of it, honey."

She ignored the giddy feeling at his sweet gesture as they followed the descending trail back into the forest. After a few moments of comfortable silence, she let out a content sigh. "This is really pretty, Gavin. Thank you for bringing me out here. It's . . . peaceful."

It was his turn to give her a cocky smile. "Have I converted you into being a nature-loving outdoorswoman?"

She snorted. "I wouldn't go that far. Let's just say that I wouldn't mind going hiking again." Her eyes narrowed. "But only easy trails like this."

"Even though you wanted to kill me at the start of the hike."

She tapped her lips with her finger. "I forgot about that."

"Too late. What do you say we make this a regular lunchtime activity?" He stopped and unzipped his pack. "I figure we have another couple of weeks or so before the weather turns to complete crap." He pulled out a foil-wrapped something and handed it to her.

"What's this?"

"Lunch. Turkey and cheddar hoagie. Lettuce and mayo, no mustard or tomatoes."

"You made me a sandwich?" She stared at him for a moment. "How did I not know you were this sweet?"

He made a face. "I'm not sweet."

She scoffed. "Not only did you pack us a lunch, but you remembered what I like on my sandwich."

"Whatever. I figured if I was dragging you out to hike during your lunch hour, I'd better feed you too." Her stomach let out a loud growl, and he narrowed his eyes. "Bean, when was the last time you ate?"

She waved her sandwich at him and took a giant bite before hustling down the trail. "Thanks for this," she called out with her mouth full. "It's delicious!"

She yelped when he hauled her backward. Her back crashed against his front, and he nuzzled the side of her neck. "Bean?"

After finishing her bite, she swallowed and muttered, "Who knew you were such a man-handling caveman?" She relaxed into him and glanced up at him in mock indignation.

"You."

The intensity of his gaze had her heart pounding, had her wanting to squeeze her thighs together to relieve the building heat. Instead, she leaned into him, pushing her hips back. She grinned when she felt him instantly hardening against her. "Not gonna lie, boss. Can't say I mind." She stepped away and shot him a wink as she continued down the trail and took another bite of her sandwich.

"Damn, woman," he groaned as he caught up to her. "Who knew you were such a tease? In fact—"

Gavin's cell phone rang, its sharp ringtone so at odds with the nature around them. "Hang on," he muttered, pulling his phone from his pocket. "Frazier."

His expression went from playful to serious in the span of

a few seconds. He met her gaze as he nodded at whatever the person on the other end was saying. "Bean's with me and I'll tell her once we hang up."

Worry had her stomach turning. After giving a couple of curt, one-word replies, he disconnected the call.

"We have to get back." Gesturing with his head for her to follow him, he continued down the trail and quickly unwrapped his sandwich. "You okay walking and eating? It's mostly downhill, nothing strenuous like the beginning."

Shaking her head, she rewrapped her sandwich. "It's probably safer if I just eat in the car."

"Sorry we have to cut this short," he said and took a bite of his food. He slowed to put her lunch back into his pack.

"No problem," she said, waving him off. "What's going on?"

"That was Xander. Everyone's okay, but someone just shot up the McClintocks' house."

Her eyebrows rose in surprise. "But they're billionaires. Isn't their house secluded and secure? How could someone get that close?"

Gavin nodded as he polished off his sandwich. "That's the problem," he said when he finished chewing. "Whoever it was dodged all the security cameras."

Her stomach sank. "Every single one?"

"Yeah." He sighed as he retook her hand. "Either someone knew where all the cameras were placed or someone hacked into the feed."

CHAPTER TWENTY-FOUR

Gavin looked around the large conference room. He was seated at the head of the long, rectangular table with Xander and Wilson to his left. On the Smartboard at the opposite end of the room was Carmichael. Looking out the door, Gavin could see all four members of the cyber team scouring through various video feeds. He knew Bean was in her office digging to see if anyone had hacked into the security feed. Everyone was working to find answers.

Glancing at his colleagues, he was thankful for the distraction. Not that he was happy someone had shot up the McClintocks' house, but happy he had something to focus on aside from his earlier verbal diarrhea with Bean. As a rule, he didn't talk about his dad. Ever. And yet there he'd been, telling her things he'd never told another soul.

When she'd asked about his family, he'd been fully prepared to give her a generic raised-by-a-single-dad story and leave it at that. Instead, her honesty about her own past and family had unleashed something in him that had him spilling his guts.

A phone ringing pulled his attention back to the Smartboard.

"Sorry about that," Carmichael said, silencing his phone. "As I was saying, Riviera and Bonson were at the hospital with Anson, and I was on my way back to the house with Rita. We were through their security gate and about to pull up under their front awning when shots were fired into the west side of the house. Polanski's security team responded, and I got Rita out of there."

"Is she okay?" Gavin asked, refocusing on the task at hand.

Carmichael nodded. "When it was clear, I brought her into the house, and she and Edward went to their secure room."

"And Polanski's team?"

Carmichael's lips pressed into a thin line. "They weren't able to locate anyone or find anything."

Xander scoffed. "You're telling me that their team of five security personnel couldn't find shit?"

Carmichael glared into the screen. "Yup."

Gavin turned to Xander. "I know you're still in the process of looking for long-term security for Rita and Anson, but where are you at with that?"

"I sent over fifteen recommendations to Edward this morning." Xander frowned. "Since the guy's insisting on keeping Polanski's team of five, I strongly suggested he hire at least three people for each of his family members."

"Think he will?"

"I don't know," Xander said with a frown. "He's still keeping Polanski as his head of security, so I don't know how good his judgement is."

Even though Gavin agreed, he asked, "Meaning?"

Xander shrugged. "Look, I don't have kids or anything, but if my head of security hired a group to protect my child, and two of the people he hired fucking kidnapped and *tortured* my kid? Let's just say my head of security would no longer be walking this fucking earth, let alone still on my fucking payroll."

Gavin's gut churned as he nodded. "Agreed."

Security was about people: reading them, doing the background work, and paying attention. How the fuck had Polanski gotten it so wrong? Something was definitely off.

Glancing back at Carmichael, Gavin asked, "Current status?"

"The cops are still here, and the feds just arrived. They're taking Edward's statement and talking with Polanski and his team. What do you want to do?"

"What's your gut telling you, Carmichael?"

His colleague glanced off-screen to the right and lowered his voice. "Something's rotten. I think Edward feels it too. When he and Rita came out of their secure room, they stayed huddled together and kept their distance from *everyone*. Except from me."

Gavin nodded and then paused as Bean entered the conference room. "Anything?"

She shook her head. "No. I don't see any traces of anyone hacking into the security feed."

"You're sure?"

Her right eyebrow arched. Hard. "Is that a real question, boss man?"

"Sorry," he said, wincing at the glare she threw his way. He cleared his throat and turned back to the Smartboard. "Owen's prepping the helo now. Let Edward and Rita know that we'll be there in thirty."

"We?" Carmichael asked.

"Everyone. Team Three got back this morning, and they'll be with me, Xander, and Wilson. They'll take over Rita's detail. You stay put until we get to you. I also have Tash en route to the hospital as we speak for an extra hand. No one is getting to that kid."

Carmichael's gaze hardened. "Damn straight, Frazier."

"Bean will be in charge of comms. I want everyone connected immediately. Call me paranoid, but I don't trust any of those fuckers on Polanski's team."

"I'll have comms up and running by the time you get airborne," Bean said, stepping fully into the room. "Everyone starts on line three. Once I get everything scrambled and secure, we'll move to another line."

A chorus of "copy that" sounded throughout the room as everyone stood.

"Bean, can I talk to you for a second?" he asked.

She nodded and then called out to Xander and Wilson, "Abbot's got the new comms at her desk. Make sure Team Three grabs them and takes extras for Tash and Team Two." She turned back to Gavin after both men saluted her. "You too, boss. Make sure you get one of the new comms. They're even clearer than the other ones and have better range."

"I will." He walked to his closet and grabbed his tactical gear. "Make sure you finish your lunch, okay?"

She leaned against his doorway and grinned at him. "Pretty sure you have more than my caloric intake to worry about right now."

Striding up to her, he peeked around her into the main work area. Seeing everyone was busy with various shit, he leaned down and quickly pressed a kiss to her lips. "Humor me. I was going to ask you to join me for dinner tonight, but . . ." He held up his tactical bag and shrugged.

"Next time." She smiled, but her gaze quickly sobered. She placed a hand on his abdomen and electricity shot through him. "Be careful, okay?"

Meeting her gaze, he nodded. "Always, B."

There was no way in hell he'd do anything to put himself

in jeopardy. For the first time in forever, he had someone to come back to.

An hour later, after introducing Team Three's Rizzo, Hanniger, and Schreiber to the McClintocks as Rita's new personal security detail, Gavin gave Carmichael the okay to return to the hospital.

Gavin was now in the McClintocks' massive home office, which they'd immediately scanned for bugs upon entering. Thankfully, no listening or recording devices had been found. Across the coffee table from him, Edward and Rita were seated beside each other on the leather couch, their hands linked tightly. Xander stood sentry at the door, while Wilson was positioned to the right of the office's window, scanning the surrounding woods where Team Three was patrolling.

"How did this happen?" Rita asked. "Polanski said none of the alarms were triggered."

"They weren't. Our IT specialist verified that the system's cameras weren't hacked."

"All due respect," Rita interjected, "but what are your IT specialist's qualifications? They could have missed something."

Gavin understood the woman's apprehension, but her superior tone grated on his nerves. "No." More like fuck no, but he was a professional, dammit. "Our IT specialist is more than qualified."

Edward frowned. "Rita does have a point. How do we know that he didn't miss anything? Hackers are very talented—"

"I'm going to stop you both right now." Irritation simmered in his gut, and he took a moment to rein it in. "My staff's ability isn't up for discussion. If you'll recall, our IT specialist was the person who was able to locate your kidnapped child within twenty-four hours *and* find the proof that members of your security detail were responsible. Our IT specialist—along with the rest of Hudson Security's cyber division—is more than capable of checking for security breaches on a video feed."

"Fuck those tech billionaire shitheads," Bean muttered in his earpiece. "But thanks for having my six, boss."

A quick glance at Xander and Wilson showed they were both sporting smirks. Looks like Bean had opened everyone's comms.

"How did these shooters evade detection?" Edward asked.

"From what we learned through our contacts at SPD and the FBI, there was only one caliber of bullet found, so it's possible it may have been a single shooter. Regardless, my guess is that whoever it was knew where the cameras were. As our team pointed out last week during our initial assessment, there are a few blind spots on your property. Whoever was responsible for the shooting managed to utilize each and every one."

They both stared at him blankly, then Edward ran a hand over his jaw. "What exactly are you saying?"

Holy shit. For a couple of tech billionaires, common sense didn't seem to be either of their strong suits. It seemed a little unfair to burst their bubble.

"Either they scoped out your property, which considering how camouflaged the cameras are doesn't seem plausible, or . . . someone on your team let them know the location of the cameras."

Rita shook her head. "But who . . ."

It should have been comical how both Edward's and Rita's eyes widened at the same time, but Gavin took no satisfaction in them realizing that it was more than likely that one of their trusted security team had sold them out.

"We don't know anything for sure at this point. It's all supposition." It was, but Gavin would bet his company someone on Polanski's team had dirty hands.

Standing, Edward began to pace. "I need to keep Rita and Anson safe."

"I need you safe too, Eddie," Rita said, wrapping her arms around her waist. Her gaze followed her pacing husband and then swung to Gavin. "What do you suggest?"

"Polanski and his team can stay here at the house."

"But you just suggested they—"

He held up a hand, quieting her interruption. "My suggestion is that once Anson's released from the hospital, the three of you move to a safe house. One of *our* safe houses."

Edward made his way to the credenza that had an assortment of liquor bottles atop it. He filled a shot glass with what looked to be whiskey and tossed it back. Shaking his head, he added a large cube of ice to a lowball glass and poured more whiskey nearly to the rim. "Rita?" he asked, glancing over his shoulder.

"No, thanks, Eddie. I'm going to head back to the hospital soon."

Edward downed half his glass before he looked at Gavin and held up the bottle of Pappy Van Winkle. "Join me?"

"No, thank you." Gavin stood and made his way toward Edward. He knew the man had been shaken by today's shooting and the possibility that his long-time security detail was somehow involved, but the last thing he needed was for Edward to tie one on. "I'll take some water if you have any."

Holding a bottle of water out to him, Edward sighed. "How did this get so fucked up?"

Gavin cracked the cap and took a drink. "We'll figure this out. We just need to keep your family safe until—"

He saw the red dot on Edward's chest at the exact moment Wilson called out, "Sniper!"

Without thinking, he tackled Edward to the ground and gritted his teeth as fire tore through his right shoulder. More shots rang out as he scanned the room. Xander, with his weapon at the ready, was crouched over Rita, who was lying face down on the floor in front of the couch with her hands covering her head. Wilson was at the opposite end of the couch, his weapon aimed at the bullet-ridden window.

"Status!" Bean shouted in his earpiece.

"I have a visual on the shooter," Rizzo replied, the strain in the Team Three leader's voice indicating he was on the run.

A single shot rang out, and Hanniger muttered, "Motherfucker."

"Report," Gavin barked. He needed to know what the fuck was going on.

"Team Three is on scene," Rizzo said. "Shooter down. Stand by."

A few tense seconds of silence later, Rizzo was back on comms. "Area secure. Shooter down confirmed. Looks like a self-inflicted GSW to the head."

Well, fuck.

With the threat contained, the tension in Gavin's body eased. Standing, he winced at the throbbing ache in his arm. "Hanniger and Schreiber, stay with the shooter. Rizzo, coordinate with Polanski—make sure he's the one who has to deal with the cops—and don't let anyone touch shit." Cognizant of the McClintocks staring at him, Gavin moved to the opposite end of the room and lowered his voice. "B, pull all video and get cyber on it. Hanniger, get a photo of the shooter's face—all angles—and get it to cyber. Find me a connection, B."

An array of "copy" sounded in Gavin's ear. "Team Two, do you copy?"

"Go ahead, Frazier," Carmichael said.

"Did you hear what just went down?"

"Affirmative. Tash is with us at the hospital, and Anson is secure."

Gavin let out a breath. At least one thing wasn't fucked up. "Good. Check in every fifteen minutes."

"Copy that."

Gavin turned toward Edward, who was now seated on the ground beside Rita. Both wore dazed looks. "Anson's team confirmed that he's secure. We've added an additional security officer to his detail as a precaution. Are you two okay?"

They both nodded, and Edward's pale face turned a slight shade of green. Pointing a trembling finger at Gavin, his mouth gaped. "Y-you've been shot!"

Grimacing, Gavin glanced at his right shoulder. His white dress shirt was crimson, and the fire running along his shoulder was irritating as fuck.

"What?" Bean's screech had him wincing. "Did he just say you got *shot*?"

"It's fine," Gavin muttered. "Barely a scratch."

"I need someone *other* than Gavin to give me an injury status update," Bean demanded. "Now!"

Xander moved toward him and slapped a folded bar towel against his shoulder.

He hissed. "Fuck you, Xan."

His friend lifted the towel away and shoved it at him to hold, then he ripped the damaged sleeve wider and frowned. "It's a bit more than a scratch, B, but it's still just a graze. He'll live."

"EMTs are on their way," Bean said. "Let me know which hospital they admit you to and—"

"No hospital," Gavin said, glancing down at his shoulder and wincing. The bullet had indeed grazed him, but it was deep and burned like a motherfucker, and he was bleeding like a stuck pig. "A few stitches and it'll be fine. I'll be back on the island tonight."

"You're so freaking stubborn," Bean muttered before clearing her throat. "Hanniger sent over photos of the shooter, so we'll get to it on this end. I'll keep the line open. Let us know if you guys need anything."

CHAPTER TWENTY-FIVE

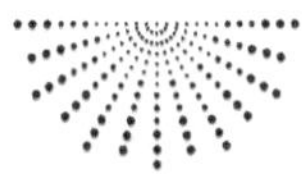

It was nearly nine at night, and holy shit, the last few hours had to have been the longest of Gavin's life. After the shooting—make that the *second* shooting of the day on the McClintock property—he'd had Team Three make themselves scarce. When the Seattle PD arrived, Gavin, along with Xander and Wilson, had stayed long enough to give their statements, each giving the bare minimum. Once that was complete and before the FBI had shown up, they'd whisked Edward and Rita away, happy to leave the time-consuming logistics and bureaucratic bullshit for Polanski to handle. Thankfully, Edward had ordered Polanski's team to stay on the property until further notice. To say they hadn't been pleased would be an understatement. And Gavin didn't give two shits.

By the time they'd escorted Edward and Rita back to the hospital to be with their son, Esme had secured a safe house and was in the process of arranging for a private doctor and the necessary medical equipment needed to continue Anson's recovery outside the hospital.

The hours that followed had been a waiting game—for

the doctors to approve Anson's discharge, for the ER to stitch up Gavin's shoulder, and for Esme to get all the moving parts settled. While all this was happening, Team Three installed additional video surveillance at the safe house, and the cyber division ran the photos of the shooter through every database available to them.

The lights of Hudson Island twinkled in the distance, and Gavin stifled a yawn. The Tylenol he'd taken at the hospital had worn off hours earlier, and exhaustion tugged at his mind. As the helo touched down, he let out a tired sigh. There was still so much to do, but the critical items had been taken care of. The McClintock family was secured at the safe house with Tash and both Teams Two and Three, along with twenty-four-seven surveillance by the cyber team.

"Thanks for the lift, Owen," Gavin said, taking off his headphones and hanging them on the seatback in front of him.

"Glad you made it back in one piece, Frazier," she replied.

He gave her a chin lift. "You and me both."

"Night, Owen," Xander said while Wilson gave her a salute.

He walked toward the main building with Xander and Wilson. The two men were not only two of his most trusted colleagues and friends, but they were two of the sharpest minds he knew.

"Answer me this," he began, running a hand over his jaw and then wincing as the movement pulled at his new stitches. "*Fuck.* It had to be my right shoulder."

"You're lucky, man," Wilson said as they approached Hudson Security's main building. "A little more to the left and it could have been bad. Could have hit the bone, nicked an artery, fucked up the muscle, or some other shit."

"True." He slowly rotated his shoulder, fire sparking at each movement, and waited for Xander to enter his security access code at the entrance. "So here's the thing, why the hell did the shooter off himself?" The question had been nagging at him for hours.

"Maybe Team Three surprised him," Xander said, holding the door open. "Maybe he didn't think he had time to run."

Gavin nodded while Xander entered another security access code for the interior door. Maybe Xander was right, but it didn't sit right. As the door silently whooshed open, they stepped into the inner sanctum. All four members of the cyber division were at their workstations, while Bean had commandeered the large ten-screen setup at the edge of their area. He could see both Tiny and MacKay on one of the monitors.

"Alvarez and Esme are checking with their contacts at SPD and FBI to see what they know," Wilson said. "Here's hoping the dead guy's the same shooter from the morning. If not . . ."

"If not," Xander murmured, "we have even more questions."

Gavin glanced at both men. "Him killing himself seems a bit extreme, don't you think?"

"Maybe the shooter was more scared of who hired him?" Wilson shrugged. "After all, both McClintock and you are alive."

Gavin frowned. "Me?"

Wilson nodded. "You sure he was gunning for McClintock?"

Maybe he was more tired than he'd realized, because he wasn't connecting Wilson's dots. "Yeah. I saw the red dot on McClintock."

Wilson's expression said he didn't buy it. "The shooter was positioned pretty far out. You sure they weren't aiming for you? Because this is twice in three fucking days you've been in the line of fire, man. Is that really a coincidence?"

"Well, shit, Wilson. When you put it like that . . ." Gavin exhaled and then pressed his lips together.

"Not much more we can do tonight, though," Xander said, slapping him on his good shoulder. "Let's check in with cyber and get the hell out of here."

The cyber team was busy at work in the center of the room. Bean was pacing off to the side, her attention focused on their wall of monitors along the edge of their work area. He took a moment to take her in. She had on a sleeveless pink sweater and a sexy, fitted skirt that hit right below her knees. Her glass-slipper heels caught the light with each step she took. There was a sight for sore eyes, and then there was Bean. Even after a long-ass day, the woman was fucking stunning. Completely inappropriate thought? Absolutely. Did he care? Not one bit.

"Holy shit, Frazier," Abbot called out, waving at their trio with her slice of pizza. "No offense, but you look like hell."

Bean spun around, and her mouth dropped open. Her gaze darted to his shoulder, and her blue eyes widened. He glanced at his clothes and fought a cringe. *Shit.* He should have thought about changing his shirt at the hospital, but he hadn't. It was still bloodstained and torn.

Her clasped hands were pressed against her lips, and the worry and despair in her shimmering blue eyes gutted him. This was *Bean*, dammit. The woman who had a spine of steel. Who, when they'd been shot at while they raced through Seattle, hadn't flinched. Not once.

He was across the room and standing in front of her in seconds. His hands reached out but dropped to his sides before he touched her. All eyes were on them.

"I'm fine, B. I swear."

Shaking her head, she closed her eyes and bit down on her lower lip. But it still trembled.

His chest squeezed, and everything inside him stilled.

Oh, hell no.

Not giving a shit about who was watching them, he wrapped his arms around her and pulled her tightly against him, dropping his lips to the top of her head. "I'm okay, honey. I promise."

CHAPTER TWENTY-SIX

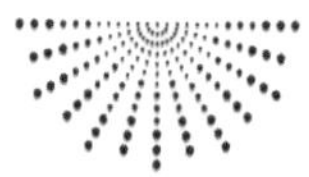

Bean spotted Gavin across the room, and her heart stopped. Completely. Her breath locked painfully in her chest, and her vision blurred with unshed tears.

Hearing he'd been shot had nearly given her a heart attack. With the comms open, she'd heard everything, so she knew he was fine. He'd just been grazed and the bullet hadn't hit anything of significance. It was a flesh wound that had required a handful of stitches. But she'd needed to see him for herself, see with her own eyes that he was okay. Unfortunately, there wasn't enough work in the world to distract her from watching the seconds and minutes tick by ever so slowly. To top it off, her team was so damn efficient that they'd not only started the frame-by-frame video analysis, but also handled the work of getting the dead shooter's picture into their various facial-rec programs.

Bean had been fine all afternoon. A little anxious and worried? Yes. As the evening had worn on, she'd grown more impatient for sure, but she'd still been fine.

Until she'd laid eyes on him.

So. Much. Blood.

She'd thought she'd be relieved to see him. And she was. But she'd belatedly realized she wasn't prepared. Not at all.

The enormous amounts of dried blood on his shirt had been like a sucker punch to the gut. He stood before her, and she couldn't look away. The white bandage covering his injury stood out in sharp contrast to the darkened bloodstains on his torn sleeve.

Her heart was threatening to claw its way out of her chest, and she slammed her eyes shut, but the bloody image remained.

He'd been shot. *Shot!*

Gavin wrapped his arms around her, and she nearly burst into tears.

"I'm okay, honey. I promise."

"You're not supposed to get hurt," she whispered into his chest.

While they'd been speeding through Seattle with some stranger shooting at them, Bean hadn't been worried. Not one bit. One, they'd been in an armored vehicle. Two, she trusted Carmichael's driving ability and her own skills to get them through the congested city. And three, Gavin had been with them.

In her mind, he was invincible. But now, seeing the dried blood, his torn shirt, and his bandaged shoulder . . . It was a chilling reminder that the man wasn't, in fact, invincible. He was just as susceptible to a bullet as the next person.

And that terrified her beyond words.

Hugging him tighter, Bean breathed him in, catching his familiar cedar and pine scent under the antiseptic smell. He ran his right hand up and down her spine while he clutched her close with his left.

"I'm okay," he kept murmuring, but neither her heart nor her head were convinced. He'd been shot. Seeing him with her own eyes, seeing how close his wound was to his chest. A handful of inches to the left, and it would have been an entirely different story . . .

Her lungs seized and a shiver tore violently through her. Holy shit, it was too much.

"Please don't cry, B."

She gasped and glanced up, not realizing she'd lost the battle with her tears. Sniffing loudly, she embraced the fear that was surging through her and jabbed him in the chest with her finger. "Don't you *ever* get shot again!"

He had the nerve to chuckle. *Chuckle.*

"I'm serious, Gavin Frazier." She jabbed him again. "You don't get to get shot. Ever. Freaking. Again."

He grabbed her finger and brought it to his lips. "I'll do my best."

She shook her head. "You have to promise me." Her voice cracked on the last two words, and more tears spilled down her cheek.

"Baby," he murmured, cupping her jaw. "I can't promise that. But I swear I'll do everything I can to avoid jumping in front of a bullet again."

Her stomach dropped. "You jumped in front of a bullet? What the hell is wrong with you? You're *not* personal security!"

A muttered curse had her glancing to her right. She'd been so wrapped up in Gavin that she'd forgotten where they were. Everyone—her cyber team, Xander, and Wilson—was staring at them with rapt attention.

"Ignore them," he whispered. "Back to work, everyone," he added in a louder tone.

Xander chuckled. "Not on your life, Frazier."

"I know, right?" Abbot chimed in. "I feel like I need popcorn or something."

Rolling her eyes, Bean turned to her team. "Popcorn? Seriously?"

Gavin dropped a kiss to the top of her head before pulling her to his chest again and wrapping his arms tightly around her. His small gesture melted her insides. The comfort of his embrace went a long way in reassuring her that he was okay. And it wasn't lost on her that he'd done it in front of their colleagues.

"All right, guys, that's enough. Witherspoon, you're on night watch?" Gavin asked, pointing to the monitors that showed the safe house.

"Yup. I mean, it's not as entertaining as all this"—he waved a hand at them and smirked—"but yeah. I'm on until three, then Tiny will be taking over."

"If there are any issues with the safe house, let me know ASAP," Bean said, still snuggled in Gavin's arms.

"Of course," Witherspoon replied, shooting her a wink.

"Let's call it a night, everyone," Gavin said, finally loosening his hold on her, though he kept one arm around her waist. "Meet back up at zero eight hundred. If you show up a couple hours earlier, I'll make sure there's food."

She glanced at him with narrowed eyes. "Bribing my team, boss man?"

"Maybe." That one word was teasing and playful, and she saw multiple sets of eyebrows lifting in her peripheral vision. Teasing and playful were two things she rarely saw from Gavin, and she knew it was something her team *never* saw.

Straightening, she smiled, happy that there was still some levity to be found after the intensity of the day. Her gaze landed on the dark-red, dried blood, and her stomach soured.

"Come on," she said, blowing out a breath. She waved at her team, took Gavin's hand, and pulled him toward their offices. "You need to get out of that shirt and get cleaned up."

CHAPTER TWENTY-SEVEN

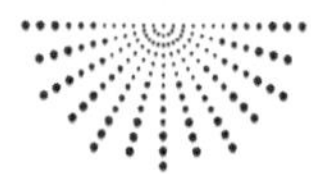

Bean was thankful Gavin didn't protest when she insisted on driving him home. Taking his SUV, their short drive was mostly silent, her mind whirling and consumed by what could have gone wrong. She knew she was needlessly torturing herself, because Gavin was fine. He was seated beside her. But still, she couldn't stop her mind from agonizing over every what-if scenario. He'd changed into a Hudson Security polo before they left the office, but the images of his torn and bloody shirt lingered in her mind.

This night could have ended so differently.

Bean glanced over at Gavin in the passenger seat. The dark circles under his tired eyes were emphasized by the moonlight.

He murmured something, but his voice was so low that she wasn't quite sure she'd heard him. "Sorry, what was that?" she asked.

"Stay with me tonight?"

That's what she'd thought he'd said. Bringing her attention back to the road, she turned into his driveway before peeking at him again. There was something in his softly spoken words that tugged at her heart. She couldn't—*wouldn't*—say no to him. Not tonight. "Of course."

As she pulled up to his garage, he pressed a button on his rearview mirror to open the door. She pulled in, cut the engine, and hurried over to the passenger side.

"I got it, honey," he murmured as he eased out of his seat.

"Don't argue with me," she said, wrapping an arm around his waist.

After unlocking the door, she hurried to the security panel and disengaged the alarm. When she turned, he stood before her. Silent.

Her breath quickened as she took him in. His jaw was clenched, and there was tension in his body, as if he were holding himself back somehow. A glance at his gray eyes showed his pupils were blown. A low rumble emanated from his chest.

She wasn't sure who moved first, but on her next breath, her back was pressed against the wall, and his body covered every inch of hers. His mouth devoured hers while his hands yanked her jacket off. She frantically tried to undo the buttons of her blouse, but her trembling hands weren't cooperating.

He pulled slightly away, his chest heaving, and tore the panels of her blouse apart. Buttons went flying, clinking onto the hardwood floors, but she didn't care. She needed this man. Desperately.

Needing to feel his hot skin against her, she grabbed the bottom of his shirt and pushed the fabric up. She ran her hands up his muscled torso, and her hand grazed the bandage on his shoulder. She froze, gasping.

"Gavin, we can't. Your arm."

"Fuck my arm." His mouth crashed against hers, and her mind went blank.

Until her hand ran over the bandage again.

She pulled away and met his gaze. Need and desire stared back at her. As much as she wanted him, she had to be sure.

"Gavin," she whispered, placing her hands on either side of his jaw. "Are you sure you're okay? I don't want you getting more hurt."

A look of tenderness crossed his face. "Yes, baby. I promise I'm okay." This time, his kiss was slow and delicate. His tongue traced the seam of her lips and she immediately opened, allowing him in. Their tongues tangled, and within seconds, their kiss grew frantic. He growled and hoisted her up.

"Wait. Your shoulder."

"Still don't care," he muttered, his mouth seeking her neck. "Wrap your legs around me."

She didn't hesitate to comply, groaning at the feel of his hardness rubbing against the apex of her thighs. "I need you." Desperation clawed at her. She needed to feel him, needed him to fill her, needed to know he truly was okay.

"I wanted to take my time with you," he murmured. "For our first time, I wanted to explore every inch of you. But, baby, I don't think I can wait."

"Don't wait." Hell no. She fused her mouth to his, sucking on his tongue the way she wanted to suck on his cock. But not now. Later. "Hard and fast. I want to *feel* you deep inside me."

"Holy fuck, B," he groaned, grinding against her. Then he stilled. "Hold on, I need to get a condom."

The way his hard cock was rubbing against her had her so close. So. Damn. Close. "I'm on the pill. Please, Gavin. Take me. I need to feel all of you."

He laid her onto the couch. Before she could sit up, he'd shoved her skirt up to her waist and yanked off her panties.

"Yes, ma'am," he said, his voice like gravel. "Baby, I can fucking see how much you want me."

She should have been embarrassed, but she didn't have time. He dropped to his knees, and his mouth was on her pussy, his tongue licking, thrusting, exploring. She nearly shot off the couch, but his arm pinned her down. Explosions rocketed within her, and tension built in her body. "You taste so damn good. I can't get enough of you."

He thrust two fingers deep inside her and flicked his tongue violently over her clit. She exploded. Detonated. Her thighs clamped tightly around his head and her body shook.

He sat up, his expression feral. "Now I want you to come all over my cock."

Her lips lifted in a smirk. "Bossy."

"Oh, baby. You haven't seen anything yet." He ran his hands from her ankles, up her calves, and over her thighs. Skimming them up her sides, he squeezed her breasts before pulling her up into a seated position. "So damn beautiful," he said against her lips before kissing her deeply. He pulled away with a growl. "On your knees, B. Hands on the back of the couch. I'm gonna fuck you hard and fast. Just like you want."

Her pussy clenched with need, arousal flooding through her. *Yes, please.*

She moved to her knees, and he stripped her of her skirt while she gripped the back frame of the couch. Leaning forward, she tilted her hips back. His hand caressed the globes of her ass, squeezing, making her even wetter.

"Look at you, baby." Gavin's voice was pure sin. He ran his cock up and down her slit, and she moaned and tilted her hips even more, desperate for him to fill her. "That's it, show me your pussy."

"Please, Gavin," she begged, not caring how desperate she sounded.

They both groaned as he pushed inside her and filled her

in one long thrust. Her insides quaked. Full. She'd never been this damn full.

"You feel so fucking good," he muttered.

She rocked her hips, needing him to move. "More. Please. Fuck me."

With a growl, he pulled his hips slowly back. The slide of every delicious inch of him set her nerves on fire. Then he surged back into her over and over again at a breakneck pace. His hips slammed against her ass, his balls slapping against her clit. She cried out and held on, taking each and every one of his hard thrusts.

"Yes, yes, yes!" Tension built within her, and she ached for release.

Then he pulled out. Before she could protest, she was flat on her back.

"Need to see you when you come, baby. Need to see your face when you take me."

The wild look in his eyes had her smiling, had her spreading her legs wide for him.

"You're so fucking beautiful," he said before claiming her mouth. Pulling away, he loomed over her. His right arm was propped on the couch by her head, supporting him. He hooked her leg in the crook of his left elbow and grabbed the back of the couch, opening her up even more.

She gasped as he thrust inside her. Every rock of his hips shot her right back to the edge. Seeing his muscles bunch as he took her—the clench of his abs, the flex of his arms—was the hottest thing she'd ever seen. He pounded into her, his eyes glued to where they were joined. "You take me so good," he muttered. "Fucking made for me, B."

Then his hips thrust even harder. He continued to pound into her, made her feel every inch of his thick cock. Her body shook, and she cried out as she came, her legs trembling as he continued his unrelenting pace.

Moments later, he thew his head back and cried out as he emptied inside her. Warmth filled her as his movements finally slowed. He eased himself down on top of her, careful not to squish her. He was still, but she felt the hammering of his racing heart, could feel him twitching inside her.

She welcomed the heavy weight of him and ran her fingers down his damp spine, reveling in the moment. Having this amazing man fill her, take her, was everything. Beyond the physical—which had blown her mind—being with him like this filled her soul.

A smile lifted her lips, and she pressed a kiss to his shoulder. "You were made for me too."

Gavin wasn't quite sure when they'd switched positions. He was lying on his back on the couch with Bean sprawled over him, her head tucked into the side of his neck.

He wasn't complaining. Not at all.

In fact, he'd never felt better.

There was post-orgasm relaxation, and then there was this. It was next-level.

It boggled his mind that Bean was in his arms, that she fit so perfectly against him. His fingers traced circles on the soft skin of her hip. This time last week, they'd just been friends on a mission to rescue a kidnapped child. Now . . .

A smile pulled at the corners of his lips, and he pressed a kiss to the top of her head. He felt her smile against his chest.

Now, they had this . . .

She kissed his pec and shifted to meet his gaze. "You know, I was thinking that—"

Gasping, her eyes went wide with alarm. "Gavin, your shoulder!" Panic laced the three words as she scrambled to sit.

Glancing at his right shoulder, he winced. Dots of crimson stained his bandage. He'd opened up his wound. "It's fine, B."

"It's not fine," she snapped. "You're bleeding!"

God, she was hot when she was all riled up. "Bean, it's fine. I have a first aid kit under my bathroom sink."

Rising, he held a hand out to her. When she took it, he pulled her up and took a moment to admire every inch of her skin. "Goddamn, now every time I look at you, I'll be picturing you like this. Naked. Sexy as hell. My come running down your thighs."

Her gaze trailed down his chest to his dick. She licked her lips, and his cock twitched. "Right back at ya, boss man."

Chuckling, he laced his fingers with hers and pulled her toward his bedroom. "Come on, little devil. Let's get this retaped, and then what do you say we go for another round?"

Her gaze darted to his shoulder, and her grin dimmed. "But—"

"No buts. This?" He raised his right shoulder. "Totally worth it."

"If you say so," she said as they entered his bedroom. She released his hand and made her way to his bathroom as he turned down his sheets and settled onto his bed. "But you're taking pain meds tonight," she called out from the bathroom. "I don't care if you don't want to or not, you're taking them."

Water ran in the sink, and after a moment, he heard the sound of drawers and cabinet doors opening and closing. He kicked himself for not taking the time to clean her up. He should be the one taking care of her, not the other way around. Next time . . .

When she returned with his first aid kit in her hands, he was peeling up the corner of his bandage. "Like I said, that was totally worth messing up the stitches."

He wasn't lying. He was still riding high from his orgasm and wasn't feeling any pain.

For the next couple of minutes, they worked together to remove his bandage. He'd popped two stitches, but it wasn't bad. As he walked her through applying a butterfly bandage, he noticed her eyelids getting heavy. She wrapped a new bandage over his shoulder and yawned.

She gathered the first aid supplies and went back into the bathroom. "I may have to take a rain check on round two. I think you wrecked me."

Gavin shifted, swinging his legs onto the bed. He pulled the duvet over his lap and froze. His heart hammered in his chest, and ice filled his veins. Holy shit, what the hell was he doing? He couldn't spend the night with her in the same bed.

His breath locked in his chest as Bean reentered the bedroom. His limbs were leaden, but he watched as she made her way to the other side of his bed. Pulling the covers down, she paused and tilted her head to the side in concern. "Is the tape bothering you? Did I make it too tight?"

Fucking hell, he couldn't do this. No matter how much he wanted to crawl into bed, pull Bean into his arms, and go the fuck to sleep, he couldn't. It wasn't an option.

Images from years ago bombarded his brain. A blond woman. Chelsea. He couldn't remember her last name, wasn't even sure she'd ever told him what it was. They'd both been out looking for a good time. Nothing more. But that night was seared into his brain. He'd never forgotten the panic and terror in her brown eyes. How her mouth had hung open in a silent scream as she'd clawed at his wrists. How she'd drawn blood on the backs of his hands.

Hands that he'd wrapped around her throat . . .

Bile turned his stomach, and he pressed his lips together. A sheen of sweat broke out over his skin. He hadn't shared a bed with a woman since that horrific night. And he couldn't now. It wasn't safe.

Bean meant too much.

"You okay?" she asked, meeting his gaze.

Whatever she saw when she looked at him had a flicker of disappointment crossing her face. *Shit! He was fucking this all up.*

She dropped the edge of the duvet and gestured to the bedroom door. "You know what, I think I'll get out of your hair." She smiled, and his stomach sank. It was one of her fake, polished smiles. "I have some stuff I have to do in the morning, so I'll just see you at the office tomorrow."

He wanted to reach for her, to grab her by the waist and haul her back to him. Wanted to cuddle her naked body close and sleep peacefully with her. Then wake her in the middle of the night and sink deep into her again.

Instead, he sat there frozen.

Unable to move.

Unable to say a fucking thing.

Not because he didn't want her to stay, but because he didn't trust himself.

She turned and glanced around. Frowning, she yanked open his dresser drawers, grabbed one of his T-shirts, and pulled it over her head. The tension in the silent room threatened to suffocate him. When she reached his bedroom door, she turned back with that damn society smile on her face. Her shoulders were ramrod straight, and her head was held high. But she didn't meet his gaze. Instead, her attention was focused on his shoulder.

"I'm taking your car, and I'll reengage your alarm when I head out." She turned but then hesitated and looked over her shoulder at him. "You going to be okay tonight?"

His stomach twisted. He was a motherfucking asshole.

Nodding, he shifted and winced at both the pull in his

shoulder and at his own stupidity. But no matter how much he willed himself to say something, he couldn't get his mouth to form the words, couldn't ask her to stay.

She opened his bedroom door, and panic surged through him, flooding every one of his senses. "Wait!"

She stilled but didn't turn around.

Seconds earlier, he'd been rendered mute. Now, fear had words spewing from his mouth. "Holy shit, Bean, I'm so fucking sorry. I want to ask you to stay, but I don't think . . . I don't know . . ."

She finally turned to face him and it was like a kick to the gut. Disappointment, sadness, and resignation all swirled in her blue eyes. With a tight smile, she nodded. "It's fine, Frazier. I'll see you tomorrow."

He scrambled out of the bed but remained standing at its edge, afraid to get too close to her, afraid she'd push him away, afraid she wouldn't. "I'm sorry. I'm fucking this all up. It's not you, I swear." The look of abject disbelief she gave him had him rushing on. "I swear to God, it's me. It's . . ." Letting out a frustrated growl, he rubbed his hands over his face. Dropping his arms to his sides, he met her gaze. The wariness staring back at him had determination surging through him. He had to get this right, dammit. "I'm a fucking idiot. When you went to get into bed with me, I froze." He waved at the rumpled bed behind him. "I couldn't fucking move. I haven't slept with anyone in years—"

"Oh, for fuck's sake, Frazier." She rolled her eyes and crossed her arms across her chest. "If you're going to lie to me, at least make it believable."

"I'm serious. Yes, I've had sex with women, but it's been a long time since I've *slept* with someone. But you . . ."

Her brow arched in challenge, and she scoffed. "I'm what? *Different?*"

"Yes! You're so fucking special. You're more important

than all the others combined." Her eyes widened the tiniest fraction. He'd surprised her. Hell, he'd surprised himself. But everything he'd said was the truth. And he was desperate for her to believe him. "I don't do sleepovers—haven't done one since I moved here—and I sure as hell don't invite anyone into my home. I want you to stay tonight. More than fucking anything. But I don't want to hurt you. And if you stay with me—in my bed—I might. I'd rather die than hurt you."

Silence ticked by for longer than he wanted. Her eyes searched his, and he feared what she saw.

"Your nightmares." The two words she uttered were a statement, not a question. Shame threatened to engulf him, but he held her gaze and nodded.

Without a word, she took his hand and turned him. She gave him a gentle shove, and he climbed back into the bed. He held his breath as she rounded the bed and crawled in beside him. "We don't have to sleep. We can just talk."

He shifted so she was tucked against him, her head on his good shoulder. He remained silent, trying to find the right words. "I'm sorry if I hurt you earlier. I didn't know how . . . or what to say."

She kissed his pec and rested her cheek back against his chest. "You can make it up to me by talking to me. As little or as much as you want."

He didn't know what to say. Didn't know where to even start. Letting out a sigh, he focused on Bean. She had one hand resting on his chest, and her fingers moved soothingly back and forth along his skin. Her touch calmed him, settled his racing heart. He took a deep breath in and let her floral scent wash over him. If he couldn't be honest with her, then what was the point? This woman had been one of his closest friends for years and meant so damn much.

"You know I have nightmares. I've gotten a pretty good

handle on them over the years, but the McClintock kidnapping stirred up a bunch of shit."

"Like I said, Gavin, you can tell me as little or as much as you want. You'll get no judgement from me."

"I know, honey." He pressed a kiss to the top of her head and sighed. "My last mission as a Delta involved this piece of shit HVT—high-value target. The guy was the head of a trafficking ring. Specialized in kids. The kicker was his base of operations was in an orphanage." His mind drifted to the afternoon they'd arrived at the village. He could still feel the sting of the insect bites and the humidity of the jungle suffocating him.

"Our team took up positions around the orphanage and the plan was to go in at zero three hundred. Take out the HVT, confirm the kill, and be done. When evening fell, a van arrived. Fifteen men got out, and the HVT was there to greet them. The kids . . ." His chest squeezed, and his throat grew thick. "We could hear the sounds of those guys fucking them, torturing them. Could see what the fuck some of them were doing through the windows. We could hear the kids crying." Their screams and terrified whimpers echoed in his brain. "But we were ordered to stand down. To wait. To not do jack shit to help them."

Wetness dropped onto his chest, and Bean sniffed. He tightened his arms around her, and he swallowed past the rock in his throat.

"We followed orders and waited until the van of men left. Waited until zero three fucking hundred hours. Then we went in. Took out the HVT and his associates, confirmed the kill, and left." He shook his head. "We left the kids. Some were dead. The ones that were still alive were in rough shape. But we had to leave them all."

He stared at the ceiling, his chest painfully tight. Tears slid down the sides of his face, and disgust coursed through him. "We were lucky that we didn't lose anyone on our team, but that mission fucked with a lot of our heads. I got out after that. So did Xander and Wilson and a couple others."

"I'm so sorry you had to go through that, Gavin," Bean whispered, squeezing him tightly. "I'm sorry the people in command were such heartless assholes."

The anger in her voice eased some of the pain in his heart. "Me too."

"That's why you started Hudson Security, isn't it?"

He nodded. "I still wanted to make a difference, wanted to help people. But I was done with the bureaucratic bullshit."

She remained silent for a few heartbeats. "I'm proud of you. Hudson Security matters. You've given us all an opportunity to make a difference."

God, this woman . . .

"I guess that was a long way of explaining that I have sleep issues. When I got out, I was plagued with nightmares. For years. I went to therapy, and that helped. But . . ."

"But?" Bean prodded when he'd stayed silent.

"The last time I attempted to stay the night with anyone was right around when I started Hudson Security. I was over on Whidbey Island and picked up a woman at a bar. Chelsea. I'd just gotten out, and she was Navy, so we commiserated over our time in the service. One thing led to another and we ended up back at her place. It was totally casual. Then I woke up in the middle of the night and didn't know where I was."

Shame swirled in his gut like a hot rock, and his pulse picked up speed. "I'm not sure what exactly happened. One moment, I thought I was still in that orphanage, and the next moment, I was straddling Chelsea, pinning her down with my hands around her throat."

It had taken him precious seconds for him to realize the woman under him wasn't a piece-of-shit sex trafficker. But it was too late. Chelsea's terror had gutted him.

"I couldn't apologize enough. I was a fucking wreck." He continued to stare at the ceiling, petrified to look at Bean, scared to see what she thought of him. "For some unknown reason, Chelsea forgave me. Not sure why. But I went into therapy after that. I was so fucking broken."

"You've never slept in bed with anyone since?"

Bean's words were soft and lacked censure. Holding his breath, he risked a peek at her. She wasn't looking at him, so he only saw the top of her head. "No. I've never wanted to. Until you. But . . . I don't trust myself."

She glanced up at him, and there was something in her expression, something he couldn't describe, something he couldn't look away from.

"I said it before and I'll say it again, Gavin Frazier. I'm proud of you."

He frowned. There was no way he'd heard that right.

She propped her chin onto his chest and met his gaze. "What you went through on your last mission was terrible. It left you with horrible PTSD. I know you didn't mean to hurt that woman, but you did."

His stomach sank and he looked away, but Bean grabbed his chin and forcibly made him face her. "But you got help, Gavin. Professional help. You did the work to get better, to manage your nightmares. You could have easily just tried to go it alone. But you didn't. It takes a lot of guts to seek help. Especially for you macho-alpha types." She patted his stomach. "And, yeah, you may have had a setback after the McClintock kidnapping, but you know the steps you need to take to manage it, right?"

He nodded.

"You could have also just shut me out earlier. But you didn't. You opened up and told me what was going on in that head of yours. I was ready to walk out thinking you didn't want me."

Everything inside him revolted at the thought. "You can't imagine how much I want you, Bean. And not just tonight."

"I want you too. And for more than just tonight." Her lips lifted into a small smile. "Thank you for talking to me, for being honest with me."

The tension in his body eased like a slowly deflating balloon. He ran a hand through her hair, unable to tear his gaze from her. "Bean, baby, I don't deserve you."

Her smile grew as she rolled her eyes. "You're a lot of things, but you're not stupid. Don't start acting like it now." Then she tucked her head against his neck.

Wrapping his arms around her, he simply held her.

As he ran his hand mindlessly up and down her spine, everything inside him settled—his heart, his soul, his entire being. He squeezed her tighter. This woman was quickly becoming everything.

"I'm still scared to sleep with you," he confessed. "I don't want to hurt you."

She met his gaze, and there was nothing but understanding in her blue eyes. "If you're really worried, I can sleep in the guest room. It's okay, Gavin."

He was shaking his head before she'd finished speaking. "I want to. Hell, there's nothing I want more than to fall asleep with you in my arms but . . . I'm nervous. If I hurt you—"

She pressed her finger to his lips, silencing him. "I have an idea. In order to have a really good sleep, you need to be totally exhausted, right?"

There was a twinkle in her eyes that had him smiling. He had no idea where she was going with this, but he was game. "Yeah?"

"How about I exhaust you? I mean, as long as you don't pop any more stitches." While she spoke, she moved off his body until she was kneeling between his legs. Her fingers skimmed over his thighs, and his cock hardened. "I mean, good sleep is vital, wouldn't you agree? Will you let me see if I can get that brain of yours to shut off?"

"Yeah." The one word came out like a croak but he didn't give a shit, because she was lowering her face to his cock. He groaned as her little pink tongue flicked the underside. He got impossibly harder, desperate to feel her mouth on him. "Please, B."

The look she shot him was sex and tenderness all wrapped in one. "Please what, boss man?"

"Suck my cock, baby. Please."

"Yes, sir."

His dick jerked at those two words. Then his brain shut off completely as she swallowed him down. The image of her sweet mouth bobbing up and down on his cock was forever imprinted into his brain.

Holy shit, this woman . . .

This glorious fucking woman.

She owned him. Completely. Mind, body, and soul. He was hers.

CHAPTER TWENTY-EIGHT

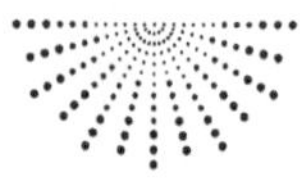

Gavin glanced around the conference room and embraced that familiar rush he got from getting shit done. Even though he was dead tired, pride bloomed in his chest from the great minds that surrounded him. Their team was beyond solid. Bean, Alvarez, and Xander were seated in various spots around the large rectangular table, and MacKay, Esme, and Tiny were joining their meeting via video call.

He was used to not getting a lot of sleep, but he and Bean had stayed up until the early hours of the morning. They'd gotten maybe three hours—easily the best sleep he'd had in years—and were back at the office by six. He wouldn't change anything from last night for the world. Well, he'd definitely change the part where he'd been a complete dumbass and had nearly fucked things up. And the entire getting-shot thing. Actually, the more he thought about it, he probably should have woken her back up for round three. After all, they hadn't tried—

Bean cleared her throat loudly while shooting him a glare that was half annoyed and half amused. Her blue eyes widened as she jerked her head toward the large screen at the front of the room.

He startled. *Oh shit.*

The room was dead silent. All eyes were on him. *Fuck.* How long had he been lost in his thoughts? Clarification: lost in his wildly inappropriate thoughts?

Running a hand over his jaw, he dropped his gaze to the table and tried to refocus, tried to recall what the hell they'd been discussing.

Nothing. Not a damn thing. The only thing he could recall was how Bean had looked—all flushed and disheveled and beautiful—as she'd ridden him hard.

His dick twitched. *Holy. Fuck. Focus!*

Clearing his throat, he glanced at the faces staring back at him on the room's giant Smartboard. "I'm sorry, Tiny, but could you repeat that last part?"

The other man nodded. "We're fairly certain that the shooter that offed himself on the McClintock property yesterday was Damian Jacoby Otton. He's a known gun for hire based out of Vancouver, BC."

"Why only 'fairly certain'?" Gavin frowned, air-quoting the last two words. *Get your head back in the game, man.*

"It looks like he had some work done on his face, so the facial-rec software couldn't make an exact match," Tiny said. "Since we don't have access to his DNA, 'fairly certain' is the best we can do. However, if you take away the chin, nose, and forehead augmentations, it's pretty close to a perfect match."

"According to some chatter I picked up on the dark web, there was a failed assassination attempt on Otton about a year ago," Bean said, glancing up from her computer. "Up until then, he was a fairly successful operative who worked predominately with a few different Russian bratva groups along the West Coast."

As she spoke, more images of Otton popped up on the

screen, some obviously older than others. The man had definitely once looked different than he did now. It was a wonder they were able to make a match at all. "There's also speculation it was one of those groups that put the hit out on him. The big rumor is that the injuries Otton incurred really messed up his vision, rendering him ineffective. He was basically blackballed after that."

Gavin could only stare at her in wonder. Brains, beauty, and a shit ton of sass. Who knew that was his type? Hell, *she* was his type. The woman was a damn marvel. A marvel who was giving him that annoyed-amused glare again.

He fake coughed into his hand and muttered, "Good intel, B."

He fought a wince. *Good intel*? Holy shit, he needed to get his head on straight. Immediately.

"Well," Xander said, "the fact that both McClintock and Frazier are still standing lends credence to the vision-being-off thing."

Gavin glanced at his friend in question, still not believing that he'd been the intended target.

Xander held his hands up. "What? Just because you don't buy that theory doesn't mean it isn't an actual possibility."

"So to add more fuel to that particular fire, I checked Otton's bank accounts," Bean said. "In his line of work, the man obviously had quite a few of them, and last Thursday, he received a deposit of fifty grand into one of his Cayman accounts. We did a dive into the deposit, and while it was a little convoluted with multiple shell companies, the money originated from Performance Exports LLC, a Washington state company that was formed last Wednesday."

Alvarez let out a low whistle. "That's not suspicious at all, is it? Please tell me you've got more info?"

Gavin could see the gleam in Alvarez's eyes. The guy was

a former detective and loved nothing more than fitting the proverbial puzzle pieces together.

"Of course, I do." Bean chuckled and met Gavin's gaze. "You wanted a connection? How about this? The listed owner of Performance Exports is Elena Nabers. She's a manager at a local auto repair shop in South Seattle. Nabers also happens to be the cousin of Bradley Smith."

Bean's eyes were sparkling, her expression indicating he should know the name. He didn't. A quick glance around the room showed everyone else was also drawing a blank. The name tickled something in the back of his mind. It sounded so damn familiar, but he shook his head. "Throw me a bone, B."

"Seriously?" She huffed out a disappointed sigh as her fingers flew over her keyboard.

Gavin shrugged. "Hey, it's a generic enough name."

Multiple photos appeared on the conference room screen. Otton's picture, a driver's license belonging to a woman he assumed was Nabers, and two others. Bean's mouse hovered over the two. "Richard Penning and Bradley Smith. They were arrested last Tuesday at the warehouse for Anson McClintock's kidnapping."

Son of a bitch. *That's* why the name was familiar. Damn, this was turning into one giant clusterfuck.

"Penning was fairly new to the family's security detail," Bean continued. "However, Smith is an extra giant piece of shit, because he was part of the McClintock security team when Anson was born."

Esme, who'd been observing on the video feed, interjected, "My contacts at the FBI are saying that Penning doesn't know much, that he was basically there to do the grunt work for a big payday. They believe Smith was the brains of the operation."

Gavin rose and paced the length of the room, absorbing

all the new information. "So Bradley Smith recruits Penning, and they kidnap and torture Anson hoping for a twenty-million-dollar ransom. But they fail and get arrested. Then the very next day, Smith's cousin—Elena Nabers—files the paperwork for this export company, sets up a bank account, and hires a sniper all within twenty-four hours. But for what? To take out Edward McClintock?" Gavin shook his head. It didn't make sense. "There's no money in taking Edward out."

"Well, before you go down that rabbit hole, there's more," Bean said. "This is the adding-fuel-to-the-fire bit I alluded to. Tiny ran Otton's photos through his own facial-rec program"—she turned to Tiny on the video feed—"it's a brilliant program, by the way, but we'll talk more about that later." She faced Gavin again. "We also gave Tiny the security footage of the man running by the McClintocks' property last week. According to Tiny's kick-ass program, there's a high statistical probability that it's the same person. Granted, without DNA, there's no way to know for sure, but I'd like to peek at the medical examiner's report on Otton, which"—her eyes narrowed as she scanned her laptop monitor—"they haven't entered into their system yet. But if Otton has a two-day-old bullet wound in his shoulder, or even a graze of some sort, it's likely he's also the shooter from our car chase Saturday night."

Gavin's frown deepened. Not because Bean had just obviously hacked into the King County Medical Examiner's system—he had every confidence she'd cover her tracks—but because he wasn't connecting the dots. He held up a hand when it looked like she was going to say more. "Wait. What exactly are you saying, Bean? Spell it out for me like I'm five." He'd heard her words, but they weren't processing.

"What Bean's saying," Alvarez cut in as he leaned back in

his seat, "is that there's a high chance that *you*, Frazier, were the target yesterday and not Edward McClintock."

He took a moment to let Alvarez's words sink in and then shook his head. "What about the earlier shooting at the McClintock house? I wasn't there for that, so there's no way I was the intended target."

"True, you weren't there for the earlier shooting," Alvarez said. "But that first shooting got you out there, didn't it?"

Gavin shook his head again, unsure if he truly didn't believe it or if he was merely playing devil's advocate. "Whoever was behind this wouldn't have known that I would go out to the McClintocks' after that first shooting."

"This place is like Fort Knox, man," Alvarez said, waving a hand at the room. "Every inch of this facility is monitored. You need to get through security to even get on the property. Then you need multiple steps of escalating clearance to get into the building. Shit, even your house is secure. The second anyone crosses your property line, notifications are sent out. If I'm a bad guy, I need you off-property to take a shot at you."

"That's fair." There was no questioning the security of their facilities on the island, but the theory that *he* was the target didn't quite sit right. "That still doesn't account for them knowing I'd go out to the McClintocks' yesterday."

"Sure it does," Xander said. "Anyone who knows your reputation knows that you get shit done. Yeah, most people have no clue we led the McClintock kid's rescue, but there's a handful of people who do. It's also no secret that Hudson Security is working in some capacity with Edward and Rita McClintock. Then someone shoots up the home of two fucking *billionaires*? Of course you're going to do a house call to check out shit for yourself."

Fine. That made sense. But . . . "That's a lot of what-ifs."

Xander shrugged. "What Alvarez said is true though. If

I'm trying to take you out, I need you off Hudson Security property."

Christ. The more he thought about it, the more it made sense. But *why*, though? He turned to Bean. "What do you think?"

"I think we can follow the money some more. We linked the shooter to Smith via his cousin, Nabers. Like I'd said, the woman's a manager at an auto shop. If you know what you're doing, it's not difficult to form a company in the state and get everything set up. It's very possible that kind of thing is within her wheelhouse. However, fifty grand is a lot. I did a brief check of Nabers's personal banking accounts. The woman's living paycheck to paycheck, and while she's single and makes decent money, most of it goes to rent and her car payment. I'm guessing if we can figure out where the fifty grand came from—because it sure as hell didn't come from any of Nabers's personal accounts—we'll find not only who's looking to take you out, but also maybe who was behind Anson's kidnapping in the first place."

"You don't think the kidnapping was just Smith and Penning? Just two disgruntled employees looking for money?" Alvarez asked.

Gavin knew his colleague didn't buy that—hell, the more they looked at it, he didn't either—but he was curious to hear Bean's opinion.

She shook her head and took a swig of her energy drink. "From everything I found, the McClintocks paid Smith and the rest of their security staff well. That warehouse you all rescued Anson from looked like a rundown POS building, but it had elaborate security. That type of setup was well above Smith's pay grade. I don't think this is some disgruntled employee trying to stick it to his former boss to get a payday. No. I think Smith is just a cog in a bigger wheel."

Alvarez nodded. "I agree. There's someone much bigger

pulling the strings. I think following the money is the best bet."

Gavin continued to pace the length of the conference room, working all the pieces in his mind. "Esme, after Smith and Penning were arrested, was anyone else questioned?"

"Penning has very loose ties to the Vancouver bratva."

Esme's response had Gavin's eyebrows nearly hitting his hairline.

"Nothing usable, though," Esme said, shaking her head. "It was his mother's college roommate's brother, or some kind of shit like that. Regardless, the FBI made some soft inquiries in Vancouver and, of course, no one knows anything."

Gavin frowned. "Usable or not, it's too much of a coincidence with Otton's ties to both Vancouver and the bratva."

"I took a look again at the intel we initially pulled on Smith and Penning," Bean chimed in. "The emails and ransom videos they sent to the McClintocks, the financial transactions . . . Everything points to them."

"Which is also pretty convenient," Alvarez said.

"Valid." Bean shrugged. "Like I said, I think Smith was a cog in a much bigger wheel. Otton, too, because why else would a freaking seasoned mercenary put a bullet in his own head?"

Wilson's words from last night echoed in Gavin's head. *"Maybe the shooter was more scared of who hired him?"*

"My two cents?" Xander chimed in. "I think Frazier stepped in a whole bunch of shit when we rescued the kid. You messed up this person's plan, and now they're gunning for you."

Gavin sank back into his chair. It made perfect sense on one level, but . . . "It seems excessive, don't you think?"

Bean scoffed. "Seriously, boss man? I can give you twenty million reasons why it isn't excessive."

"Well, fuck, when you put it that way . . ." He rubbed a

hand over his chin and smiled at the sparkle in her blue eyes. "Now we have more damn questions."

"Yeah," Xander said, "but we also have a pretty damn good link between the kidnapping, Frazier foiling it, and someone trying to off him."

"Holy crap, can we please stop talking about Gavin getting killed?" Bean grumbled as she pointed at him. "The guy has a bullet hole in his arm."

Xander snorted. "It's just a fucking graze."

Bean leveled Xander with a fierce glare that had Gavin wincing. Hell, a quick glance around the room showed *everyone* was wincing.

"Care to repeat that, Xander Bonetti?" Bean asked.

Wisely, the man shook his head. "No, ma'am, I don't. I was just trying to be funny."

"Well, you're not. So enough with the talk about Gavin dying." Her chin lifted ever so slightly, as if she were silently challenging Xander. And damn if that little gesture didn't warm everything inside him. "Understood?"

Xander saluted her, looking properly chastised. "Yes, ma'am."

"All right, children, settle down." Gavin chuckled. Yeah, the woman was a damn marvel. "Thanks for having my back, B. Next steps?"

Bean flashed a sweet grin that socked him right in the chest before she turned to the Smartboard. "Tiny, I'll send you what I have so far on Smith's and Penning's financials. I'd like a fresh set of eyes on it. Feel free to dig deeper if something catches your attention. I'd also like you to look into the warehouse where we found Anson. Find out who owns the property, because there has to be a reason they brought him there specifically. Feel free to pull Abbot and Oliphant in to help if you need it." She turned back to Gavin. "I'll tap into the ME's system to see if Otton had a shoulder injury that would be a match to something our shooter from the car chase might have. I'll also add all the photos of McClintocks' security—both past and present—into the facial-rec tracking system I have that monitors the island. Just as a precaution. That way, if any of them step foot on Hudson Island, we'll be notified. I'll also have cyber go over the video surveillance footage from the car chase and both shootings again. Alvarez?"

"I'll touch base with my SPD contacts and see what they found at the McClintocks' yesterday. See what intel they passed on to the FBI, if they're keeping anything under wraps, and if they have anything new on or from Polanski's team." He turned to the Smartboard. "Esme, you and I can touch base and compare notes as well."

"I'll check in with Teams Two and Three," Xander said. "Make sure everything's kosher with the McClintocks at the safe house."

"If they need anything, let me know," Esme said from the video feed. "I can have whatever they need brought to them within a couple hours."

"Well, damn," Gavin said, leaning back in his chair and looking at his teammates. "Looks like you guys have it all handled."

"Damn straight, boss. You just sit there and look pretty," Bean said with a wink as his colleagues chuckled.

"Besides, man," Xander said, "fairly sure you're on lock-down now."

Gavin frowned.

"You know the saying third time's a charm?" Xander asked. "Well, there won't be a third time for anyone to shoot at you again. Do us all a favor and stay on-property—either here or at your place—until we figure out what's going on. With Team Two, Three, and Tash at the safe house, we're stretched thin."

"Also," Bean added, "the driver is still unaccounted for."

His gaze swung to hers. "What?"

"We're almost certain that Otton was not only the jogger going past the McClintocks', but also the shooter from after the charity gala. But what about the driver from the car chase? We have zero footage of that person. It could be anyone. So I agree with Xander. Until we figure out more, you're on lockdown."

Part of him scoffed. Lockdown? Yeah, right.

He opened his mouth to say so but hesitated when he met Bean's gaze. There was a silent plea in her blue eyes, and damn if he wouldn't do just about anything for her. "Okay. Though *lockdown* sounds a bit harsh, don't you think?"

His heart squeezed at the relief that flashed over her face. Sticking close to Hudson Security was a minor inconvenience, one that in the grand scheme of things didn't matter. The last thing he wanted was her worrying. She had enough on her plate.

"All right," Gavin said, addressing the group. "We have our assignments. Well, I don't, so let me know if I can help—"

A quick rap on the conference room door had him turning.

Mel stood in the doorway with a frown on her face. "I'm so sorry to interrupt. Gavin, we have an issue at the security gate."

Alarm surged through him as their receptionist stepped fully into the room, her brow furrowed. "What's going on, Mel?"

Wringing her hands together, she let out a sigh. "I have a woman at the security gate demanding entry to meet with you. She's not on your calendar and I told her that we can't let her in without an appointment. She threw a fit and is now refusing to move her car. She's blocking the gate and says she's not leaving until she sees you. I'm so sorry."

He shook his head. "Nothing for you to be sorry for. Did she give her name?"

"Constance Whitman." Mel's frown deepened. "Or maybe it was—"

"Whitcomb?" When the young woman nodded, Gavin didn't bother biting back a groan.

"I'm pulling up the security gate feed now," Bean said, her fingers tapping on her keyboard.

Within seconds, the live video feed from the security gate was up on the Smartboard. Sure enough, there was Constance Whitcomb in her Mercedes-Maybach with her arms crossed over her chest and a pinched expression on her face.

"Fuck," he muttered.

"What do you want to do, boss?" Bean waved at the screen. "I can turn on the gate speaker from here if you want."

"No." This was the last thing he wanted to deal with. He glanced at Alvarez and Xander, both of whom were shaking their heads.

"Don't look at me," Xander said and pointed to Alvarez. "He's met her before, too, bring him."

"Nope," Gavin said. "She only knows Alvarez from the SPD, not here. Frankly, the less contact she has with Hudson Security people, the better. You're up, Xan."

"Motherfucking hell," he muttered.

"Mel," Gavin said as he moved to stand behind Bean. He bent at the waist to peer over her shoulder at her laptop screen. Constance Whitcomb was seething. "When you get back to your desk, you can go ahead and let her through the gate. Let her know where to park. Xander, wait for her outside and escort her in, then wait with her in the Fishbowl until I get there." The small, glass-walled six-seat conference room was off the lobby and was used for meetings with people who weren't cleared to enter their inner sanctum.

"Yeah," Xander said with a groan, rising from his chair. "The last thing we want is that woman wandering around the lobby."

"But the lobby's secure," Mel said, confusion echoing in her voice.

"Trust me," Xander said. "If you'd met her, the last thing you'd want is her milling about. The woman's atrocious."

"Isn't that the damn truth," Mel muttered.

Gavin's eyes narrowed. "She yell at you?"

Mel waved at Constance's image, which was still up on the Smartboard. "I wasn't exaggerating when I said she threw a hissy fit. But honestly, her insults were pretty basic. I've heard better and way more creative from my little high school cousins."

Gavin blew out his breath. It had been apparently too much to think his interactions with Constance Whitcomb were over. Piece of fucking work. "Thanks, Mel. And I'm sorry you had to deal with that."

"No worries." She shrugged. "It's all part of the job."

"It's actually not, but thank you for coming to get us." He shook his head as Mel left the room. "Xan," he called out, stopping his friend at the door. "Make sure Constance doesn't fuck with Mel. She doesn't even get to look at her."

Mel was the youngest employee they had on staff. Only twenty-two. Not only was she like everyone's baby sister, but she was the actual little sister of Hanniger on Team Three.

Xander lifted his chin. "You don't even have to ask, brother."

Heaving out a loud sigh, Gavin placed his hands on Bean's shoulders. Touching her, even in this casual way, grounded him. He glanced at the Smartboard at his colleagues who were still on the video call. "MacKay, Esme, Tiny, let's plan on catching up the same time tomorrow. But if any of you need anything before that, I'm available."

After they said their goodbyes, Bean disconnected the video call.

"If you need help with Whitcomb, let me know," Alvarez said from his seat across the conference room table. "I know the woman can be a lot, and all joking aside, I can help however you need."

"Thanks. I may take you up on it depending on what she wants." Gavin squeezed Bean's shoulders. He looked down at her. "I know it goes without saying, but please make yourself scarce while Constance is on-site. She only knows you as my girlfriend from the charity gala *and* under a different name. I don't want her connecting you to here."

"Of course." She patted his hands that were still on her shoulders, and her eyes darted to the video feed where Constance appeared to be yelling at the security gate speaker again. The corners of Bean's lips lifted into a smirk. "Good luck with her, boss man. Something tells me you're gonna need it."

CHAPTER TWENTY-NINE

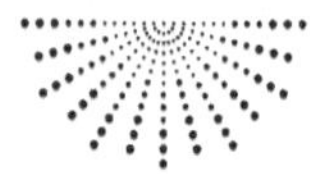

"Gavin Frazier, it's so lovely to see you again." Constance blasted him with a smile that Gavin knew was supposed to be sexy. Or seductive. Or some other shit. It was none of the above. Holy hell, this woman had to be fucking kidding.

Stepping into the conference room, he nodded to Xander, who stood near the glass door with his arms crossed over his chest. Gavin slid the glass door shut behind him. Constance was seated at the head of the rectangular table like she was queen of the fucking castle. Everything about the woman had him bristling.

"Just so we're clear, Mrs. Whitcomb—"

"Constance, please," she cooed. "There's no need for formalities."

A shiver of revulsion raced up his spine. "Constance. Let's get one thing straight. You do *not* get to yell at any of my team members. The only reason I allowed you into our office today is because I respect your brother. But that's it, that's your one free pass. If you want to come here again, you schedule an appointment like everyone else." Her shoulders straightened, the seductive look faded, and a snooty do-you-know-who-I-am look took its place. "Now, what did you want to see me about?"

"I need to know where my brother is."

He sat in the chair on the opposite end of the table from her and shook his head. "I'm afraid I'm not at liberty to provide that information."

Her nose lifted ever so slightly. "It's imperative you tell me where he is. I think he's in danger."

"That's precisely why I'm *not* telling you where he is."

A satisfied smirk crossed her face. "So you *do* know where he is."

Holy shit, this woman. "You already know that or you wouldn't be here. Now is that all?"

"I'm not leaving here until you tell me where my brother is." She crossed her arms and lifted her chin with that superior look.

He was done. "Mrs. Whitcomb, if you think that I will not have you physically removed from my property, you are sorely mistaken."

Her shoulders dropped, and she let out a sigh. As far as acting went, it was an okay performance of acquiescence, but he knew the woman was full of shit.

"Gavin, I'm sorry I'm coming across as difficult." Understatement. "I'm just so concerned about my brother. I heard about the shootings at their home and went over there as soon as I could. But the only people at the house were Adrian and his security team, and even he has no idea where you've taken my brother and his family. I'm just beside myself."

Gavin was pretty damn sure if there'd been a couch in the conference room, she would have staged a faint of some kind. "Mrs. Whitcomb, I'm not telling you where your brother is."

"Can you at least tell me if he's okay? Are Rita and Anson

with him? Is little Anson okay?" Tears welled in her eyes, and he had to acknowledge the chin tremble was very convincing. But he'd been told how she'd acted at the hospital after Anson had been admitted. The woman didn't give a shit about her nephew.

"I'm not telling you anything." He rose and caught Xander's gaze. "Now, will you be leaving on your own accord?"

Part of him wished she'd throw another fit just so he could toss her ass out.

Instead, she stood, running her hands over her hips, appearing to smooth out her skirt. He caught the glint in her eye though. The way she cocked her hip out slightly. *Holy fuck, give me patience.*

"I'll be staying at the Pacific View Resort for the next few days. I'd love to treat you to dinner while I'm here." Her gaze trailed lazily up and down his body. "For business, of course. I'd love to talk with you about that security opening you have next year. In light of everything that has happened with my brother, I'd love to pick your brain about what security measures I can take while I wait for your schedule to open up."

"I'm busy with my girlfriend this week."

"Ahh, the brown-haired woman from the charity gala?" He didn't respond. "Well, she seemed lovely. Very fashionable." She pursed her lips, and her gaze traveled to Xander, giving him the same once-over. "Perhaps your second-in-command here would be available to provide some information about your company's services."

"No one is available, Mrs. Whitcomb." Gavin slid open the glass door and gestured to the lobby. "Mr. Bonetti will escort you to your vehicle."

She stepped toward him and then paused in the doorway, stopping directly in front of him. Her shoulder brushed against his chest. "If you hear from my brother, please let him know I'm worried about him. Please have him call me. It's urgent."

Gavin remained silent, his expression blank. He wasn't saying a damn thing to the woman. Instead, he caught Xander's gaze over her head and lifted his chin.

"This way, Mrs. Whitcomb," Xander said, taking her elbow and steering her through the lobby past Mel, who was on the phone at the reception desk, and out the front door.

The moment the door closed behind them, Gavin let out a breath. Holy fuck, that woman was something else.

"Gavin," Mel said, urgency in her tone. "Bean needs to see you immediately."

Entering his security code, he waited impatiently for the door to the inner office to open. The second he stepped through, Alvarez was there. His friend's expression was stony and it sent a bolt of worry through him. "What is it?"

"Whitcomb had a listening device on her."

Ice shot through his veins. "What?"

They hurried down the hall and into Bean's office.

"The Fishbowl cameras were on during your meeting," Bean said. "I'm not sure if you recall, but a few months ago for shits and giggles, I added bug sweepers to that room." His brows rose, and she shrugged. "It's a damn good thing I did, too, because Whitcomb had some kind of listening device on her. Unfortunately for us, it was battery operated, so I wasn't able to hack into it."

"Could it have just been her phone the sweeper was picking up?"

Bean's eyes rolled. "Please, boss, do you think I buy the shitty detectors? I have three different kinds in that room. But to answer your question, no. I picked up her cell phone signal and this was completely different. She had a bug of some kind on her."

"Fucking hell," he muttered, stalking to Bean's desk. Grabbing the landline, he hit the button for Hudson Tactical.

"Wilson," a deep voice answered.

"It's Frazier. I need you to follow someone ASAP. Constance Whitcomb. Xander just escorted her from the building." He gave Wilson a brief recap of their conversation in the Fishbowl and informed him that she was wearing a listening device of some kind. He scanned Bean's monitors, seeing the information they had on Constance. Bean pointed at her screen and then at the phone, and he nodded. "Bean's sending you the intel we have on Whitcomb to your cell. She's staying at the Pacific View, and I want to know what the fuck she's up to."

"On it," Wilson replied. "I'll check in in thirty. Out."

Gavin set the phone into its cradle and scrubbed his hands over his face. "What the fuck is going on?"

He startled when small hands settled on his stomach. His eyes popped open and Bean was there, looking up at him with concern on her face.

"Breathe, Gavin."

He did as he was told and glanced at Alvarez, who was still in the room. "You heard our bullshit conversation in the Fishbowl. What the hell is this woman up to?"

Alvarez shrugged. "I'll ask around. My brother and his wife run in that same Seattle philanthropic circle as the Whitcombs and McClintocks. I'll see if they've heard anything about her. Because you know what those high-society types love more than their fancy parties? Gossip."

Bean slid her hands from his abs to his sides and squeezed. The small gesture was both reassuring and intimate at once. "I've asked Tiny to dig deeper into Constance— her schedule, financials, who the hell she's sleeping with. If there's dirt to be found, he'll find it. As much as I hate to admit it, the guy's damn good at what he does."

The corners of Gavin's lips lifted at her irritation. "Good. But he's not nearly as good as you, of course."

She glanced up at him with a growing smirk, wrapping her arms around him in a tight embrace. "Damn straight, boss."

"Jesus, kids, I'm still in the room," Alvarez said, clearing his throat. "But I'm leaving."

Bean chuckled. "Sorry, not sorry?"

Alvarez gave them a chin lift as he left and shut the door behind them.

Gavin let out a sigh and pressed his lips to her forehead. "Thanks for being so kick-ass at what you do. If you hadn't added those bug sweepers—"

"Stop. Turn your brain off for a second, okay? There's nothing else we can do right now. I have cyber tracking her car, and I've sent the info to Wilson. Alvarez and Tiny are doing their things and looking into her. What do you say we take a brain break and go for a little hike?"

The vise he hadn't realized had been squeezing his chest released. "That sounds like a great idea. We can hit Jackson Cove and—"

"Sorry," she interrupted, shaking her head and stepping away from him. "You're still on lockdown, buddy. We can do one of the easy trails by Tactical."

His brow furrowed, though he was fighting a grin, and he hauled her back against him. "Buddy?"

Mischief danced in her eyes as she shrugged. "Figured that sounded better than dumbass."

Laughing, he dropped a kiss on her lips. Before it could get heated, he pulled away. "Does this mean you've given some thought to taking one of Wilson's outdoor survival classes?"

She snorted. "Hard pass, boss man. Hard pass."

"But you'll admit that hiking is fun, right? A good way to clear your head?"

Her eyes rolled hard. "I admit nothing. Now, are we going or are you gonna keep yapping?"

He yanked her close for another kiss, this one deeper. He'd make an outdoorsperson out of her yet.

CHAPTER THIRTY

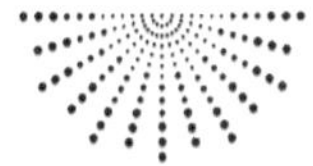

Half an hour later, Bean had changed into leggings, a long-sleeved shirt, fleece vest, hooded down coat, and, of course, her new hiking boots. It was a crisp and dreary gray afternoon that threatened rain. Basically, a typical October day in the Pacific Northwest. She and Gavin made their way past the Hudson Tactical facility toward the trailhead she'd explored with Wilson last week. She bit back a chuckle. *Explored* was probably a bit of an exaggeration. It had been more like a very leisurely stroll where she was sure her friend wanted to gouge his eyes out.

She peeked at Gavin and the humor in her fled. He was focused ahead of him, but the crinkle between his eyebrows was on full display. His mind was elsewhere.

"You doing okay, boss?" she asked, popping the top of her energy drink and taking a swig.

He glanced down at her and cringed. "How do you drink that?"

She held the can out to him. When he shook his head, she shrugged and took another drink. "It's good. It's like a liquid Jolly Rancher. I'll have you know, I used to drink the full-sugar ones. This bad boy has zero sugar. So it's not *that* bad for me."

"I wouldn't go that far," he murmured.

"To be fair, I did drink a big bottle of water this morning."

His lips pursed. "After how many cups of coffee and energy drinks?"

She chuckled. "Fair point, but one bottle of water is better than none, right?"

"True." A tired smile ghosted his lips as he stuffed his hands into the pockets of his down jacket. "I just worry about you, B."

She sobered at his words, at the dark look that flashed over his face. "I know, and I appreciate it. But I promise I'm trying to be better about eating and properly hydrating." Well, hydrating in general. But whatever. "Believe it or not, this is only my second can of the day. Before that whole passing-out incident, I would have usually already had at least four." More like six or seven. On top of the three to four cups of morning coffee. But the way the guy was grimacing at her admission, she didn't want to give him a heart attack.

"What else is bugging you, boss?" When he gave her a pointed look, she rolled her eyes. "*Gavin.* You're worried, and I know it can't just be about my energy drink consumption."

He remained silent as they passed the easy trail she'd taken with Wilson. They veered to the right, and he held a branch up for her to walk under. "All of it. The shootings. The not knowing. Constance freaking Whitcomb. The fact that we're stretched so thin with the McClintocks at the safe house."

"Are you thinking of hiring another team?"

"I probably should, but it's so damn hard to find good people. The teams we have are solid, but we basically have them booked out through the middle of next year. I don't want to have anyone burnout." He let out a weary sigh and scrubbed his hands over his face. Dropping his arms, his shoulders straightened, and he inhaled deeply. "I don't want to talk about that though. We're here to clear our heads. Tell me something non-work related. Maybe something about your childhood. I know you said you spent most of it at boarding schools, but did you have fun? Get into trouble?"

Bean made a face. "You met my mother. Fun wasn't a high priority. But I suppose my childhood was fine." She fought a cringe. That had sounded horrible. It hadn't been bad, just . . . different. "Looking back, I definitely had an unusual upbringing. Boarding school at four. Done with high school by twelve. Two undergrad and two master's degrees by eighteen." She shrugged. "But at the time, I didn't really know any better. It wasn't until I was around thirteen that I realized I was an anomaly."

He took her hand and squeezed. "You had friends and stuff, right? You were happy?"

Her chest tightened, and she frowned. Happy? That old feeling of not fitting in settled heavily in her gut. She wanted to be honest with Gavin, but she also didn't want to be a complete downer. "I think the better word is focused. Determined. The boarding school I went to had kids of a variety of ages. When I started, I was the youngest, so it was hard to talk with the other kids. I'd mentioned Marie—"

"The cook who gave you your nickname."

A small smile bloomed, both from the memory of the woman and the fact that he'd remembered. "Yeah. Other kids came and went, but she was the one constant. I talked with her a lot. Picked her brain on what adult life was like. Watched sitcoms in the evening with her."

"She was like your mother figure?"

Bean heard the warmth in his voice and nodded. Marie was the one who'd baked her cookies for her birthday, the one she'd run to when she'd been twelve and thought she was hemorrhaging, thought she was dying. Marie was the one person she kept in contact with from her childhood.

"At my school, since kids graduated high school at different ages, once you started your college courses—if you were too young to live on-campus at your university—you were transitioned into the boarding school's 'college' dorms. It was hard to make friends. At that point, even though most of us were going to Stanford, everyone was kind of doing their own thing."

Gavin looked at her in utter bafflement and appeared to be choosing his words carefully. "That sounds . . . impressive, for sure. But, honey, that sounds . . ."

"Boring?" She chuckled because, holy shit, it did sound boring. Luckily, she'd never known anything different, so she'd never noticed how lonely her childhood had been. "I obviously had a hard time relating to other kids. I mean, do you know what happens when you take a group of socially awkward, too smart, introverted kids and put them in a room together?"

He shook his head.

"Absolutely nothing. We didn't talk to each other or engage in regular teenage mischief—or what I'm assuming teenage mischief is based on what I saw on TV—but I swear, I did have my share of fun. When I was thirteen, I got really into RPGs."

Gavin's jaw dropped, and he stopped dead in his tracks. A look of horror crossed his face. "Rocket-propelled grenades?"

She blinked. Twice. Then she burst into laughter. "Oh my God, Gavin, it's obvious you weren't a nerd as a kid. Role-playing games. You know, online computer games? *Ever-Quest, World of Warcraft, Gothic*—that kind of thing."

"Holy shit," he wheezed, slapping a hand to the center of his chest. "You had me worried there for a second. I mean, what the hell kind of fancy-ass school lets *teenagers* play with heavy-duty weapons."

She shook her head, wiping a tear of hilarity away. "It was a school for super nerds. The only warfare was simulated."

"Thank God for that." He mimed wiping sweat from his brow.

The small gesture warmed her heart, and she couldn't help but smile at him. Playful Gavin was quickly becoming one of her favorites. The way his eyes crinkled at the edges and the deeper lines bracketing his mouth softened his face was everything.

"Speaking of weapons . . . I'd really like it if you took some of our weapons training courses." She opened her mouth to complain, but he held up a hand. "I know you've been putting it off since you've been so busy. But with Tiny coming on and you delegating more to the cyber team, I'd like you to consider it."

He gave her his most pathetic puppy-dog look.

She rolled her eyes but chuckled, shaking her head.

His expression grew serious as he held her gaze. "Bean, it's important to me that you're safe. That you know how to defend yourself. At least think about it. Please?"

Gah! Of course, he had to go and be all sweet, had to make her insides all gooey.

It's not that she had anything against their company's courses. In fact, she'd heard great things about them. It's just that she'd never handled any sort of weapon before. She could chop up vegetables as well as the next person, but that was as far as her knife skills went. She'd also never held a gun. Therefore, she knew she wouldn't be good at it. And, yes, she understood that was the whole damn reason for the courses and lessons, but she hated not being good at something. If she wasn't good at something, she put it off for . . . Well, forever if she had to.

Gavin's kicked-puppy-dog look was back and dialed up a few notches. She bit back a smile. "Fine. I'll think about it."

"That's all I ask and I'm taking that as a win. Now, were you good at these computer games you played?"

She slowly turned her head to him, one eyebrow arched high. "Is that a real question, Frazier?"

He winced, holding up his hands in mock surrender. "No. Not at all. It was a lapse of judgement. My stupid mouth saying stupid things."

"I figured as much." She gave him another pointed look. Good Lord, he was cute. "But in response to your stupid question, obviously, I was very, very good at those games."

"Obviously," he said, sending her a wink.

She grinned up at him and hooked her arm through his as they continued up the trail. Who knew hiking with Gavin Frazier would be this fun, this relaxing. "What was cool about the games was that they were all online. I picked a persona and no one knew I was a thirteen-year-old girl living at a boarding school and working on her first computer science degree. I wasn't the weird kid. I just got to play and just . . . be."

"I'm glad you had that outlet."

"Me too. For as long as I can remember, it was easier to relax when I was behind a computer screen. I've never done well with people."

"You deal with people just fine, B."

She shook her head. "It may appear that way, but on the inside, I'm usually a nervous wreck."

"When you first started at Hudson Security, did me and MacKay make you nervous?"

"No. You two were fine. But I'd heard about you guys from Esme first, and I knew you guys were solid if Esme trusted you. That woman barely trusts anyone—especially back then."

"Valid point." His lips pursed, and his eyes narrowed, but he remained silent.

She knew that face, that I-want-to-ask-but-I-don't-know-if-I-should expression. "Go ahead and ask whatever's on your mind."

He was quiet for a few more moments before he spoke, as if weighing his words. "Now that we have a larger crew at the office, are you okay with that? The last thing I want is for you to be uncomfortable at work. I want to make sure it's always a safe space for you. Anything less is unacceptable."

Holy. Freaking. Swoon.

Her insides melted. If she weren't holding on to his arm, she'd be a puddle of goo at his feet. Who knew this man could be so sweet . . .

The intensity in his gaze—a mixture of protectiveness, care, and desire—had her gulping. But she had to be completely honest with him. "I've lived an unorthodox life. Until I came to work for you, I'd never truly felt secure. For the first time in my life, I have a place that I fit."

He pulled them to a stop and faced her, taking both her hands in his. "You're more than your job, B. You're more than your brains and your beauty. You're the whole damn package."

Heat raced over her face, and she bit her bottom lip, her gaze dropping to the center of his chest. This man . . .

She let out an unsteady chuckle. "Now you're making me nervous in a totally different way."

He stepped toward her, eliminating the space between them, and wrapped her in his arms. Tipping her chin up with his finger, he gazed down at her, heat and tenderness swirling in his eyes. "Good to know. Because you make me nervous in the best way."

Her stomach flipped as he pressed a kiss to her lips.

Before things could get too heated, he pulled away, took her hand, and continued up the trail. "Do you still play?"

It took a moment for her brain to connect the dots. *Games. Right.* "I try. It's been a bit hectic the last few months, so I haven't had a lot of downtime."

"I'm sorry for that. I know we put a lot on your plate."

She shrugged. "Yeah, but it's what I want. To keep busy. Letting go and delegating has been . . . hard." Her nose scrunched. More like excruciating. It took everything she had to not micromanage her team. To not make sure they were doing things the right way. *Hey, control freak!* "However, I will admit—out loud—that Tiny's really good. Better than I thought, actually. MacKay made the right call bringing him in."

Gavin stopped in his tracks and stared at her like the proverbial deer in headlights. Then he laughed. And laughed. And laughed.

She crossed her arms over her chest, lips pursed as she waited for him to be done.

After way too long, he finally quieted down to little snickers. "Holy shit, B, did it hurt when you said that? Because, baby, your face just now?" His finger made a circle in the air around her face. "Swear to God, you looked like you were either gonna puke or punch something."

Her hands hit her hips, and she glared at him but the corners of her lips twitched. Shaking her head, she huffed out an indignant sigh. He was too damn cute for his own good.

Before she could think of some smart-ass comeback, Gavin swooped her up into his arms so they were face-to-face, her chest pressed tightly against his. She clutched his broad shoulders, her feet dangling in the air. A flush tore over her cheeks, and she may have squeaked.

"Holy shit, B. You're so fucking hot when you're all grumpy, you know that?"

He crushed his mouth to hers and every nerve in her body caught fire. She moaned and parted her lips. His tongue thrust into her mouth, and she welcomed it, welcomed him. She couldn't get enough of this man.

"Damn, baby, I need to make you grumpy at me all the time."

"Is that so?" she asked, wrapping her legs around his waist and rocking against his growing erection. His moan had satisfaction surging through her. *She'd* done that. And she wanted more . . .

A bird cawed, and she pulled away, breathless. He had one hand under her ass to support her, and the other buried in her hair. She wasn't sure how long they'd stood there devouring each other, but her heart was racing and everything was unsteady. This man destroyed her senses.

And by his equally heaving chest and wild eyes, it appeared to be a reciprocal destruction of senses.

When Gavin finally spoke, his voice was like gravel. "As much as I want to push you up against the nearest tree and sink deep into you . . ." He shook his head, and his eyes darted up to the trees.

It took a split second for understanding to sink in. When it did, she gasped and heat flooded over her face. "Oh my God," she muttered, dropping her head into the side of his neck.

He cleared his throat. "Yeah . . ."

Laughing, she met his gaze and framed his face in her hands. "Yeah, is right. Pretty sure we just traumatized everyone in cyber for life." She glanced up and scanned the trees. "Do you even know where the cameras are out here?"

As he lowered her to her feet, she pulled him down for

one final kiss. Because she could. And cyber had already gotten a show, so what did it matter?

With a growl, he nipped at her lower lip before straightening. "No clue. I know Wilson wanted to make sure there weren't any blind spots." He glanced up and scanned the trees. Then he waved, calling out, "Sorry! Feel free to delete all that."

Snickering, Bean hooked her arm through his. "You're a nut. It's doubtful anyone picked us up on the cameras." He arched an eyebrow at her, and she winced. "Yeah, I'll make sure that whoever is monitoring the game cameras erases that little part." She cleared her throat. "Well, secret's out about us, huh?"

She cringed and wanted to hit herself over the head. She'd hoped the words had come out casually, but the way Gavin stilled had her stomach twisting. She suppressed a disappointed sigh. Things had been going so well, but she had to go and make everything awkward. *Typical, Bean. Typical.*

Bean's words had Gavin pausing. They'd been said casually, but there'd been a nervous edge in her voice. And that wasn't going to fly.

"Are you okay with everyone at the office knowing we're together?" he asked.

"Um, yeah. It's fine. I mean, if you're okay with it?"

He turned to fully face her. He wasn't sure what had just happened. One second, they were making out and joking about getting caught on the cameras. Now, she was unsure. Awkward. Nervous.

This was *Bean*. The most kick-ass woman he knew. She should never be any of those things.

Spotting a felled tree, he pulled her toward it and sat.

Patting the bark next to him, he waited until she was seated. "I know we've moved about a million miles an hour here. Hell, I haven't even taken you out on an official date—"

Her eyes widened in surprise, and his stomach sank. After everything they'd talked about the other night, did she think this was just a quick, casual fuck? Holy shit, if she did, then he was an absolute asshole.

"Look, B, I know we jumped into this pretty fast and—"

"We've been friends for eight years."

"Yeah, but this?" He cradled her face in his hands and kissed her. He took his time tasting her lips, her tongue, then her lips again before pulling back. "This? This is new. And we went pretty fast. Like I said, I haven't even taken you out, which is all on me. That's my fault. And just so there's no miscommunication, that's what I want. To take you out. To date you. To be with you."

She looked at him with tentative eyes, like she wasn't sure she quite believed him.

"Is that something you want too?" His voice caught on the last three words. *Please say yes.* He wasn't sure what he'd do if she wanted to keep things casual.

With wide eyes, she gave a slight nod, and the tight band around his heart eased. He ran his thumb over her lower lip. Knowing her past, her history, he vowed right then and there that he'd do everything in his power to make her see how amazing she was.

"I don't know if you want to put a label on what's going on between us, and we don't need to."

Her eyes narrowed. "If *you* had to choose a label for us, what would it be?"

"You'd be my girlfriend. My partner. My woman. I'd also add my lover"—he shook his head and cringed—"but that word has always creeped me out."

She laughed, as he'd intended. "It creeps me out too."

"But we don't need to label this if you're not comfortable with that. I want to be with you. You want to be with me?" When she nodded again, this time with a small smile lifting her lips, he continued, "I hope you know that I respect the hell out of you. You've always mattered to me. And now?" He took in the arch of her eyebrows, the sharp cut of her cheekbones, the way her irises shifted from clear blue to nearly navy at the edges. His chest squeezed tightly. This woman was everything to him. "Now, you matter so damn much."

She leaned into him and sealed her lips to his. Not caring about the cameras, he explored her mouth slowly, as if they had all the time in the world. Hell, if he had his way, they did. They'd have their entire lives.

A sharp trill had him groaning. His phone vibrated in his pocket.

She chuckled. "Is there a phone in your pocket or are you just happy to see me?"

He laughed. With one hand, he hooked her behind the neck and pulled her in for a hard kiss. With his other hand, he pulled the phone from his pocket. "Aren't you the comedian," he muttered against her lips.

"Humor and sarcasm when I'm nervous. It's a thing." She shrugged. "What can I say?"

"Only good nervous around me, right?"

The smile that spread over her lips warmed his heart. "Right. Now answer your phone."

"Yes, ma'am," he said, bringing his phone to his ear. "Frazier."

"It's Alvarez. We need you guys back at the office. And as a heads-up, I don't know what you and B are up to, but cyber's hooting and hollering like twelve-year-olds. Be prepared."

Rolling his eyes, Gavin replied, "Thanks, man. We're on our way back now." Rising, he glanced around the trail and held a hand out to Bean. "We're about twenty to a half hour out." His eyes narrowed at the noise on the other end of the phone. "What the hell was that?"

Alvarez chuckled. "That was a collective 'Aww' from cyber. You must have done something that met their approval."

Shaking his head, he let go of Bean's hand and glanced up at the trees. With a giant smile, he raised his middle finger. He chuckled at the raucous laughter he heard coming through his phone.

CHAPTER THIRTY-ONE

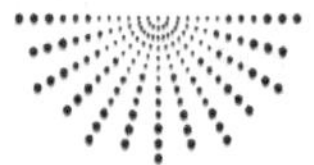

After some ribbing from cyber—because apparently, they were all still middle schoolers at heart—and still dressed in her hiking attire, Bean entered the large conference room and greeted Xander and Alvarez. She took a seat at the head of the rectangular table and opened the lid of her laptop. In under a minute, Tiny was on the room's wall-sized Smartboard.

"Sorry to cut your hike short," Alvarez said with a smirk. "But I figured you'd want in on this. It's nothing substantial, but it's interesting. Tiny?"

"Like Alvarez said, this is all preliminary, but it does raise more questions. On Saturday night after the car chase, Bean asked me to look into Constance Whitcomb's finances. I did. At first glance, everything was fine. She and her husband, Roger, have a substantial joint checking account, and he has a number of individual investment accounts. Truly, everything looked normal. But when I dug deeper, I was able to see the structure of their joint account. Both their names are technically on it, but Roger completely controls it. A stipulation in their private banking contract is that he's the only one authorized to spend on the account. Any transactions initiated by her have to be preapproved by him. She does have an individual account, and it appears that Roger has a recurring transfer going to it from their joint account for her monthly allowance. The transaction memo is literally 'Constance's Allowance.'"

Bean frowned. "That's a bit archaic." Not that she was a fan of Constance's or anything, but that whole control-your-wife's-money thing was gross and antiquated.

"Agreed," Tiny said. "However, her allowance is forty grand, so I'm pretty sure she isn't complaining. The forty grand is deposited into her individual account on the first, and she blows through a good chunk of it on shopping, spa trips, and vacations. However, as of last month, that monthly transfer stopped. Then yesterday—two days after the charity gala—a hundred and fifty grand went from her individual account back to the joint account. As of this afternoon, she has two hundred bucks sitting in her account *and* her credit cards are frozen."

"So she's broke?" Gavin asked. "But she said she was checking into the Pacific View Resort today. That place isn't cheap."

"Hang on." Tiny looked to the side, and the sound of his typing rang through the speakers. "She's using a McClintock Family Foundation credit card."

Bean pushed her laptop forward and leaned her elbows onto the table. "What about her own money? I mean, she's McClintock's sister and she works for the foundation."

"Her paychecks get deposited into that joint account with her husband. When I searched her SSN, it showed that she has one bank account with her brother. However, it's an 'and' account that requires both parties to sign to access the funds.

Neither she nor Edward have touched that account in over a year. It looks like all her available cash is tied to her husband."

Bean pursed her lips. "Did she do something to piss off her husband?"

"I have a theory on that," Alvarez said. "You know how I said this high-society group loves gossip? Well, they did *not* disappoint. I checked with my brother and his wife, and there's a rumor going around their circle of friends that Constance's marriage is in trouble, that old Whitcomb has finally had enough. It's no secret that he hasn't divorced her because of her ties to McClintock, and that he's turned a blind eye to her many affairs. Not that he's been a saint either. He's been known to screw around with lots—"

"Nope," Bean said, holding up a hand and shaking her head. "Please stop. I do *not* need the mental image of that man screwing anything."

Alvarez chuckled. "My point is that there are whispers that Constance is sleeping with her stepson. That Whitcomb found out, and instead of divorcing her, he's freezing her out financially."

"Well, shit," Gavin said, running a hand over his chin. "That jives with her current financial situation."

"I took a peek at their prenup," Tiny said. "There's no provision for cheating on either of their sides. However, if he initiates the divorce, she gets six million as a settlement. If *she* initiates the divorce, she only gets five hundred grand."

Bean's mouth fell open. "Why the hell would she agree to such a shitty prenup?"

"My guess? Forty grand a month," Alvarez said.

Xander scoffed. "So Whitcomb's just going to stay married to her to basically fuck her over. I mean, it's one thing if she's cheating with random people, but cheating on him with his actual son?"

"Where is she now?" Gavin asked.

"Wilson checked in before you guys showed up," Xander said. "He said she went directly to the Pacific View, checked into her room, and has been there ever since. He's hanging around until things quiet down, then he'll put some of our tiny cameras up near her door so we can monitor her."

Speaking of cameras . . . Bean pulled her laptop toward her, opened the video she'd received from cyber, and shared it on the Smartboard. "This is video of Constance on the ferries this morning. Nothing exciting. She boarded at the Mukilteo Ferry Terminal. Once her car was parked, she went up to the coffee stand, talked to the person in line behind her, grabbed a coffee, and went back to her car." Bean sped through the surveillance footage. "She disembarked at the Clinton Ferry Terminal, drove through Whidbey Island, then hopped on the next ferry at Coupeville to Hudson Island. This time, she stayed in her car for the entire ferry ride. After she disembarked, she drove straight here. No stops. Like I said, nothing exciting."

Gavin sighed and leaned back in his seat. "So where does that leave us?"

"With more fucking questions," Alvarez said. "Aren't you glad we called you guys back to the office for this?"

Bean chuckled and glanced at the screen. "Tiny, can you look into Roger Whitcomb's son?"

"On it."

"Wasn't Roger's son at our table at the charity gala?" Gavin asked.

Her brow furrowed. "I think so, but I can't picture him."

"I feel like we're missing something," Xander said. "I have no clue what though."

"Tiny," Bean said, "did you find anything on the warehouse where they took Anson?"

"Not yet. Ownership on the property is a clusterfuck. In

the past three years, it's changed hands over twenty times. Sometimes it's the same entity but with a different name, other times it's a completely separate company. I have a program running to pull all the entities and their owners and registered agents. It's slow going though."

"Well, crew," Gavin said, "back at it, I suppose. Let's check back in tomorrow morning."

As Tiny disconnected, Bean rose and stretched.

"I have about another hour or two of work," Gavin said. "Have dinner with me tonight?"

"I'd love to," Xander said, deadpan.

"I'm in too," Alvarez added. "Can I bring the fam?"

Gavin shook his head. "You can both fuck off."

Chuckling, both men made their way to the door, waving their goodbyes.

"So," Gavin began as he stood and placed a hand at the small of her back. "Dinner tonight?"

"Are you cooking?"

"Uh . . . seeing as I'm not really in the mood for ramen, yes."

His teasing smile had butterflies taking flight in her stomach. Yup, Playful Gavin was so damn cute.

She narrowed her eyes. "Are you saying I can't cook?"

"Not at all, because I'm pretty sure *you* said that." He stepped toward her and pulled her against him, looping his arms around her. "Now give me a kiss so we can get back to work and then get the hell out of here."

She rose up on her tiptoes and pecked him on the lips.

"Nope," he growled. "Try again. And make it a good one."

She tsked. "Bossy."

"I'll be happy to remind you later just how bossy I can be." His arms tightened around her. "Now kiss me, B."

She rose up onto her tiptoes again, and he met her

halfway and crashed his lips to hers. There was nothing sweet or playful about his kiss. No, it was hot and demanding. Like he was marking her, claiming her. And it lit her on fire. As much as she loved Playful Gavin, this other version was definitely becoming a favorite.

CHAPTER THIRTY-TWO

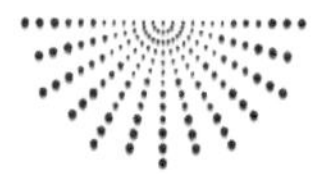

Bean tightened her ponytail and glanced at herself in her office's full-length mirror. She'd changed out of her black pantsuit and red Ferragamo heels and into her hiking wear. Who would have thought that midday hikes were good for her brain? Her mind was sharper, her caffeine consumption was down, and she'd been sleeping better.

She rolled her eyes. Okay, while the first two points may have something to do with the hiking, the third point was due to an entirely different type of exercise.

Namely, Gavin.

A flush warmed her body as she recalled "dinner" last night. They'd barely made it two steps into his home when they'd attacked each other. Clothes had gone flying, and he'd taken her hard against the wall. Then on the dining room table. And then on the couch. They hadn't gotten to eat actual food until nearly ten, but they sure as hell had feasted on each other.

After that, they'd made it to his bed, where they'd taken it nice and slow and fallen asleep in each other's arms. She'd woken at four-thirty—earlier than usual—but not from

Gavin having a nightmare. No, she'd woken to his head between her legs. Suffice it to say, the man's mouth was magic, and it was a lovely way to start the day.

The alarm on her phone dinged, pulling her from her thoughts. If she wanted to actually hit the trail, she needed to get a move on. With one last glance at her reflection, she grabbed her puffer coat and went in search of Gavin.

The door to his office was open. Bean knocked on the doorframe and peeked her head in.

"Ready?"

He winced as he hung up his phone. "I'm sorry, baby, but I have to take a rain check. I need to call Edward and Rita. They want to talk about Polanski's team."

"That's fine," she said. "Do you need me to sit in?"

"Nah. Xander and Wilson are joining the call with me. We won't need your crew until we know exactly how they want to proceed."

"Sounds good. I'll see you later, then?"

He nodded. "Have dinner with me tonight?"

She grinned and waggled her eyebrows. "Would dinner happen to be code for anything else?"

He leaned back in his chair and locked his fingers behind his head. The smile he sent her was pure sex. "Oh, we'll have actual food tonight, but you better believe I'll be eating you for dessert."

Her stomach flipped. *Yes, please.*

Her mouth opened to reply, but she froze at the gagging noise behind her.

Xander squeezed past her and into Gavin's office. "I think I actually threw up a little in my mouth."

He flopped into one of Gavin's guest chairs with a grimace. "Just so we're clear, I have no issues with the two of you. Hell, you guys are fucking cute and I'm happy for you both. But this shit?" He pointed a finger at her and then at Gavin. "Gross. It's like hearing your parents having sex."

Bean chuckled. "Well, maybe if you didn't sneak up on people, you wouldn't hear what you're not supposed to."

Xander's mouth gaped. "You're standing in the doorway."

Gavin shrugged. "Could have been worse."

"Yeah, I've already walked in on you two making out." He shuddered as he glanced around. "Everything in here's been disinfected, right?"

Bean rolled her eyes. "I'm out of here. I'll be back in about an hour or so. Two max."

"Well, shit. Look at you, Miss Outdoorsy," Wilson said from behind her.

Chuckling, she struck a pose. "Who'd have thought, right? But I'm sticking to the easy trails."

"Good for you," Wilson said, patting her on the shoulder as he entered the office and took the seat next to Xander. "Mark my words, you'll be joining me on my eight-mile treks before you know it."

"Don't hold your breath." She snorted. "On that note, I'll leave you guys to it."

"B," Gavin called out, and she turned back. "You have your phone on you?"

She patted the pocket of her leggings. "Yup."

"Call me when you get back to the trailhead."

She arched an eyebrow, and he held her gaze, arching an eyebrow right back.

Sometimes his bossiness wasn't as cute. "You do recall that the entire area is monitored, right?"

"Yeah." Xander chuckled. "You guys traumatized the entire cyber team. They were talking about how it was like watching their mom and dad make out."

Wilson chuckled. "I heard about that."

Gavin sent both men a glare, which they both ignored. He

focused back on her, his sharp jaw clenching. "I recall, but humor me? Please."

She rolled her eyes. It wasn't a big deal, but apparently, she liked needling him as much as he liked to needle her. Because that jaw-clenching thing he did? Pretty hot. "Fine," she said with an exaggerated huff. His eyes narrowed, and she shot him a wink before turning.

An hour and a half later, Bean was back in her office, unlacing her hiking boots. She had to admit, she was pretty damn proud of herself.

Who would have thought she'd like the great outdoors? Not her. That's for damn sure.

She hated to admit it, but Gavin had been right. There was something balancing about wandering around the woods. Everything was so big out there, and that reminded her to slow down. Her programs would still be there when she got back to the office. A part of her felt guilty for taking time away for herself, but she was pretty sure that was the workaholic, control freak talking. The fact that she'd even felt any sort of anxiety for taking a break was telling. She really needed to work on the whole work-life-balance thing.

Baby steps, right?

After changing out of her hiking clothes and back into her work outfit, she pulled the hair tie from her hair and brushed it out. Satisfied she looked work ready again, she grabbed her laptop and headed to the large conference room. As the first one to appear for their meeting, she dialed up Tiny. Moments later, his face appeared on the screen.

"How are you, Tiny?"

"Good. You?"

"Can't complain." Her eyes narrowed at the smirk that crossed his face. "What's that look for?"

"Nothing." He chuckled as she continued to glare at him. "Cyber put together a montage of yesterday's hiking highlights for me. Said to consider it a welcome-to-the-team kind of thing."

She dropped her head into her hands. "Kill. Me. Now."

He laughed. "Don't worry, Bean. They love you. Though I'm not gonna lie, it's . . . interesting being a part of a larger team."

She glanced back at him and smiled at the baffled look on his face. "It's odd, right? But don't worry. They'll grow on you."

"Who'll grow on you?" Gavin asked as he walked into the room with Xander and Alvarez behind him. Gavin made a beeline to her and dropped a kiss to the top of her head before taking the seat beside her. "Good hike?"

Warmth heated her cheeks and she nodded, clearing her throat. "Yeah, and apparently, cyber did a montage of us hiking yesterday and sent it to Tiny."

"Of course they did." Gavin shook his head. "How's it going, Tiny?"

"Good. I mean, not as good as you guys, but what are you gonna do?" The man chuckled, but before Bean could say anything, he continued, "I have an interesting update on Branson Whitcomb if you guys are ready?"

Gavin glanced at Xander and Alvarez, who both nodded, and leaned back in his seat. "Go for it."

"For background," Tiny said, "Branson Whitcomb just turned thirty-one and is the only child of Roger Whitcomb. His mother was Roger's third wife, Miranda, who passed away five years ago from breast cancer. Branson's living in a condo in downtown Seattle that was owned by his late mother."

Bean tried to recall what the guy looked like but drew a

blank. As if reading her mind, Tiny shared a picture of Branson on the Smartboard. She nearly snorted. His dark-blond hair looked like it was in need of a haircut, but it blew in the wind just so. He was dressed in khaki shorts with an unbuttoned linen shirt and was barefoot and leaning on the rail of some yacht. There were Gucci sunglasses on his face and a champagne glass in his hand. The Mediterranean Sea sparkled behind him, picturesque villas dotting the background. He looked like the stereotypical vacationing trust-fund douchebag.

Of course this guy was sleeping with his stepmom.

But now that she could put a face to the name, she remembered him from the gala. He'd sat at their table next to his father and hadn't said a word. He'd simply scrolled through his phone the entire evening—not bothering to lower its volume—with an unending glass of whiskey.

"Branson began drawing from his trust at twenty-five," Tiny said. "Five hundred thousand a year—a lump sum for that first year, and monthly installments after that. At thirty, it bumped up to seven-fifty. When he reaches thirty-five, it'll be a million a year from then on. It sounds great, but unfortunately for him, his father is the account trustee, and he froze the accounts shortly after Branson's thirtieth birthday. Branson's been living off what was in his account, but during the last six months, his funds have been dwindling fast. Very fast."

"Drugs?" Alvarez asked.

Tiny made a face. "He's most likely a recreational user, but for the amounts we're talking about, my guess is gambling. He took a few trips to Vegas and Monte Carlo the year before with friends, but six months ago, he was in Vegas and blew through about a quarter mil. Ever since, he's been hemorrhaging money. In the last six months, there have also been four large deposits into his account of a hundred grand each—all cashier's checks. Without fail, a few days after each deposit, the money is gone."

"Can you trace the cashier's checks?" Xander asked.

Tiny glanced at her. "Bean?"

She wrinkled her nose. "Yeah, but it'll take some time. Extra safeguards have to be put in place to ensure we don't raise any flags. There's also really no way to make any of the information we get admissible."

"In my experience," Tiny added, "if the money is from the mafia, triad, bratva, or whatever group, the bank's not going to have a record of it. Those transactions never hit their books."

"That's fair," Gavin said, tapping his chin with his finger.

"Any updates on the warehouse property?" Bean asked.

"Not yet," Tiny replied. "But just going by the number of companies involved in this parcel of land, I can guarantee you that this warehouse isn't used for anything good."

She raked her hands through her hair in frustration. They had more information, but instead of any answers, they just had more questions, more puzzle pieces that they couldn't get to fit.

"We talked to Edward and Rita earlier," Gavin said. "He's concerned about his sister. Polanski called him to let him know that Constance was at the house the evening of the shootings. At first under the guise of concern, trying to get Polanski to disclose their location. According to Polanski, when she realized he didn't know, she changed tactics and tried to get him to loan out one of Edward's security guards to her."

Bean made a sound of disgust. There was something so wrong with that woman.

Gavin shrugged. "Of course, this isn't new information to us, but according to Edward, it raised some red flags. The guy's paranoid as fuck right now—"

"As he should be," Alvarez interrupted. "After what happened to his son, who can blame him?"

"True. However, it was Constance's concern that worried him. They don't have that kind of relationship. He said that up until a month or two ago, he and Constance—and I quote—tolerated each other at best."

A chill crawled down Bean's spine. "A month or two ago? Right around when her husband froze her accounts?"

"When it's rumored her husband found out she was sleeping with his son?" Alvarez added.

Letting out a sigh, she mentally tried to adjust the puzzle pieces. They were missing something that was right in front of their faces.

Her computer dinged. Sitting up, she pulled up her notifications. "Well shit," she muttered, throwing her screen up on the Smartboard for everyone to see. "It's my facial-rec software from the Hudson Island ferry."

Surveillance video began to play. She clicked on it, pausing the video on a man getting into his car on the lower deck of the ferry. She quickly pulled up another image—a driver's license photo—and added it to the screen.

"This is Marcus Driskel. He tripped my facial-rec program because he's a former McClintock security guard." She glanced at her notes. "Looks like he was a part of Rita's security detail but was let go when they cleaned house after Anson's kidnapping."

"What the hell's he doing on Hudson?" Xander grumbled.

She pulled up different video angles until she got a clear shot of his license plate. "I'll have cyber track his car. We can see if he meets with Constance."

"Not to be a wet blanket or anything," Alvarez said. "But what if Constance hired him? You said she'd inquired about personal security—not only from Polanski, but from you as well. What if she legitimately hired this guy?"

"It could be something innocuous like that." Gavin's jaw clenched, and he shook his head. "But something's telling me that's not it. At least, that's not all of it."

Bean knew she wasn't alone when she said she trusted Gavin's gut feelings. Hell, they all did.

Frustration clawed at her insides. Again, more info and no answers.

"Okay," Xander said. "Say she's hired this guy as her bodyguard. Her accounts are frozen. How's she paying for him?"

Bean shrugged. "Probably the same way she's paying for her stay at the Pacific View. Through the foundation . . ." Her eyes narrowed. The McClintock Family Foundation. In under a minute, the foundation's bank register was up on the Smartboard. Seriously, whoever was in charge of their bookkeeping passwords needed to be shot.

She scrolled through the expenses. Checks for catering and photography, charges for countless restaurants and cafes. Thousands at Prada, Louis Vuitton, and Hermes.

Disgust coursed through her. "For a nonprofit, they sure spend a hell of a lot of money on not so nonprofity things."

"B, why don't you have cyber pull all those transactions and print them out?" Alvarez suggested. "Have them go back two full years. We can divvy it up and go through it all."

She slowly grinned. "Like good old-fashioned detective work?"

"Exactly. The more eyes the better, right?" Alvarez rose. "I have to cut out early, but this'll be the first thing on my to-do list tomorrow."

"Date night?" Xander asked, then he frowned as he glanced at his watch. "Er, date late afternoon?"

"They're having a talent show at Daisy's daycare, and Scarlet and I plan to be front and center. Be prepared, brother," Alvarez said to Xander with a grin. "Daisy wants to invite you over to the house this weekend so she can show you her song and dance routine."

Bean grinned. Alvarez's stepdaughter was quite possibly the cutest almost five-year-old she'd ever met. And the little cutie was *enamored* with Xander—she'd even dubbed him Xandy. Aside from her parents, Xander was quite possibly the little girl's most favorite person.

"Count me in," Xander said. The big lug clearly adored the little girl right back.

As they said their goodbyes to Alvarez, Bean shot off an email request to cyber for copies of the transactions. They had a kick-ass team, dammit. Between all of them, they had to find something. Right?

CHAPTER THIRTY-THREE

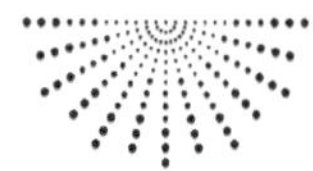

"Damn, woman. Your shoulders are tight."

Bean sighed into her mattress as Gavin pressed an especially tight spot near her neck. "It's your fault."

"And how is it my fault?"

"You promised me dinner but then mauled me the second we stepped into my house."

"Don't think I heard any complaints from you," he muttered with a low chuckle.

"Oh, no complaints. Just stating a fact. My shoulders are tight from food depravation." His hands moved down the sides of her spine, and she bit back a groan.

"Not quite sure that's how it works, baby, but okay."

She heard the smile in his voice and it warmed her heart.

For the next twenty minutes, Gavin worked her back and legs until she was a limp noodle. Her legs were especially tight from hiking. Not that she'd done anything strenuous, but she'd gone from basically zero activity to three days in a row of hiking. It was embarrassing she was this out of shape, but it was what it was.

"You still with me, B?" he asked as his thumbs dug into her lower back.

"Uh-huh," she groaned, blinking her eyes open. Then her stomach chose that exact moment to let out a loud grumble.

He snickered. "Well, lucky for you, I put the food I brought over into the fridge before you mauled me for round two." His hands fell away, and she rolled onto her back. His gaze heated as he took in her naked breasts.

"Don't think I heard any complaints from you," she teased, throwing his earlier words back at him.

"Damn straight you didn't." He leaned down, sucked her right nipple into his mouth, and released it with an audible pop. Then he did the same to her left before he straightened and hauled her up with him. "Dinner. Actual food this time. I gotta keep your energy up."

Dinner consisted of giant chicken Caesar salads with extra croutons.

"Things are not looking good for Constance," she said while they ate. "How do you think Edward's going to react about his sister—"

"Nope." Gavin pointed his fork at her. "No work talk."

She rolled her eyes. "To be fair, it's more than just work talk. It's a there's-a-high-probability-that-Constance-Whitcomb-is-somehow-involved-with-you-getting-shot talk. Kind of important, if you ask me."

A soft smile graced his lips. "I want to know what's going on as much as you do, but right now, it's me and you. It's time to shut off everything else."

She pushed her empty plate away from her. Now *that* she could get behind. Or rather, have him get behind her. "What exactly do you have in mind?" she asked with a devious grin.

He chuckled. "While I like what's going on in that dirty mind of yours, I was thinking of something else."

Her eyebrows hit her hairline. "Oh, really?"

"Oh, we'll get to what you were thinking later, but first, what do you say you show me one of the games you play?"

She didn't think her eyebrows could get any higher, but she was pretty sure they were on the top of her head. Had she heard him right? "You want to game with me?"

"Sure. I don't know if I'll be any good at it. I've never really been a computer game player."

She snickered. "Yeah, the fact you call it 'computer game player' says a lot."

"Be nice." He pointed a finger at her and winked. "I introduced you to hiking, and you like it."

She wrinkled her nose and then huffed out a sigh. "I do. It's relaxing."

His grin could only be described as victorious. "Well, maybe I'll like computer game playing."

"Okay. But we'll ease you into it. You've heard of *Fortnight*, right?"

"I've heard of it, but that's it." His embarrassed grin was adorable.

"Well, we'll play *Battle Royale*. It's pretty straightforward. You pick a character and shoot shit until you're—hopefully—the last one standing. I figure that may be right up your alley. If the middle school crowd can figure it out, I'm betting you can too."

"Thanks for the vote of confidence," he muttered as he followed her to her workstation.

She wheeled over a second chair and quickly set him up at her computer. Sitting beside him, she powered up her extra laptop. Excitement had her fingers tingling. Knowing Gavin, he'd be a natural—the guy was annoyingly good at everything he tried. But if he actually liked it, holy crap, she couldn't help but think of how much fun they could have.

As the opening notes to the game rang out from her speakers, she quickly showed him how to maneuver in the game. Of course, it was no problem for him, and she chuckled at the determination on his face. You'd think he was about to perform a tracheotomy.

"We'll work as a duo," she said with a grin. "That way, you'll at least have a shot of not getting killed in the first twenty seconds."

He gave her a cocky grin, leaned in, and kissed her. "Let's do this, baby."

CHAPTER THIRTY-FOUR

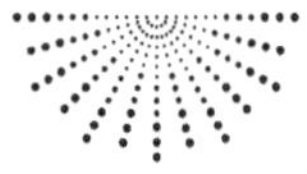

"Holy shit, my eyes are crossing," Gavin grumbled, scrubbing his hands over his face. After a relaxing evening with Bean getting slaughtered at *Fortnight*, they'd spent the rest of the night in her bed, relaxing in a completely different, more satiating way. Like clockwork, they were both up early and back at the office by seven. He had to be honest though, the rinse-and-repeat was a lot more enjoyable with her by his side.

"No kidding," Xander said, leaning back in his chair.

They'd been going over the McClintock Family Foundation's bank transactions since they'd arrived at work, and it was now a quarter past noon. He and Xander were currently seated at Team Two's workstation. With the team out of the office, he and Xander had figured they'd mix up their scenery from the large conference room to the main room. The view out the floor-to-ceiling windows was nice—gray and overcast with an occasional miraculous sunbreak—but it was still fucking tedious work.

Abbot cleared her throat as she walked by. "Imagine how much more of a pain in the ass it would have been if I'd just printed all that shit out for you guys like you'd wanted so you could do your old-school investigating."

"Point to you, Abbot," Gavin said, giving her a salute. "Thank you."

The cyber team's lead had balked when she'd received their request to print out two years' worth of banking transactions for the McClintock Foundation. Bean had quickly thrown them under the bus, telling Abbot they wanted to go through the documents line by line with pens and high-lighters, like an old-school investigation. Which, to be fair, was exactly what they'd wanted to do.

Abbot had flat-out refused. In under five minutes, she'd emailed Excel spreadsheets of all the foundation's transactions to him, Alvarez, and Xander. She'd even included separate tabs with the transactions sorted by date, vendors, and transaction amounts, because she'd figured they would ask her how to do that shit anyway.

She hadn't been wrong.

Paper pushing with contracts and agreements was one thing. Spreadsheets of mind-numbing data? Not his favorite.

They'd hooked up their laptops to Team Two's oversized monitors, and Gavin had been looking into a few of the companies that the foundation had made large and multiple payments to—those that weren't retail stores.

A throat clearing had him looking up. "Is Bean around?" Alvarez asked, approaching the station where he and Xander were working.

Gavin shook his head, a grin blooming on his face. "She went for a hike."

Alvarez's eyes narrowed. *"Bean?"*

He chuckled. "I know, right? Some program of hers was doing something. I don't know exactly what, but it pissed her off. She needed a break."

"Why aren't you with her, seeing as the two of you are joined at the hip?"

He flipped off his friend.

"Oh, please, tough guy," Xander muttered. "He was getting ready to go with B, but McClintock called. So the poor baby here had to let his lady go by herself."

"Christ," Gavin muttered, slouching down in his chair.

"Please, dude," Xander scoffed. "You were full-on pouting when you took McClintock's call."

"Whatever." Weak comeback? Absolutely. But nothing his friend had said was wrong. He'd much rather be out hiking with Bean than staring at a spreadsheet with these two. He glanced at Alvarez. "Anyway, why are you looking for Bean? What's up?"

"Maybe nothing, but I was looking at some of the foundation's charges for the charity gala, particularly for the catering and event planning. The charges totaled just over a hundred grand and seemed excessive, so I tried to find out more about the companies. But I couldn't find anything. No websites, no Yelp reviews, no socials. Which is odd for companies that charge that much, right? I was hoping Bean could do her magic and see where these companies are based."

That was odd. "Let me see if Tiny's available." Gavin grabbed his phone, and after the second ring, the other man picked up.

"Hey, Frazier. What's up?"

"Bean's out of the office for the next hour or so. Are you free to look up some stuff for us?"

"Of course. I can patch in to one of the Smartboards. What conference room are you guys working in?"

Gavin glanced at his and Xander's monitors. "Uh . . ." *Shit.* "How about I get Abbot to set us up on this end and have her let you know where to connect."

Tiny chuckled. "Sounds good. I'll be on standby."

"Thanks, man." Gavin disconnected and called out, "Abbot. Can you set us up in the large conference room and get Tiny up on the Smartboard?"

She gave a brisk nod. "You got it, Frazier. Bring your laptops to the conference room and I'll handle everything."

They followed Abbot into the conference room. Gavin had learned a long time ago when anyone in cyber told him to do something, it was best to just comply. It took Abbot less than three minutes to get everything set up. Another minute later, Tiny joined them on the Smartboard via video call.

"While you were getting set up," Tiny said, "Alvarez shot me the names of the two companies he was looking at. Five Stars Catering and Sunset Event Planning. A quick search shows both companies are registered in the state of Idaho with no registered agent on file. However, what's interesting is that they both have the same mailing address. A PO box in Federal Way, Washington. Would you, uh, like me to check to see who opened the PO box?"

Gavin narrowed his gaze. "Are you as good a hacker as Bean says you are?"

"Abso-fucking-lutely."

Gavin grinned. The man hadn't hesitated one bit. "Then by all means, do your thing."

"I can't believe I didn't see this earlier," Alvarez said, shaking his head. "I assumed the catering charges over the last month and a half were just for the gala. But then I remembered it was at the Four Seasons, and they do their own in-house catering. So why pay a separate catering company fifty grand? And the event planning charges are another fifty grand."

"Don't beat yourself up, man. An outside catering company could still be hired to do a specialty cake or desserts or some shit. Something that the Four Seasons doesn't provide," Gavin said. "However, for a company to charge fifty grand for that and *not* have a website or social media of any kind? *That* doesn't add up."

"Well, holy shit, gents, we got a hit," Tiny said. "The person who opened the PO box was the one and only Elena Nabers."

A chill crawled up Gavin's neck.

Nabers was the same person who created Performance Exports, the company that paid Otton to shoot him, and she was now linked to the McClintock Family Foundation, whose president was Constance fucking Whitcomb.

He frowned. "Can you check in Idaho's system to see if Nabers also created the catering and event planning companies? Better yet, can you search both the Washington and Idaho records for any other companies she's opened?"

"On it. This may take a little bit of time, though."

"Thanks, Tiny." Gavin turned to Xander and Alvarez. "So we finally have a connection."

Alvarez nodded as he ran a finger over his laptop screen. "According to the transaction list, last Wednesday, a fifty-thousand-dollar check was deposited by Five Stars Catering. That's the exact amount that hit Otton's account the next day from Performance Exports LLC."

Anger simmered in his gut. Letting out a breath, he turned to Alvarez. "Can we get the feds or SPD to bring Constance Whitcomb in?"

"If we can get confirmation that Nabers also opened the catering and event planning companies—which are obviously bogus—I think the feds would be more than happy to ask Constance a few questions. They'd still need more info to link Whitcomb to the shootings, but the embezzling from the foundation is pretty clear-cut. I'm guessing they'd be interested in picking Nabers up as well. That deposit into

Otton's account—if Bean and Tiny can package what we have so it's admissible—is pretty damning."

Gavin ran a hand over his jaw. "I don't want to spook Constance though. We need time to get all our ducks in a row. Right now, she's still at the resort, but once she's on the move . . ."

"What if Quinn happened to pull her over for . . . expired tabs or something?" Xander shrugged with a devious glint in his eyes and gestured to Tiny. "I mean, what if there's no record in the Department of Licensing that she renewed her vehicle registration and that little renewal sticker on her license plate wasn't there?"

Gavin glanced at his friend and nodded, a smile playing on his lips. "That would be unfortunate for her."

Sheriff Quinn O'Conner was a solid law enforcement officer who they all had great respect for. He was a Hudson Island local son and friend to many of them. He was also a former fed, and as sheriff, he was by the book and fair. If they were discussing their intel-gathering tactics, they were extra careful around him. They didn't want to put him in an awkward position, and they made damn sure any intel they turned over to him was fully admissible in the court of law. Gavin knew it couldn't be easy having a private security company operating on the island, so they tried not to rock the Hudson Island Sheriff Department's boat and provided them with assistance if they needed it.

Xander grinned. "I'll check with cyber on where Whitcomb and her bodyguard are at and I'll . . . figure something out."

"I'll give Quinn a call and see if he can meet us here. It's probably time to give him a heads-up on all this shit anyway." Gavin turned to the Smartboard. "Tiny, I'm heading back to my office, but let me know when you've got something on Nabers and those companies."

"Copy. Talk to you gents later."

Tiny disconnected the call and Gavin gestured to the now-blank Smartboard. "I like him." He pinned his two friends with a glare. "But if you ever tell Bean that, I'll deny it and find a way to make your lives hell."

CHAPTER THIRTY-FIVE

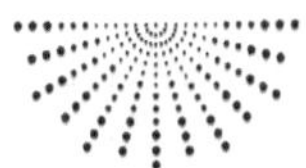

Following the concrete path, Bean zipped up her jacket as she rounded the Hudson Tactical building and came to a halt. In the distance, a group of roughly twenty people stood at the trailhead in a semicircle around Wilson and Joe Buchanan, the head of Hudson Tactical. There were a few women mixed in the group, and they all looked to be law enforcement types. Disappointment had her frowning.

As she made her way over to the group, Wilson caught her eye and gave her a chin lift. While Buchanan continued to address the group, Wilson made his way toward her.

"What's up, B?"

"I should be asking you that question." She nodded to the group. "The trails off-limits today?"

"Yeah, sorry. They're in from Southern Oregon for an outdoor firearm safety and training session." Glancing back at the group, his lips pursed. "You're not gonna want to be roaming the woods while they're doing their thing."

"Noted." She wrinkled her nose. The last thing she wanted was to head back to her office and deal with her glitching programs. Unless . . . She glanced at her watch.

"Uh-oh." Wilson chuckled. "What's that look for?"

"Just figuring out if I have time to swing out to Jackson Cove for a quick hike."

A grin spread over his face. "Look at you, Miss Quick Hike During Her Lunchbreak." A grin spread over his face. "Who the hell are you and what have you done to our desk jockey?"

"You're funny," she said, deadpan.

"That I am, my friend. But I have to ask, do you know which are the easy trails out there?"

She nodded. "Gavin took me out there on Monday."

"You have your phone on you?"

"Yes, Dad," she said with an exaggerated sigh.

He held his hands up. "Hey, I had to ask. The last thing I want is Frazier pissed at me because he can't get a hold of you."

She rolled her eyes. "Dramatic much?"

A sharp whistle cut through the air and they both glanced at Buchanan, who waved at her.

"That's my cue," Wilson said. "Be careful out there."

Her gaze flickered to the group and then back at him. "You too."

Ten minutes later, Bean entered the parking lot of Jackson Cove State Park. She pulled into an open spot next to a Subaru Outback and cut her engine. As she got out of her Audi, she snagged the water bottle she'd filled with her favorite sugar-free peach energy drink—baby steps, right?—and took note of the four other cars in the lot. She zipped her car keys into her jacket pocket and set her phone's timer for thirty minutes so she'd know when to turn around, then she tucked the phone into the pocket of her leggings and grinned. *Look at me, all outdoorsy!*

She made her way to the main trail. A part of her wanted to take the gorgeous route that overlooked the water. However, she recalled how steep the beginning of the trail was. The last thing she wanted was to slip and twist her ankle, so she veered to the other easy trail that Gavin had pointed out.

Taking a deep breath in, she let the forest scents soothe her. She focused on the uneven trail and the sounds of critters scampering away. The tension in her shoulders eased. Never in a million years would she have guessed that *she* would go out for a lunchtime hike. But being out here settled her. The sounds, the scents, the solitude. They were like a reset button for her brain.

After a few minutes, the sound of voices carried over the quiet forest. Glancing up the trail, she saw flashes of orange and yellow along the switchback. She coughed loudly, attempting to alert whoever was out there of her presence. That was a thing, right? The voices paused before resuming. Ahead of her, two women in brightly colored jackets appeared from around the bend. They looked to be in their sixties. Both were wearing small backpacks and using walking poles.

Wait. Did she need walking poles? This was supposed to be an easy trail.

Bean shifted her water bottle from her right hand to her left. The backpacks were probably a good idea though. They were pretty cute too. Who knew the great outdoors had such cute accessories . . .

"Good afternoon," one of the women called out.

"Hello," she replied.

"Lovely afternoon for a hike," the other woman said as they approached. "Just so you know, it gets pretty muddy about a quarter mile up by the waterfall. Have a good hike."

"Thanks for the heads-up," Bean said as the women passed. "Enjoy your day."

Look at me being all peopley and making small talk with strangers. She wanted to pat herself on the back.

After a moment, her smug smile faded, and a familiar worry simmered in her belly. A worry she'd worked her whole adult life to overcome. Well, maybe not *overcome.* Because did anyone ever fully overcome the worry of not being enough, of not measuring up?

She'd accepted long ago that she'd never be good enough for her parents, so she'd worked to become good enough for herself. Yes, her social skills were lacking, but what she lacked in social skills, she made up for with her hacking skills. *You're one of the best in the freaking world. Don't forget that.*

Work had become her life. She was proud of that, because she was damn good at what she did. But Gavin's words from the other day echoed in her mind. *"You're more than your job, B. You're more than your brains and your beauty. You're the whole damn package."*

Was she though? She didn't question her knowledge, her brains, or her computer skills. She was self-aware enough to know she couldn't get too cocky, and she worked to continue to improve, to constantly learn, and to stay sharp. Having Tiny on board would be good for her. It would push her to not get lazy and complacent.

But while she was confident in her intelligence, there was no doubt that her social skills were subpar. And no one would ever call her well-rounded. So was she good enough for Gavin? Truly?

Their physical relationship was new and beyond amazing. On one hand, it boggled her mind that she got to kiss him and touch him. But on the other hand, it felt like they'd already been together forever. It was so natural, so right.

Gavin knew her—flaws and all. She didn't have to hide who she was with him, but she wasn't quite sure if that was a good thing or a bad thing.

He was their leader and was great with people. Could she be the partner he needed? Could she stand beside him at functions like the charity gala? If she were being honest, the mere thought gave her hives. But that was part of the deal, part of what he did as the face and head of Hudson Security.

Again, his words sounded in her head, pushing down some of the worry. Even more than his words, though, she recalled their talk in the woods and all the moments they'd had up until she'd left for her hike today. She thought of the way he looked at her . . . His gaze always held that potent mixture of affection, protectiveness, and flat-out desire.

Her heart warmed. Perhaps they could find a compromise. Some kind of middle ground. Hell, maybe she could bribe Esme to go to all those events with him instead.

A smile lifted her lips, and a new feeling filled her belly. One of butterflies and hope and . . . love. Yes, she was scared. She'd never had a relationship that mattered. However, she'd never backed down from a challenge, and she wasn't starting now.

She took a cleansing breath in and let the crisp forest scents do their thing. She exhaled and slowed her pace as the trail narrowed. The women she'd passed earlier hadn't been wrong. The next five or so feet were a muddy slog. Glancing around, she spied a large stick off the side of the trail. Grabbing it, she poked at the mud to see how deep it was. Thankfully, it wasn't too bad. Using the stick for balance, she carefully made her way through the mud. Her footing gave way and she yelped, but thankfully, her handy-dandy stick kept her from face-planting.

When she reached firm land, she pumped her fist in the air. "Hell yeah!"

With her walking stick in hand, she continued up the trail. Gavin and Wilson were definitely going to hear about her amazing newfound stick-finding abilities. Maybe she'd sign up for one of those outdoor survival classes after all.

A loud crash sounded to her right.

She froze.

Holding her stick like a baseball bat, she scanned the forest. Another rustle kicked her pulse up a notch. Everything was silent except for her racing heart. Then a deer burst through the trees and stopped on the trail in front of her. She locked eyes with the animal and tightened her grip on the stick.

Holy shit, do deer attack?

The deer huffed out a breath and looked in the direction it'd come from. Two smaller deer popped out of the trees and stood next to the larger one. Lowering her stick, she shook her head as the big deer gave her one last look before they all pranced away.

"Yeah," she muttered, slapping a hand over her still racing heart. "You're definitely signing up for Tactical's class."

She continued her hike, and after a few more minutes following the twisting trail, the faint sounds of a waterfall echoed through the trees. The whoosh of gently rushing water grew louder with each step until she rounded a curve. To her right, about a few dozen yards away, was a beautiful waterfall tucked against the rocks. The trail narrowed and continued away from the waterfall. She stopped and admired the view, absently wondering if there was a little river or lake somewhere higher up in the hills.

Twigs snapping behind her pulled her from her thoughts. She glanced behind her and shook her head. Nothing. Her imagination was getting the best of her. Or rather, her newfound fear of wildlife was getting the best of her. More sounds of rustling filled the air, and her gaze swung up the trail.

Tightening her hold on the stick, she turned. *And we're done.* She may be proud of her mini-outdoorsy achievements, but nope. It was time to head back.

Heading down the trail, every noise and every rustle of leaves had her head on a swivel. She carefully trekked through the muddy area and was relieved she didn't lose her balance. She jerked to a stop when some small critters darted out of the trees on her left and flew across the trail. With a hand over her heart, she took a deep breath. *It's just another deer family. You're okay.* When she got back to the office, she was definitely going to leave this part out of her solo-hiking story.

More twigs snapped to her left. She jerked and scanned the dense forest, holding her breath. It was definitely time to get out of th—

Her eyes narrowed at a shadow in the distance, and her stomach clenched. Was that a person?

Ice shot down her spine and the fine hairs on her arms rose.

Run!

She took off down the trail, her heart threatening to beat out of her chest. She risked a glance behind her. No one was there, but she didn't slow. Everything inside her screamed to keep moving. As she turned her attention forward, a blur to her left startled her.

Something hard slammed into her, knocking her off her feet. She tumbled off the side of the trail and down the mossy embankment. Momentarily dazed, she glanced up at the figure looming at the edge of the trail. There was a man dressed in olive-green pants, a black coat, and a ski mask. It looked like he was trying to find a way down to her.

Holy shit, not good. Not good at all.

Grabbing her walking stick, she jumped up and took off and cut to the right, zigging and zagging through the trees until she could no longer see where she'd tumbled off the trail. Spotting a group of fallen stumps, she crouched behind them and prayed he wouldn't be able to find her.

Bean's hands trembled, and her mouth had turned to dust. She held perfectly still, not knowing how long she sat crouched behind the logs. It could have been seconds. It could have been minutes. Bile rolled in her belly when branches broke and twigs snapped.

The man's movements were getting louder, closer.

She remained frozen, terrified to move.

After the longest five heartbeats of her life, his steps receded as if he were moving away from her. Still, she didn't move.

Then her alarm went off, the chime vulgarly loud in the quiet forest.

Her heart shot up her throat as loud footfalls raced toward her.

"You can't hide from me," the man said in a singsong voice.

Popping up from behind the stumps, she gasped at how close he was. She darted to the right. Using every ounce of strength she had, she swung the walking stick like a baseball bat. She aimed for his knees and made contact, the reverberation like a live current running up her arms.

He cried out and crumpled, clutching his left knee. She tried to run past him, but he lunged at her. She spun around and ran in the opposite direction. She peeked behind her, and her stomach rolled. The bastard was still staggering after her.

"I wasn't going to hurt you," he called out. "Now all bets are off, bitch!"

Her lungs were burning, but she kept running. She

yanked her phone from her leggings pocket, but her hands were shaking too much to turn off the alarm.

Her foot caught on something, and she stumbled. Her arms pinwheeled and both her phone and walking stick went flying.

She hit the ground with a thud, her hands scraping against rocks and dirt, somewhat breaking her fall. The man was gaining on her. She quickly scanned the area around her, but didn't see her phone.

Move!

Fear had her scrambling back up, and with her heart in her throat, she ran deeper into the forest.

CHAPTER THIRTY-SIX

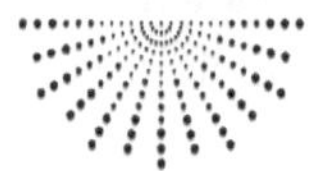

"Is there a reason we're having this meeting at your office instead of over food?" Sheriff Quinn O'Conner asked as he settled into a guest chair opposite Gavin's desk. "I mean, don't get me wrong, Frazier, your setup here is impressive and all, but I'd much prefer meeting over a meal like usual."

"No doubt we all would," Xander added with a laugh. "But Frazier's in lockdown."

Quinn's eyebrows rose. "Care to clarify that?"

For the next ten minutes, Gavin updated Quinn on everything. The rescue of Anson McClintock, the gala and car chase, the two shootings at the McClintocks' home, and the subsequent information they'd uncovered.

"I wanted to keep you in the loop," Gavin said. "I don't know how fast the feds will move on this."

Quinn snorted. "Feds moving fast? You're kidding, right?"

There was no love lost between the local sheriff's department and the FBI's Seattle office.

"Exactly," Gavin said. "Constance Whitcomb is staying at the Pacific View, but should she decide to leave, we were hoping you could keep an eye out for her car."

"And why exactly would I do that?" Quinn asked, leaning back in his chair.

He looked at his friend for a moment. "Do you really want to know?"

Quinn grimaced and ran a hand over his face. "No. Make that fuck no."

Yeah. That's what he'd thought. Chuckling, Gavin glanced at his ringing cell phone. Tiny's name showed on the display. Holding up a finger, he rose and brought the phone to his ear.

"Hang on," Gavin said by way of greeting. Excusing himself, he stepped into the hallway and shut the door behind him. "All right, go ahead."

"Nabers is the one who created Five Stars Catering and Sunset Event Planning. In addition, she's created Sherman Photography—another vendor that appears multiple times on the foundation's bank register."

The McClintock Family Foundation had been established to provide access to technology and STEM education and experiences to underserved communities, and Constance was using it as her personal bank account. That was disgusting enough, but knowing she was most likely responsible for her own nephew's kidnapping and torture was beyond fucking appalling.

Gavin shook his head. He'd do everything in his power to make sure she was brought to justice. "Thanks for the intel, Tiny. Everything needs to be admissible. Once it is, call Esme and let her know. Pass along what you have so she can let her FBI contacts know."

"On it. This woman's going down. Also, that thing with the Department of Licensing has been taken care of. Later," Tiny said before hanging up.

He pocketed his phone and looked out at cyber's work area. Countless monitors were busy with activity. Restless energy buzzed through him. They were so damn close to bringing Constance Whitcomb down.

"Abbot," he called out. When she glanced over, he made his way toward her. "Where's Whitcomb right now?"

She turned to her computer. After a few keystrokes, numerous security feeds filled the screen. "Still at the Pacific View. She and the bodyguard resurfaced from their room not too long ago. Looks like they just got seated in the dining room."

"Thanks," he said. "Keep an eye on her, please."

"You got it," she said, calling over Oliphant.

Leaving them to it, Gavin reentered his office. He nodded at Alvarez, who'd pulled up an extra chair beside Xander. Taking his seat behind his desk, he met Quinn's curious gaze. "We have confirmation that Constance Whitcomb is embezzling money from her family's nonprofit foundation. There's also a high probability that she was involved in the kidnapping of her nephew, along with the multiple shootings."

Quinn's eyebrows rose. "No shit?"

"We still have to dig a little deeper for the proverbial smoking gun, but it's there somewhere. Esme will be informing the FBI with what we've found, but you know as well as I do, those fuckers are slower than molasses."

Quinn remained silent and then nodded. "I can have Deputy Chase go out and post up at the resort." With his elbows on the armrests of his chair, Quinn steepled his fingers and brought them to his lips. "If Constance leaves the resort, what do you think Chase should be on the lookout for? Hypothetically speaking, of course."

"He could stop her for expired tabs." Gavin shrugged. "Hypothetically speaking."

Quinn chuckled. "Of course—"

Gavin's cell phone rang. "Sorry," he muttered. He didn't

recognize the number but brought his phone to his ear. "Frazier."

"The almighty Gavin fucking Frazier," a man said, disdain clear in his voice.

Everything inside Gavin stilled. Glancing at his colleagues, he quickly put the call on speaker. "Who the fuck is this?"

"Wouldn't you like to know?" The man tsked, clearly enjoying himself. "How about this? I have your girlfriend."

Ice shot through his veins, and his vision tunneled on his phone. "What the fuck did you just say?" he hissed.

He desperately wanted to reach through the phone and strangle this fucker. Demand he tell him what the fuck he was talking about. Instead, he had to sit there and watch as Xander, Alvarez, and Quinn sprang into action. Alvarez shot out the door with his phone to his ear. Quinn moved to the opposite side of Gavin's office, quietly speaking into his phone. Xander shot to his feet, his attention locked on Gavin.

The man on the other end chuckled. "Got your attention, didn't I? Well, asshole, I have your girlfriend. Pretty little thing, and she looks great in those skintight leggings of hers. You have two hours to round up ten million dollars. I'll call with transfer instructions."

Gavin knew there was a protocol for keeping the caller on the line, but for the life of him, he couldn't remember what it was. The only thing on his mind was Bean. "How the fuck do I know you're not lying?"

"I was planning on sending you a video of her before I send you the transfer instructions. I'm nice like that. Consider it like a before and after. If you don't send the money, I'll send another video of me cutting off one of her pretty toes. Perhaps one for each fifteen minutes you're late with your payment. Once her toes are gone, I'll move to her fingers. Talk soon, asshole."

The call disconnected.

Gavin stood staring at his phone. A dull roar filled his brain. His heart hammered in his chest, and his breaths came in pants. Gripping the edge of his desk, images of Bean flashed in his mind like a slideshow. Then the images were tinged with red, and the noise in his head intensified. With a deafening cry, he flipped his desk. He stalked to the bookcase on the side of the room and upended it. Rage poured out of him in a howl.

He turned to the Smartboard mounted on his office wall and grabbed the edge, but strong arms clamped down around him.

"That's enough, Frazier," Xander shouted.

He stilled. Not because the other man had his arms pinned, but because he was about to clobber his friend.

"Brother or not," Gavin seethed, "you have one motherfucking second to let go of me."

Xander let go but shoved him hard.

Off-balance, Gavin fell onto his couch.

Xander got right in his face, and it took everything he had to not punch his friend.

"Dammit, Frazier, focus! We don't know if he actually has her. Cyber's tracing the call and searching for her phone."

"She's hiking out by Tactical," he said, his voice raw.

Xander shook his head. "Tactical has a group doing firearms training. Wilson said she was heading over to Jackson Cove instead."

He shot up from the couch. "Let's go—"

Xander stepped in front of him and slammed a hand to his chest to stop him.

He sucked in a breath. "I swear to God, Xan, I will fucking lay you out right now."

"Pull yourself together!" Xander shouted in his face, spit

hitting him. "You cannot lose your shit now, man. Bean needs you. She needs all of us. So fucking focus."

Gavin's chest squeezed painfully, as if someone had reached in and ripped out his insides—lungs, guts, heart. All of it. *Holy fuck, this can't be happening.*

He wheezed out a breath and bent over, his hands on his knees.

"She's everything to me," he whispered. "I love her so damn much and I've never even told her." Bile rose in his throat at the thought of anything happening to her. "I can't fucking lose her. I can't."

Xander's hand slapped down on his left shoulder and squeezed. "And you're not going to, brother. We all love Bean. She's like everyone's sister. We know how you feel about her, man. You'll get the chance to tell her how much you love her. To her face."

Gavin straightened and sucked in a breath. Fear and rage twisted inside him, leaving his hands trembling. If he had to burn down the goddamn world to bring back Bean in one piece, so be it. But Xander was right. In order to do that, he needed to get his shit together.

He blew out another breath and flexed his hands. He met his friend's gaze and swallowed past the lump in his throat. "Bean means the fucking world to me."

"I know. But you aren't going to be any use to her dead. We need a fucking plan. When you've got yourself under control, meet us in the conference room and we'll get to work."

Gavin glanced around his destroyed office and nodded. "Thanks. Appreciate you, brother."

Xander lifted his chin. "I've always got your back, man. Always."

.   .   .

Ten minutes later, everyone was gathered in the large conference room with Esme and Tiny on the Smartboard. The door was open, and the cyber team hustled in and out.

Gavin frowned. Abbot was seated in Bean's usual spot, which was just all kinds of fucking wrong. He paced the length of the room. His mind was in a whirl, and his heart was twisted in a painful knot.

Taking in his colleagues, the tension in the room was thick. He took a moment to calm himself down. *Keep your shit together, dammit.* "What do we know?"

"Constance and her bodyguard are still in the resort's dining room," Abbot said. "Bean's phone is turned off, but it last pinged at Jackson Cove State Park. The tracker on her phone showed her off trail about a quarter mile in."

Quinn cleared his throat. "Deputy Chase is standing watch at the resort and will detain Whitcomb the moment she starts driving. I've updated him on the situation and that —" He frowned when his phone rang. After answering, he remained silent as he listened to the person on the other end, his frown deepening.

Gavin's gut rolled. Something was wrong.

"Fucking hell, Chase," Quinn growled. "Do *not* let Constance Whitcomb out of your sight. I'm on my way." He disconnected his call and looked at Gavin with fury in his eyes. "One of the guests in the dining room had an allergic reaction. Chase confirmed it was Whitcomb's bodyguard. The EMTs just got there, so he's not sure what the bodyguard's status is." He headed to the conference room door. "I'll update you when I find out more." He turned and met Gavin's gaze. "Call me if you need extra manpower or people to help search. Whatever you need, Frazier."

He lifted his chin. "Thanks, man. I will."

A second after Quinn left, Wilson and Buchanan entered and quietly took seats at the table.

Gavin blew out a breath and scrubbed his hands over his face. Holy. Fuck. "What else do we know, people?"

"The call you got came from a burner phone," Abbot said with a frown. "However, it pinged last near Jackson Cove. The same as Bean's did. Unfortunately, there's no tracker on his phone, so we can't get a more exact location than that."

"I might have something!" Oliphant called out from his workstation outside the conference room. He rushed in with his laptop in his hands and took a seat at the table. His fingers flew over his keyboard, and within seconds, his laptop screen was on the Smartboard. It showed video surveillance from a ferry. "I was going over the frame-by-frame analysis of the Constance Whitcomb footage and here"—he paused the video—"she talks briefly to the person in the coffee line behind her. And if you zoom in on his face . . ."

Gavin's eyes narrowed at the grainy image. The hairs on the back of his neck rose. "Is that . . ."

"Branson Whitcomb," Oliphant answered.

Holy motherfucking shit.

"Just to double-check, I ran this image and one of him I pulled off his Instagram through Tiny's facial-rec program, and it's a match. Then I saw this photo on his social media." Oliphant added another photo to the screen. It was Branson on the beach with a young woman in a tiny white bikini tucked against his side. "That chick is the infamous Elena Nabers." Her driver's license photo was added to the screen. "I also double-checked her photos through Tiny's program. It's another match."

Witherspoon rushed into the room. "I got Branson's vehicle info from the ferry. It's a rental but registered under his name. The Jackson Cove trailhead cameras show his car's still parked in the lot. Bean's car is still there as well." He held up a large box and set it on the conference room table. "Here are the comms. I know Bean usually takes the lead, but between me and Abbot, we'll have everyone's back."

Gavin's heart was beating wildly in his chest. He wanted to rage, wanted to scream, wanted to tear Branson Whitcomb limb from fucking limb. But this wasn't about him, dammit. Bean needed him. Needed them. He glanced at the time and then met the gazes of each of his teammates. "We have an hour and fifteen minutes until this fucker calls me. Let's go get our girl."

CHAPTER THIRTY-SEVEN

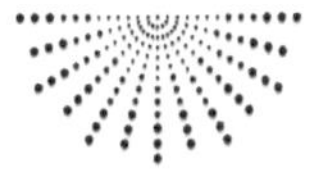

Bean stifled a whimper as a cramp had her right calf spasming. She didn't recall how long she'd run for, but it had to have been at least a couple of hours since she'd first encountered the man on the trail. For the longest time, she'd heard him stumbling after her. She knew she should have tried to cover her tracks, but she didn't have the first clue about what that kind of thing entailed. When she no longer heard him, she thought she was making her way back to the trail, but no.

She was hopelessly lost.

On the plus side—because she was desperately trying to find any sort of plus side—it was still light out. That was something. The heavy forest canopy cast creepy shadows all over the place, so she was thankful it wasn't the dead of night. Regardless, she was seriously rethinking her newfound like of the great outdoors. The only thing she was certain of was that the second she got out of this mess, she was signing up for Tactical's survival course. And not the easy one. The big one that covered weapons and booby traps. Because holy shit, she had no clue what she was doing.

She winced when her calf spasmed again, but she was too afraid to stretch her leg out. In her search for the trail, she'd stumbled upon the hollowed-out tree she was currently hiding in. Literally. She'd tripped and fallen, smashing into the tree. Her impact had caused a family of something or other to scurry out. She'd quickly checked to see if it was truly vacant, and when nothing had attacked her, she'd crawled in. The space was tall enough for her to sit upright, but she had to bring her knees to her chest to remain hidden. Both her ass and legs were currently protesting her position.

She wasn't exactly sure how long she'd been hiding, but she'd heard the man walk by twice. Unfortunately, she knew she couldn't stay hidden forever. She was certain her absence must have been noticed by now, but she'd lost her phone and wasn't wearing any sort of tracking device. There was no way Gavin or her team could find her. A shiver tore through her. If she didn't get out of her hiding spot, she was going to die in the woods. Exposure, animals, the crazy man chasing her, or a freaking heart attack. There were no good options.

Slowly straightening her legs, she took a moment to rub her aching muscles. Then she waited. Her feet were poking out from the tree, and she took it as a good sign that no one grabbed her. After a few more moments, she carefully scooted out of her hiding spot. She frowned as her body protested every movement. Gnawing on her lower lip, she scanned the area around her and willed her racing heart to steady.

No such luck. She was still lost.

She took a tentative step, her ears peeled for any kind of noise. But there was nothing but quiet forest sounds. Or what she assumed were quiet forest sounds.

Not sure which direction to walk in, she moved in the opposite direction of her hiding spot's entrance. She recalled hitting it and scampering backward as the critters fled and made a beeline toward her. Yes, that was the way she'd come.

Her stomach clenched tightly. Right?

After walking a handful of yards, she paused and tilted her head to the side. There was a sound that was different . . .

She closed her eyes and concentrated on the sound. It was like . . .

Her eyes flew open. The waterfall!

If she could get to the waterfall, she could find the trail from there. Her pulse quickened and she picked up her pace. She recalled that the trail had only been a few dozen yards away from the waterfall. If she got to the base of the falls, maybe she could make her way—

Bang!

The tree beside her exploded. A sharp sting slashed across her cheek. Covering her head with her arms, she took cover behind a large rock. Another bang sounded, and she bit back a yelp. Rock fragments rained down over her.

"Come out, come out, girlfriend," the man called out. "You and I need to have a talk. Besides, there's nowhere for you to go."

Her lungs seized. The crazy man wasn't wrong. "What do you want?"

"I just want to talk."

Bullshit. "Who are you?"

"Look, we can do this the easy way or the hard way. It's your choice."

She remained silent and tried to listen for his movements. The only thing she could hear was her thudding pulse and her erratic breaths. She shuffled to the side to peek around the rock and—

A fist slammed into her face, knocking her onto her back. Her vision wavered as the man's booted foot connected with her hip. She curled into a ball, but he was on her. Screaming, she bucked and writhed to no avail. He pressed her face into the dirt, his knee on her neck. She winced as he yanked her arms behind her, and fire tore through her shoulders.

Her blood turned to ice. The man had tied her wrists together.

He yanked her upright, and she couldn't hold back a groan. Every part of her body throbbed. She wiggled her hands and relief had her shoulders sagging. He hadn't zip-tied her, and whatever he'd used was loosening with every movement.

"Stay," he muttered, shoving her against the boulder she'd hidden behind. He grabbed his gun, which he'd dropped on the ground, and waved it at her.

"Who are you?"

Again, he ignored her question. Instead, he fiddled with his phone one-handed. She took a moment to commit his figure to memory. Though he wore a ski mask, she saw enough of his skin to know he was white and had dark-blond hair poking out of the bottom edge of the mask. He was taller than her—which didn't say much—but he was a few inches shorter than Gavin's six-two. The guy was deceptively strong and had a lean runner's build.

She narrowed her eyes when he glanced up, pointed his phone at her, and chuckled. "Say hi to the camera," he said in that stupid singsong voice.

The fucker.

With another guffaw, he tapped his screen and grinned, pointing the gun at his phone. He must have switched the camera to selfie mode. "As you can see, asshole, I have your girlfriend. I'll be calling you in twenty minutes, so you better be ready with the money. Ten million. Chop-chop, or else I'll chop chop your lady friend." He ended the video and sent her a smile that had chills racing up her spine.

There was no way she'd heard that right. "You're ransoming me for ten *million* dollars?"

His smile grew wider. His teeth were glaringly white against the black ski mask.

Holy shit, this guy is psychotic.

"Oh, I'll push for more, but ten mil will be fine for now." He texted something, the video presumably, and then pocketed his phone.

As she continued to work the binding on her wrists, Bean's mind whirled, trying to place him. He didn't have an accent and spoke with a pompous air. She *knew* she should know who he was, but his voice wasn't familiar. If she could get him to talk more, maybe he'd say something to jog her brain.

Minutes passed before she spoke. "Look, mister, I don't know who you think I am, but trust me, I'm not who you're looking for. *No one* is going to pay ten million for me."

He scoffed. "Oh, so you're not Gavin Frazier's girlfriend?"

Her heart stopped, but she managed to keep her face neutral. Or at least she'd hoped so. *Think, Bean!*

"Everyone's always underestimating me," he said, slowly pacing in front of her and waving his gun as he spoke. "They think I'm a fuckup. But you know what? I'm a fucking *genius*. A genius who's going to have an extra ten million in twenty minutes care of Gavin fucking Frazier. That asshole owes me."

The man stalked back and forth like a caged animal. Minutes ticked by in silence as her eyes tracked his every movement. The binding on her wrists was nearly undone, and a plan formed in her mind. It was half-assed and certainly risky, but it was all she had.

There was no way in hell this guy knew what kind of relationship she and Gavin had. *She* barely knew. The only people who'd seen them together romantically were people she trusted with her life.

"Look, I'm telling you, Gavin isn't going to pay ten million for me. He's not serious about me. We fuck. That's it. He's not going to shell out that kind of money. Aside from fucking, he and I barely know each other."

Even though everything she said was a lie, the words she spoke still turned her stomach. Because she and Gavin weren't just fucking. Somewhere along the line, she'd fallen in love with the man. And she knew he felt the same way about her. Though he hadn't said the words out loud, she'd seen it in each and every one of his actions. Every damn thing he'd done, his every touch, his every gesture had showed her how much he loved her. There was no doubt in her mind that he'd pay any amount to get her back. Just like she'd do the same for him.

It pissed her off that this asshole was trying to take that away from her. She wasn't sure if Gavin and her teammates were going to be able to find her, so it was up to her to try and save herself.

The man shook his head, making a disgusted sound. "Please. I was there when you two were all over each other. And he confirmed it two days ago. I heard it with my own ears. You two are more than just a booty call."

The puzzle pieces were all there, but they weren't fitting together . . .

"Then you saw and heard wrong. Gavin and I aren't an exclusive couple."

"Sorry, but I'm not buying it. You see, no man can resist my lover, but he did. Twice. That's how I know the two of you are serious. Ten million serious." He laughed as if he'd made a joke and tucked his gun into the front of his pants.

Glaring at him, she hoped he'd accidently shoot his own dick off. *Who the hell is this assho—*

It clicked.

All the puzzle pieces finally clicked into place.

Branson. Fucking. Whitcomb.

And Constance—his *lover*.

Bean didn't bother holding back her cringe. Yet another reason to hate that word. *Stay on task, dammit!*

She eyed him up and down, putting every ounce of disgust in her gaze, which wasn't hard. "I hate to break it to you, but you're wrong yet again. Gavin fucks plenty of other women. Maybe he was able to resist your lover because he didn't want to dip his dick into some dirty, used puss—"

Her head flew to the side. Pain exploded along her jaw. Managing to keep her hands locked together behind her, she nearly toppled over, but Branson grabbed her by the throat, righting her.

Holy shit, who knew the asshole could move that fast? One second, he was standing a few yards away, and the next . . .

She refused to squirm when his fingers tightened around her throat. Yeah, she'd probably pushed too far, but she didn't care. Meeting his gaze, she wheezed out, "You can't kill me until you get your money. Or are you unfamiliar with how extortion works?"

His hand dropped from her throat, and he backhanded her. "I know what the fuck I'm doing, bitch!"

She leaned into the boulder and worked her jaw from side to side. "Do you? Because you need some kind of leverage—"

He yanked the gun from his waistband and took a menacing step toward her, crowding her space. "I know what the fuck I need! He fucked up our first plan and he'll pony up every fucking dime." He jabbed the gun into her ribs on the last three words.

She held herself completely still. *Shit.* Her plan to get him talking, to press his buttons until he was distracted enough so she could somehow disarm him may not have been the best idea.

Fuck it.

He may be bigger than her, but she sure as hell was smarter. "And how do you plan on getting your money, huh?" Holding his gaze, she shrugged. "Pretty sure you missed that call time you mentioned in your video."

His eyes narrowed, and he spun away from her. He tucked the gun back into his waistband and reached for his phone. Yanking her hands apart, she rushed him. Jumping onto his back, she locked her arms around his throat as they fell to the ground. He bucked beneath her, but her mind replayed every self-defense video she'd watched, every mixed martial arts fight she'd seen, and she held on.

He managed to pull out of her hold and scrambled to stand. She wasn't as fast. He came at her while she was still on her back. Her feet came up and landed against his chest, pushing him away with everything she had. She launched him backward, and two loud pops had her freezing.

She gasped as his body jerked to the side. He landed on his back, arms spread out, and he groaned.

Before she could take her next breath, there was movement all around her. Multiple dark figures swarmed from out of the trees and converged on Branson who was writhing on the ground, moaning and cursing. She scooted backward, desperate to get away. Strong arms enveloped her, and she tensed. Her mouth opened, a scream ready in her throat, when the arms tightened around her.

"Bean, honey, it's me."

She stilled at the familiar voice.

Gavin.

Every bit of tension in her body liquified. She twisted, burying her body deeper into his arms. The sharp edges of his tactical vest dug into her chest, but she didn't care. Her trembling arms wrapped around him, and she buried her face in the side of his neck.

His arms tightened around her and emotion threatened to overtake her. Until this moment, she hadn't realized how scared she'd been, how worried she'd been that she'd never see this man again.

He'd come for her.

CHAPTER THIRTY-EIGHT

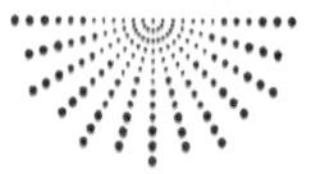

Once again, everyone was gathered in the large conference room, and Gavin scanned the faces of their group. Xander, Wilson, Buchanan, and the entire cyber team were seated around the large table. MacKay, Tiny, and Esme were on the Smartboard. It was nearing eleven at night, and Quinn, along with three FBI agents, had just left Hudson Security's offices.

Despite the hour, there was a buzzing energy fueling the group. Because Bean was sitting with them. She was beside him, the fingers of her left hand laced with his. Of course, that didn't prevent his amazing woman from typing on her laptop one-handed.

She was okay. A little bruised and battered—which had him howling—but she was good. If only his heart could believe it.

Finding her deep in the forest of Jackson Cove State Park had been relatively straightforward. Once they'd had her general location, they'd headed to that sector of the park. Abbot had launched Bean's thermal drones and it hadn't taken long to locate her. Their team—him, Alvarez, Wilson,

Buchanan, and Xander, with Witherspoon directing comms and Abbot flying the drones—had quickly and silently trekked to get her. The hardest part had been waiting for the right moment to move. He'd nearly lost his mind as he'd watched that asshole hit her. Multiple times. Thankfully Xander had taken over as team leader or else Gavin would have been arrested for gutting the fucker.

The last five-plus hours since they'd found her had been absolute chaos. The FBI had descended, along with Quinn's team. Between Bean getting checked out by the EMTs and then doing interview after interview with the feds, Gavin hadn't had a moment alone with her. There were a million moving pieces that still had to be dealt with, but none of them mattered.

He squeezed Bean's hand and studied her profile. The left side of her face was bruised, and there were a few small scratches along her cheeks and forehead. But the corners of her lips curved up while she continued to type.

She glanced at him. "What do you say we get this mission debrief over, boss?"

The exhaustion in her eyes tore at his gut. He brought her hand to his lips and pressed a kiss to each of her bruised and scraped knuckles. He'd come so damn close to losing her.

Giving her a nod, he wrapped her delicate hand in both of his and turned to the group. "All right. What do we know?"

"We know that Wilson's still a fucking crack shot," Xander said with a grin. "Two bullets. A through-and-through in each shoulder. Impressive."

Gavin lifted his chin at Wilson, eternally thankful for his friend.

"Both Constance and Branson are in federal custody," Esme said from the Smartboard. "Branson had a pit stop at Harborview Medical Center in Seattle to get his shoulders stitched up, but I'm told they're both now at the federal detention center in SeaTac. I believe they're currently getting processed."

"That's correct," Tiny said. His eyes narrowed as he glanced at something off-screen. "Looks like with Branson it's kidnapping, extortion, and murder for hire. Charges for both Bean's case and Anson's. For Constance, all the same ones plus embezzlement and an attempted murder charge."

"Attempted murder?" Bean asked.

She glanced at him with shock in her beautiful blue eyes, and Gavin could only shrug. This was news to him as well.

"While you guys were out on Bean's rescue mission, there were some developments," Tiny said. "Abbot?"

"Marcus Driskel," she said, adding photos of the man to the Smartboard. "As we all know, Constance just hired him as a bodyguard. He was formerly with McClintocks' security and was part of the group that was fired after Anson's kidnapping. Tiny looked through his financials, and let's just say there were some red flags."

"According to my contacts," Esme said, "Driskel and Constance were dining at Pacific View this afternoon and she poisoned him. He has an anaphylactic allergy to tree nuts, and she snuck a mixture of pulverized cashews, almonds, and walnuts into his food. The only reason Driskel didn't die right then and there was because there was another diner at the restaurant who had two EpiPens on them. That and the EMTs were just down the road. He got lucky."

Gavin frowned. "Why did Constance poison him?"

"Because Driskel was also the driver she hired to take you out after the gala," Esme said. "Otton is dead, and Driskel is the last loose end tying that incident back to her and Branson. I was told that Driskel made a deal with the feds. He said she legitimately hired him for security protection this week. Said he was skeptical but needed the money since she didn't pay him for the car-chase situation. Apparently, when he arrived at the resort and met with her, it turned into a fuck fest. Obviously, he didn't realize she was planning to off him."

"Esme also got some intel on the warehouse property where you found Anson," Tiny said.

"Of course she did," Gavin said with a smirk.

Bean chuckled. "I swear, woman, you're magic."

"What can I say?" Esme shrugged. "Tiny passed along the companies affiliated with the site and a couple of the names sounded familiar, so I did some digging. Long story short, the property belongs to a Triad group operating out of San Francisco. I checked with my various contacts and they confirmed that Branson had some gambling debts, and the Triad bailed him out. He promised a payoff plus extra interest for use of the property." She winced. "Obviously, the guy's going to run into some problems when he hits federal prison, because he didn't hold up his end of the bargain."

Gavin didn't give a shit about what would happen to Branson. As far as he was concerned, the fucker deserved everything that came his way. He just hoped that if the Triad went after him, they'd make him suffer. Heartless? Absolutely. Did he care? Not at all.

"Then there's Elena Nabers," Abbot added. "She was also taken into federal custody today. According to her social media, messages, and texts, she was in some kind of relationship with Branson. She basically did whatever he wanted in exchange for lavish vacations, expensive gifts, that sort of thing. He never gave her cash, so we didn't see anything hit her financials, but there are numerous photos posted online of the two of them vacationing together. While looking through some of her photos on social media, something interesting popped out." Abbot added another photo to the Smartboard. This one was of Nabers in a black cocktail dress with an older, dark-haired man in a suit. "Tiny, care to take this one?"

"That guy," Tiny said, "is DJ Madison, a current *trusted* member of Polanski's team."

"Motherfucking hell. *He's* the fucking inside guy." Gavin scowled but took no satisfaction in being right about there being a traitor among Polanski's team.

Tiny nodded. "Looks like it. We found multiple large deposits into his personal account from Sherman Photography, one of the bogus companies Nabers created. He was taken into federal custody today as well."

"Holy moly," Bean said, leaning back in her chair. "I knew you guys were awesome, but *damn*. You all took it next-level."

Abbot grinned and waved at the rest of the cyber team. "What can we say, B, we learned from the best. Over the last few hours, I think all of us asked ourselves, 'What would Bean do? What would she look into next?' Besides, there was no way in hell you weren't coming back to us. We had to make sure we had all our ducks in a row for you."

Bean's eyes misted, and Gavin squeezed her hand. "You have to admit, honey, you *are* pretty amazing."

She glanced his way and a tear slipped free. She hastily swept it away and gave a watery chuckle. "You guys . . . Thank you so much for everything. Thank you for finding me."

It took everything Gavin had not to haul her into his lap. Instead, he yanked her chair closer to his and wrapped an arm around her shoulders.

"Everyone here loves you, B," he whispered, pressing a kiss to the side of her head.

"Not to add to the waterworks or anything," Alvarez said. "But I'd just like to say that I'm really proud of you, B. You handled yourself well out there."

"But will you please sign up for our outdoor survival class?" Buchanan cut in with a grin.

"Yes," Wilson chimed in. "Pretty please?"

Bean laughed, wiping away another renegade tear. "Believe it or not, when I was hiding in that hollowed-out tree, I told myself that was one of the things I'd do if I got out of that mess."

Gavin squeezed her shoulders. The thought of her not getting out of that mess turned his stomach.

"Well, you did get out," Xander said. "And you did a damn fine job. Though I must say, egging Branson on about Constance was risky. However, the bit about that woman's dirty, used pussy was fucking hilarious—"

"Hey!" Gavin glared at his friend as laughter filled the conference room.

Xander held up his hands. "What? *She* said it, not me. I'm just repeating. Besides, it was hilarious. Risky, but hilarious. And I, for one, am in complete agreement with B." Xander glanced at Bean and then nodded at Gavin. "He almost lost his shit though."

Alvarez smothered his laugh with a fake cough. "Anyway, good job out there. We all know you're fucking smart, and no one is surprised you outwitted the fucker and got him to turn his back on you."

"Again, totally thought Frazier was gonna lose his shit, but what can you do?" Xander shrugged, grinning. "You're his woman, B, so you can't fault the guy, right?"

She glanced at him, grinning. "Your woman, eh?"

"Damn straight." He winked at her, tipped her chin up with his finger, and pressed a quick kiss to her lips. "All right, everyone out. I'm not gonna tell my woman just how much I love her in front of all of you."

"Oh, come on," she said, her tone teasing as chuckles

broke out in the room. "I love you, so what does it matter if they're all witnesses?"

His heart locked in his chest, and his gaze bored into hers. She stared at him with a look of love he still wasn't sure he deserved. But he was taking it, dammit. Taking her. Forever.

"Everyone, get out," he growled.

Laugher filled his ears as his teammates cleared out. Bean waved and thanked them all, but he didn't take his eyes off her.

The moment the room was clear, he pulled her onto his lap and pressed his forehead to hers, unable to speak. The fear and worry, the hours of not knowing where she was or if she was okay were lodged in his throat like a rock blocking his words.

She was safe in his arms, but he still couldn't quite believe it.

Her soft hands cupped his jaw, and his eyes filled with tears. Closing them, he savored her touch.

"I love you, Gavin. Thank you for coming for me."

His chest squeezed with emotion. Her words, her touch eased the panic gripping his heart. "I love you so much, B. I was so scared I wasn't going to get the chance to tell you, to show you how much I love you."

She pulled her forehead from his and tilted his face up so he met her steady blue gaze. Her thumb brushed away a tear he hadn't realized had fallen. "But you have shown me in so many ways. I know you love me. I was too busy getting stuck in my own head, but your love fueled me today, made me want to fight, to not let him win."

She pressed a kiss to his lips, and more tears spilled down his face. God, this woman . . .

He crushed her to his chest and held her tightly, memorizing her scent, the feel of her in his arms. He never wanted this moment to end.

"I love you so damn much," he whispered, dropping his face into her neck. "So much."

"I love you, too."

With a sniff, he pulled away and took a deep breath in, wrangling in his emotions. "You're going to have to bear with me though. I'm not sure I can let you out of my sight for a while." He shrugged and gave her a lopsided grin. "I'm basically going to be your shadow."

She smiled and pressed another soft kiss to his lips. "That's fine." Then her eyes narrowed. "Wait. How long are we talking?"

"Forever, baby. You're stuck with me forever."

She laughed. "We're going to compromise on the shadow part."

"And the forever part?" He held his breath.

Her expression softened, and his heart expanded. "You've got yourself a deal on the forever part." The smile she gave him was blinding. "Now shut up and kiss me."

A grin split his face. "Yes, ma'am."

He was more than happy to do her bidding. Forever.

EPILOGUE

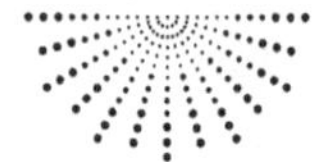

B ean shot off an email to cyber about the update she'd written for their background-check program and shifted in her chair. "Gavin, I'm working," she complained, pushing him away.

Okay, fine. He was peppering kisses along her neck and her complaint was half-hearted at best, but still. It had been a week since the Whitcomb incident, and she'd been splitting her time between the office and home. Her injuries had been relatively minor—bumps, bruises, and a couple of sore ribs—but the less she moved, the better.

"You're always working," he grumbled. "I think you need to take a break."

"Like you don't work just as much as I do." Her muttered words turned into a sigh as his tongue did something amazing to the sensitive skin behind her ear. She tilted her head to the side to give him better access and dug her fingers into his hair. "Yeah, but—"

"No buts," he murmured, wrapping his arms around her waist. "Take a break with me."

"Jesus Christ, horndog," Xander groaned from behind

them. "Can't you leave the woman alone for five damn minutes?"

Gavin straightened, spinning around with his hands on his hips. "Why the hell are you in this house, Xan?"

Rising, Bean laughed and patted Gavin's stomach. "I told you that I'm working." He glared at her, and she laughed harder.

"Sorry, dude," Xander said. "I have a meeting with your lovely lady, so you're getting kicked out."

She shrugged and flashed Gavin her most innocent smile. "It's true, boss. I'm going to have to kick you out."

He gave her a thoughtful look. "What's your meeting about?"

She didn't bother holding back an eye roll. "It's about *your* request to look into possible applicants for a new security team."

He held her gaze for a moment, nodded, and then turned to Xander. "I'll give you a hundred bucks to reschedule to tomorrow."

Xander threw his head back and laughed. He stepped toward them with his hand out, fingers wiggling. "Deal."

Her jaw dropped as Gavin fished out his wallet and slapped a crisp hundred into Xander's open palm.

"You crazy kids stay out of trouble." Xander patted Gavin on the shoulder and headed to the front door. "See ya tomorrow, B."

When the door shut behind him, she turned to Gavin with her arms crossed over her chest. "That was kind of rude, don't you think?" But it was also kind of funny, though she wouldn't admit that out loud.

Gavin shrugged. "He'll get over it. Besides, I wanted to talk with you."

She scoffed. "Pretty sure your lips on my neck had nothing to do with talking."

He arched an eyebrow at her, a look of mock indignation on his face. "You're not the only one capable of multitasking, you know."

She couldn't have stopped the grin on her face if she tried, because damn, he was cute.

"Remember how we talked about that forever thing?" he asked.

"Yes, but we agreed that whole shadow thing was a no-go. I mean, I love you, but the hovering is a bit much." The grin she sent him had him chuckling. However, she wasn't kidding. The hovering was a *lot*.

"Well, what do you say we move all this"—he motioned to her workstation—"to my place?"

Her heart tripped. "What are you saying?"

"I'm saying I'd like you to move in with me." She opened her mouth to speak, but he talked over her. "And the only reason I'm suggesting my place is simply because it's bigger. I'd be more than happy to move in here, but we'd probably have to build on. Or we could build a new place. I mean—"

She pressed her finger to his lips. God, this man was too cute. The nervous-talking thing was something that absolutely slayed her.

"However, there's one thing that's not making the trip over," he mumbled against her finger.

She narrowed her eyes.

"This." He tugged on her sweatshirt. "You're beautiful and stunning, but this is gross."

She barked out a laugh and glanced down at her 49ers sweatshirt. "Sorry, buddy. It's part of the deal. No sweatshirt, no me."

He threw his head back and groaned. "You're killing me, B. I'm more than happy to compromise on anything, but this"—he tugged the hem of her sweatshirt again—"it hurts my heart."

Ridiculous. The man was ridiculous.

Biting the inside of her cheek to keep from smiling, she arched an eyebrow at him. "Oh yeah?" She pointed at her top. "This hurts your heart?" She whipped the sweatshirt over her head and tossed it over her shoulder with a smirk. The bra she wore was purely decorative, the cups a sheer pink that covered nothing. "How's your heart now?"

His gray eyes heated as he took every inch of her in. A grin split her lips when he muttered something that sounded like a growl.

She cleared her throat and placed a hand on her hip. "I'm sorry, what was that?"

He met her gaze, and the desire staring back at her had her body heating. "Fine. You can bring the sweatshirt—"

"Oh, can I? How magnanimous of you."

He stepped toward her, that mischievous look coloring his face. "But every time you wear it, I get to toss it on the floor."

Her laugh turned into a yelp as he lunged at her. With a strength that shouldn't have surprised her, he tossed her over his shoulder—careful not to put any pressure on her sore ribs—and slapped a hand on her ass as he circled the room. He laid her gently down onto the couch, his playful gaze sobering as he leaned over her.

"Move in with me? I'm just joking about the sweatshirt. I don't care what you wear or where we live. I just want to be with you. I want to hold you at night and wake up with you in the morning. I want that every day for as long as I'm breathing."

Her heart pinged, and she framed his face in her hands. This sweet man was everything.

"I love you, Gavin."

He pressed a kiss to her lips.

"I love you too." The corner of his mouth tipped up. "So is that a yes?"

Nodding, she laughed. "Of course I'll move in with you."

"Thank God." He grinned at her, relief evident on his face, along with his love. Then his eyes twinkled with mischief as he lowered his head. "Now, where was I?"

ENJOY THIS BOOK?

Reviews & ratings encourage other readers to try out a book & I would love your help spreading the word! If you could take a quick moment to rate and/or leave a review on your favorite book site—Amazon, Goodreads, and/or Bookbub—I would be forever grateful! Thank you!

ALSO BY CHRISTINA SOL

Want more of Gavin & Bean?

Sign up for Christina Sol's Newsletter for a free bonus scene.

www.christinasol.com

The Spotted Dog Series

Redemption

Reclaiming

Returning

The Hudson Island Series

Shattered Vows

Shattered Illusions

Shattered Dreams

Shattered Secrets

The Hudson Security Series

Out of the Shadows

ACKNOWLEDGMENTS

To my wonderful readers, thank you so much for taking the time to read Gavin & Bean's story! For me, writing a book is always nerve-wracking. And starting a new series? Multiply those nerves by a million. So I truly appreciate the support you've shown! For those of you who expressed your excitement for Gavin's story—please know that's what pushed me through some rough where-is-this-story-even-going writing moments. lol. I'm eternally grateful to you all!

To Heather, Shelli, Jen, and Danielle, I can't adequately put into words how much your feedback, honesty, and support is appreciated! Thank you so, so, SO much!

A huge, heartfelt thank you goes out to my family, friends, and fellow writers who have provided so much encouragement. You all mean so much!